A TIME TRAVEL

BOOK 3 OF THE RECKONING

# RECOIL

# D.M. TAYLOR

ISBN: 978-1-7345442-7-5 (E BOOK)
ISBN: 978-1-7345442-8-2 (PAPERBACK)

Cover Design by 100Covers.com
Interior Design by FormattedBooks.com

Quantum
Entanglement
Publishing

*This book is dedicated to those who believed in its future even when I questioned it. That kind of support can't be scientifically engineered.*

# CHAPTER 1

## TADEN

I bent over and hurled again, sick with the vision of Danika whisking President Berthold from the entryway of his staged assassination.

Danika's betrayal was the straw that broke the camel's kneecaps.

I'd come to look at the inner strength and poise of this woman as the force I wanted to carry my own tide. I trusted her motivations and held a deeper respect for her than I had held for any other woman in my life—which, I suppose, was a high pedestal to place any one person atop. Dr. Pasterski, Ruth, Dakotah, and President Moore. All of these astounding women I had set beneath Danika Farkas.

The moment I saw her—from my hidden spot on that staircase—revealed as a traitor, I greeted regret like an old friend. Ms. Farkas had hired me into this secret government organization. It was her signature on the dotted line of my career as a physicist of time travel. Her deadlines and imposing expectations pushed my labor of love into reality. I feared her, but I also loved her. If she really did orchestrate the dictatorship of President Berthold, and was involved in his plan to release an endemic, why did she even bother to save me from my untimely death? I'd already delivered the time travel she so desperately wanted to determine the fate of our world at the outcome of The Reckoning. Danika no longer needed to keep me around as a pawn in her game—to idolize her even further.

The physical effects of time traveling back to the present, coupled with the images of betrayal that Abel and I had just returned from, left me with no more forward momentum.

"I need a minute here."

Abel glanced around the empty lot. We hadn't gotten any further than behind the building complex that held Danika in the past timeline. She'd just be finding the gunshot wound Abel delivered into President Berthold before our Timed Released Bands sent us home.

"Do you think you've got anything left in your stomach?" Abel asked, his hand on my lower back. "I'm worried you're going to become dehydrated."

"I think that's the end of it." I wiped my mouth with the back of my hand. The waves of nausea and regret were passing from me, only to be replaced by my next visitor—one I knew well. One that wouldn't be leaving anytime soon. Grief enjoyed its time snuggled up next to me and refused all other visitors.

"No one would believe it, Taden." Abel paced next to me, his fingers raked through his hair. "No one," he repeated for good measure.

Abel was trying to console me. He knew I would jump into chastising myself for not having seen the writing on the wall.

I'd become skilled at this particular reflective behavior, having been betrayed so deeply by Marius after ignoring the many blatant red flags. I was already mentally combing through countless Danika memories, assaulting myself to identify each and every warning sign that stared me in the face—all of which I must have refused to see.

"I just can't…" My lip quivered, the words stuck in my throat. "I can't believe I fell for this again."

"Taden. Don't do this to yourself. We *all* know Danika. She deceived all of us." His forehead pulled into intersecting lines of concern. He brushed his thumb across my cheek to catch the droplet that slipped out before I resisted the urge to crumble.

"It's too much." I rose from my hunched-over position in attempt to suppress my nausea. "I can't do this anymore." My emotions dragged me to the edge. Locking my hands behind my head, I tilted my face to the diluted gray sky.

Abel stepped closer to me. "Do you need to let it all out?"

How did he manage to make his voice so soothing? He'd proven his ability to calm me with his words and the sounds that accompanied them. He'd done it again and again.

This is how Abel learned to meet me at an emotional crossroads. Abel Mihal was the type of guy who wanted to bring peace. He loved helping people get emotionally unstuck. Since becoming closely connected to the three women he worked with at the National Institute of Science and Technology, he often reminded me what he learned from us.

"Sometimes, people don't want a solution." He looked me right in the eyes when he said this to me. "Most of the time people just want to be heard, want to vent, want empathy."

He held his arms up just wide enough that I could read the invitation for him to hold me. His embrace was like nothing else on the planet. How could just his arms stabilize my breathing and blood pressure?

Over the decades of us working together at the NIST, we'd come to know that Quinn, Jaxson, Dakotah, and I were definitely problem-solvers. This meant we were also the type to work through our emotional responses to life. We'd learned each other's nuances of responding to triggers. Well, not so much Jaxson. He was mostly placid.

Abel had asked me for the distinction of whether this was a "release" moment or a "let's figure it out and solve it" moment.

My arms fell at my sides, and I looked him square in the face before I let out an animalistic scream. My emotions had taken me to the edge and so I jumped. Thankfully, I couldn't see Abel's face through my teary vision. Relief pulled my body to the ground. With my forehead pressed into a patch of prickly weeds poking through crumbled pavement, I replayed every single loss I'd experienced in the first three decades of my life.

I saw my grandma's funeral, my dad's memorial, my mom's last moments, the flashes of almost losing my sister to drugs, the first man I ever loved choking the life from me, my soulmate abandoning me in time, and now Danika.

Abel's hand was on my back, moving in slow steady circles. "It's gonna be all right," he said. "Get it all out. Remember to breathe."

He demonstrated the breaths for me to follow. I nodded and pulled in a gasp, following his instructions as if they were essential to my survival.

"That's right. Deep breath in." He sucked his breath in with exaggeration and held it as he continued coaching. "Deep breath out." He released it with a push of air.

If he were anyone else, I would've gotten defensive and annoyed. Even if it were Ruth, my sister, I'd probably have responded to the suggestion of taking deep breaths in a negative way. But I followed Abel's lead—only with a tenth of the tenacity he mentored for me. I didn't have the energy to devote to calming myself that purposefully. Regardless, I did find comfort with Abel.

After getting to my feet, I reached for his hand. My fingers laced through his. My breathing still irregular, I looked directly into his gaze. He was, no doubt, the love of my life.

Blinking rapidly, I muttered to myself, "It's nothing. This is all nothing." I sucked in another gasp. "Nothing."

His brows rose into his hairline, indicating I hadn't mastered the calmness he coached. Abel was watching me break, and he knew it.

"I've got you," he said, squeezing my hand.

"Please." I heard the begging seep from my voice. My eyes found his again. "Don't let me go."

And there it was. All my sadness and heartache cozied up to the fear that had become my parasite. I was afraid of losing another person I loved—whether to death, betrayal, or abandonment. And some part of me worked to protect myself from the inevitable way I would have to let go of each person I would ever love.

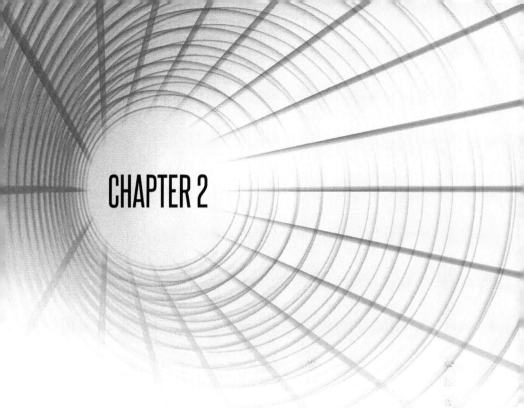

# CHAPTER 2

With my elbows propped on the table in our data office, I reviewed the notes I'd rescued from the abandoned asylum.

Listening to the rhythm of Dakotah's keyboard clicking, I ruminated aloud, "I referenced the DNA of a descendant."

"Hmm?" Dakotah asked, peering over the top of her computer screen.

I dangled my notes above the table. "Me in the past suggested that we'd need to get DNA from a descendant of the traveler to send them into the future."

Her chin jutted. "*You'd* need to have a child."

Twisting my earring in endless loops, I tried to figure my way into the future without the one thing I'd need to get there: *my* child.

"I don't know how strong this theory is yet," I said.

"The only way to know is to test it," Dakotah said, pushing her lips together.

"Are you insane?"

"I'm just sayin'." She shrugged. "If you're not going to put a bun in the oven, what's another idea for testing this theory?"

I ignored her and read more of my notes aloud to redirect the focus back onto time travel. "The link a descendant's DNA adds to the time traveler's DNA is younger," I said, tapping an imaginary timeline on the table. "The younger DNA strand pulls the older DNA strand in the opposite direction of a backward time travel loop." I circled my index finger forward on my invisible timeline to track the concept. "Instead of moving matter through the past as far back as the DNA's age, it travels forward into the future as far as the age of the DNA."

"Now, we just need a kid," Dakotah chimed. She returned her focus to her computer screen and resumed tapping on her keyboard.

"I could test the theory using *any* of our agents. Several of them have children."

"It's true." She didn't falter in her constant tapping. "But we both know you're not about to hand this moment over that easily."

I grinned and confirmed her suspicion with a single nod. I was acutely aware of how *not* excited I was about the idea that the first time traveler to step foot into the future could be someone other than me. A quiet pondering filled the office, accompanied by Dakotah's keyboard rhythm.

"You're about to wear a hole in my floor," Dakotah scolded. Her voice scattered my musings.

"Sorry," I said, stopping mid-step. "I didn't even realize I was pacing. I feel like I'm right on the…oh!" I yelped.

Dakotah startled in her chair. "What? You got it?"

I pointed at her with a wide grin. "I think I might have an idea. I've gotta go get this written on the board," I said, backing toward the exit. "Thanks for listening!"

By the time I got to my office, my brain had fully conjured an enticing concept of going into the past to bring someone into their future using a descendant of that person's DNA. I scribbled this pathway out on my office window, which doubled as a sketch board.

The leap from that idea to my mom was instantaneous. Lost in a reverie of all the things I would say to her when I finally got to see her, I startled when Abel knocked on the other side of my window.

"You gotta see this," I mouthed through the glass, waving him inside.

"I know that look." He came through the door. "You've got something big, don't you?"

"I think I do. Look." I pointed to the scribbles I'd poured out.

"Ah, offspring. Mmm hmm." His fingers bent, pressing his knuckles into his lips while he studied my mind map. "Who are you thinking about bringing from the past?"

My cheeks flushed, and I quickly averted my eyes. I was sure he'd already guessed at my hope.

"Taden?"

"So, it can only be you and me. We must keep this breakthrough a secret. Danika can't find out we might've solved how to get into the future."

"I agree," he said, turning from the window to face me. "That doesn't answer my question, though."

"If it's down to just you and me, that only leaves the option to bring one of our parents forward," I said, my face burning crimson.

"Okay… keep going," he said, his disapproval already written all over his face.

I stood erect. "I want to be the first person in the future."

"I would expect nothing less," he said.

"I figure that narrows the field down to two people, maybe three."

He waited for me to continue with curiosity. I anticipated his quiet resignation as I pointed a finger for each of the possibilities. "My grandma. Which I think is a terrible idea. How would I explain all of this to her? My dad. He's tricky because of him and Dr. P. Having to explain their relationship to a younger version of him would be awkward. Plus, I don't like bringing a younger version of him to this timeline and having him interact with the present-day version of himself. It's just a messy situation." I let my voice drift off as I fixed my eyes back onto the scribbles on my window.

"That leaves the third possibility," he reminded me.

"You know who I'm going to say."

"I do," he confirmed.

"But you're going to make me say it anyway?" My voice hinted at an accusatory tone I didn't expect. Was I trying to blame him somehow? Why?

"I think you should say it out loud so you can hear yourself make this suggestion." He stood firm in his presumption.

My throat constricted and oxygen struggled to make its way in. I swallowed back the anger I was tempted to unleash.

"You don't want me to see her?" My desperation was pitiful.

He dropped his chin but held my eyes with his. "I want you to heal."

"I'm well aware that this idea is not helping me let go of her." I wrapped my fingers around the base of my eraser and swiped the board clean of the notes. They were burned into my memory already, anyway. Abel put his hand on mine, stopping the eraser as it reached the solution. We both paused there, looking at the words: *age of descendant's DNA determines distance forward in time.*

"But this is not only about my personal desire to see her again. We need her to test this theory. I have *her* DNA."

"You're not wrong," he said. His hand was still on mine. "It would certainly prove or disprove the theory."

An inhale of relief washed through me. I turned from the window to face him again.

"You don't think it's a terrible idea?" I asked him, skeptical he was only humoring me at that point.

"No, I don't think it's terrible." He put his finger on the tip of his nose as he carefully chose his next words. "I don't think it's the only idea, though."

"Who else?" I asked, throwing my hands up. "There's no one else, Abel."

"I could bring one of my parents from the past," he offered in earnest.

I collapsed into the chair behind me, rubbing the back of my neck. "They're still alive. It's the same as if I brought my dad from the past."

"It's similar, yes, but we know that facing another version of yourself from a different timeline doesn't make the world implode. Why are you using that excuse as a legitimate reason?"

"I have concerns that the interactions between different versions of one's self can severely alter a timeline. We are trying to make as few waves to the timelines as possible."

It was complete crap, and he knew it. There were no concerns of the sort.

"Bringing your deceased mother from the past?" He asked me this question like he was stepping onto an iced-over pond, unsure if the weight of his question could be held. "This is the proposal for making as few waves as possible?" He remained tentative in his query, his voice becoming softer with each new opposition to my claim. "It would be a major shift in our timelines." He squatted down in front of me and put his hands on my knees, almost whispering. "Have you thought through the consequences? Would she stay here? Would we be trying to avoid her death? How would that play out?"

Abel was ambushing me with his barely audible questions, and they were all legitimate. If I was going to entertain this idea, I should be willing to address them, but I couldn't bring myself to answer any of his concerns. If I did, I'd have to reconsider what I'd already decided I would do.

"Can we table this for a few days?" I looked back to the window, wiped clear of all but the essential link into the future. "I need to think."

He straightened up and leaned over me. He pressed his lips between my brows. With my lids closed, I gave in to the gentleness he offered. I wanted to draw into the stillness of the moment and away from the drama unfolding. I didn't want to face the test this future circle-back moment with my mom had presented.

It shouldn't be a surprise to anyone who knew me that all I ever wanted was to see my mom again. But I suppose it would be a surprise to anyone who knew me that I still hadn't learned my lesson from trying to obtain that wish.

· · · · · ⚬ ⚬ ● ● ● ⬤ ● ● ● ⚬ ● · · · ·

# CHAPTER 3

"Oh, hey! Good morning," Dakotah said as she slowed her walk past my office.

I startled from the deep trance I was in, staring at my computer screen. "I didn't hear you come in."

"You're here early today." She glanced at the clock. "Or are you here late?"

I forced my lips to pull upward into something that would resemble a smile.

"I see," she said under her breath. "Did your idea from yesterday pan out?"

She approached my computer to look at what I'd been working on. I quickly minimized the screen that displayed the cancer research, my nervous energy evident in my rapid blinking. With her hands on her hips, Dakotah's eyes fell on the time-travel algorithms still on my screen from the evening before.

"It was a dead end," I said, sucking in my cheek for emphasis.

"The whole night?" she asked, squinting at me.

I nodded. "Waste of a night."

She waited. I felt the opening for an admission, but I ignored it. It was harder, though, to ignore the tightness—her silent invitation to talk—left in my chest. I wanted more than anything in the world to tell her about my brilliant idea to bring my mom here. I was sure Dakotah would get it. She always made me feel like she understood my plight. But I had to wonder, in light of Danika's betrayal, could Dakotah be too perfect? And could that be a part of her role to gain intelligence on behalf of Danika and whatever she had going on with President Berthold? Even if Dakotah was legit, I couldn't open up to her. I had to keep her safe from the information Danika was after. My loneliness was easily distracted by the idea of having my mom back.

"Are you doing all right?" Her voice was full of accusation as she crossed her arms. "You seem a little..." She paused again. "*Off* lately."

"What do you mean?"

"Ever since we got all the Marius drama figured out...is there something lingering?"

Feigning disgust, I said, "Please. No. That's ancient history. It's been months since he's been gone, and I feel total peace with the situation."

"You're sure nothing is bothering you?" she asked.

I shrugged and pulled on the fake smile again. Her brows rose, acknowledging my detachment. We said more to each other in our body language than I had allowed in our conversations ever since I found out about Danika.

"You know where to find me if you want to talk," she said, putting her hands on her hips. "You know I respect your space, but I'm starting to worry about you."

My fake smile gave way to the faintest trace of a genuine one.

"I know," I said.

She took that as her cue to leave.

Once she was out of eyesight, I clicked on the minimized screen to resume reading the updated statistics I'd found for my mom's cancer survival rate. Since her death fifteen years earlier, it had almost doubled.

"Incredible," I muttered, already formulating the plan to bypass my mom's death.

· · · · · · · ● · · ● ● ● ● ● ● · · · · ·

# CHAPTER 4

My theories could only be discussed with Abel, as no one else—not Dakotah, not even Ruth—was to know that I had possibly cracked the code into the future. Abel and I had concluded keeping them unaware of Danika's corruption was the best way to keep them safe.

After the changes made from our time travels during The Reckoning and each event Abel traveled back to adjust afterward, we'd learned that the alterations had wide-spreading effects. While we were capable of undoing some truly awful scenarios like the spreading endemic that President Berthold unleashed in a fit of rage, time travel left scar tissue within our timeline. Even more consequential than the fractured memories time travel planted in our timeline, it seemed that for every changed event a fee was owed to the universe in exchange. My working theory had developed into a life for a life. If we saved a life that wasn't meant to be saved, we owed the universe in some way—that it would collect. Unless the concept of reuniting with my mom was a gift from time in payment for removing the terror of Berthold, I worried that the choice to bring her back would cost me. In my gut, I feared I could be failing this test the universe had once again brought to my door.

I found myself pulling back on all fronts, no longer openly sharing what I freely gave to Abel. It was as if by closing one door, I had to close them all. The confusion and overwhelmingness of these feelings that grew within should've been the litmus for my choices.

But every morning, I got out of bed filled with this new source of aching like I was prematurely grieving a loss that had not yet happened. I'd look over at Abel, at his chest gently rising and falling in peaceful sleep. His lips pressed firmly together as he dreamed—I imagined—of saving the world. And I wanted to reach out to him, make him understand that I needed to do this. Once and for all use the time travel I'd discovered to see my mom. I needed this very selfish thing, no matter the cost. But then I imagined what that cost might be.

I'd remind myself what it felt like to have him leave. I was already preparing to let him go again. Would he leave me if I went against his warnings regarding my mom? If he did, it would be justified. If he didn't, would time take him from me? Isn't this what the universe was trying to teach me? To let go?

In my pursuit of future time travel, I was going to have to make some type of sacrifice. I would either be giving up the notion of bringing my mom home or I'd be giving up something in exchange for cheating her death. There wasn't enough data to prove my theory, but there wasn't enough to disprove it either.

Regardless, we had to solve future time travel for the same purpose as originally intended: we needed to see what terror lurked ahead of us and stop it in our present. That seemed like the only way to bypass the toll charge of an altered timeline—to make the changes in the present. To do this, I would have to get into the future. And to do that, I'd have to make some difficult choices about how I went about getting there. I had a premonition of the season I would soon enter, and pulling inward was how I would survive it.

Every morning I made the choice not to gravitate into Abel's arms, I pulled myself further away from Ruth, too. I had also erected walls around my conversations with Quinn and Dakotah. None of them could know what I was conjuring.

Eventually, it wasn't even about their safety. After a while, it was only about my longing.

· · · · · ● ● ●● ● ●● ● ● · · · ·

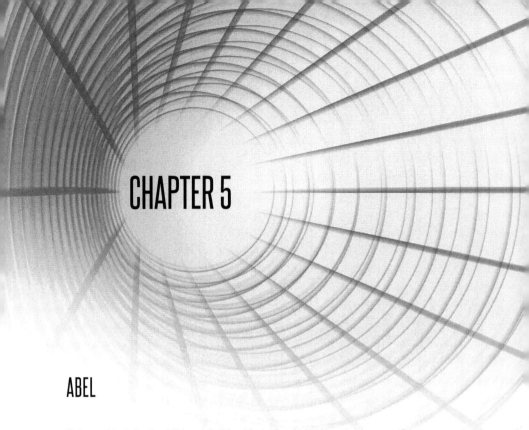

# CHAPTER 5

## ABEL

"We need to talk about this again," I said as I handed over a steamy mug.

She accepted the offering, setting her tablet aside and leaning back onto the headboard of our bed she hadn't yet left from the night before. Her tousled hair and oversized pajama shirt were just as much of a turn-on as when she was dressed to the nines.

Taden pretended she didn't know what I was referring to.

"Your mom," I reminded her. "I don't see how this won't alter our timeline in a major way. Considering how her death affected all of our lives so dramatically."

She acknowledged my point with a single tilt of her head as she gulped down the brown liquid, but she still refused to participate in dialogue on the subject. I felt somewhat like a drowning swimmer. I wasn't used to Taden emotionally shutting me out.

"You know I don't want to deprive you of closure with your mom," I said. "That's not what this is about. I only want what's best for you."

"I know." Her lips moved as if she was going to express the thoughts ambling around in her head, but then they stopped.

"How about we turn our attention away from who we are going to test the theory on and focus more on figuring out when we hope to begin testing?"

I paused and placed my hand on her knee. "In light of what we now know about Danika."

"I think we should've already made our move," she declared.

I heard a thread of accusation in her statement. It was becoming a habit to hear that tone in her voice. I didn't much like it. I nodded in agreement, wanting her to know we were still on the same team.

"Okay. Yes. I think you're right. We probably should've already started testing this plan. Which brings us back to the issue. We really are going to have to go head-first into this."

She suddenly sat upright and rigid. Her eyes fixed on me like she was a fierce competitor, ready to accept the challenge.

"Okay. I agree," she said.

"Okay," I repeated with a heavy exhale. "Let's just back away from the issues surrounding your mom and time travel and look more closely at considering how this would impact your dad. It would definitely affect his relationship with Dr. Pasterski."

I saw a glimmer of surprise cross her face. Had she really not considered her dad in this?

"Here's another scenario I've run through my mind," I went on. "If you bring your mom here, and she doesn't die from cancer, Ruth would potentially not remember a life where she died but would instead know her absence as what? A disappearance?" Punctuating the brevity with silence, I continued. "Only you would have the memory of your mom's death, because you would be the only time traveler on that timeline change." I laid down on my back next to her. "I wonder how that would affect Ruth's life choices. Better yet, how would you handle being the only one with that particular memory?"

"Well," Taden stretched out her pondering on the most substantial point I'd been able to conjure on the subject, "Ruth wouldn't have become addicted to drugs for starters, so I imagine it'd be worth the trade-off."

"True. That's possible. But also, she might not have gone to New York and launched her very successful career," I countered.

"Or she might have chosen something even better and maybe she would have found the love of her life—who she bypassed while she was strung out in her bedroom for a year."

I grasped that Ruth was not the angle to use as a reasoning chip. Taden was much more receptive to the alterations that would affect her dad, and even the lonely memory of a life without her mom.

"You wouldn't spend as much time with Dr. Pasterski growing up. That could have the potential to change whether you even develop time travel. That's an awfully big risk."

"Is it?" she asked. "How about this?" She pulled her legs up and set her coffee cup in the center. "What if we pulled her from her timeline and saved her—*here*—with modern cancer treatment? We wouldn't have saved her life in her own timeline. To them, it wouldn't much affect any new outcomes because she still wouldn't be a part of her actual timeline."

"I'm not sure I follow," I said.

"Essentially, the events in that timeline would unravel the way they had. Just, instead of my mom dying from cancer, she would go missing. I would still grow up without my mom, but we'd skip her agonizing death."

My mouth gaped. "I don't know what to say." I shook my head, hoping the words would come to me. She folded her arms, looking away from me. "You're a woman who—despite any rash decisions you make—always makes incredible sense. The root of your logic is in place, and in that way I'm able to support even the most ridiculous theories you conjure."

Slow, silent minutes passed between us.

"But this? This is the first time that I can't meet you where you're at," I added.

The distance these words placed between us was palpable. Still, I stammered, trying to make her see reason.

"Don't you see that if Ruth lives a life with your mom abducted, and then finds out you were responsible, how that would destroy the two of you?"

Taden shook her head. Was she really going to shut me out?

"How about you?" I asked, trying a different angle.

"What do you mean, how about me?" she replied.

"How will you respond to finding out you were the villain?" Her brow furrowed. "Think about it. You'd grow up with an abducted mother to—one day—learn you were the abductor."

The path that got her here, all the emotional work she'd done to get here was clear. But she was refusing to see the ground she'd already covered. How had she come so far, just to turn back around? Couldn't she see the things she would lose by doing this?

"What if I only brought her here for a few minutes?" she suggested. "She could return home right away. No harm done. No ripples made."

"If that was your intention, why would it even need to be your mom? It would make just as much sense to use any of our parents or grandparents," I countered.

The debate raged on between us for hours. Eventually, she conceded.

"I get it, Abel." Lying flat on our bed, she wiped her face with the palms of her hands. "It's a bad idea. You don't think I know it?" She turned to her side, facing away from me. She felt far away. "It's fine."

Her words were gently giving in, but it felt like a deeper insurgence to get to her mom. She dug her arm under the pillow and pulled it closer to her cheek.

"I'll talk to my dad tomorrow. If he agrees, I'll begin running some minor tests with him."

She had said the words I was trying to pull from her, but it didn't feel like a consolation. I scooted my body next to hers. Strands of her red hair stuck to her cheek. As I slid my fingers across the loose pieces, moving them behind her ear, I felt her body tense.

The shock of her response to my touch flooded me with painful frustration, but I would not be driven by my own insecurities.

"I can see you're in the weeds, and even though we aren't seeing eye to eye I'm here, and I don't appreciate the way you're shutting me out." I slid my arm down her side and tucked it across her ribs. This time she settled into my embrace.

"My dad is a good candidate," she agreed. "He already knows about time travel, and we can trust him not to tell anyone about going into the future." Then she covered my hand with hers and tucked her fingers between mine.

"I wish I could make this easier for us," I whispered.

"I know," she said. "Me too."

· · · · · · ● ● ● ● ● ● ● ● ● · · · · · ·

# CHAPTER 6

## RUTH

Feeling lonely in my apartment, again, I grabbed my phone for the seventh time in the last thirty-five minutes. I'd falsely hoped to find a text, an email, or any personal notifications that said someone was thinking about me, that someone wanted to be here with me. That for one night, maybe, I wasn't alone.

I re-read the last text I'd gotten from President Moore. It was still a weird thought that she was my friend Mary. It was even weirder to know that in another timeline, she was more. I still opted to think of her as my Maria.

Marius had just proposed. She'd sent me a picture of the insanely giant diamond on her hand.

"I wanted you to see it before reporters got a hold of it," she had texted. I was happy for her. Truly, I was. But I couldn't deny that I was heartbroken for myself.

I guess I'd never really faced the fact that I was hoping Mary would see me the way Maria saw me. That I would feel her arms around me again someday.

I shook the memory of Maria from my head, threw my phone on the couch, and before I even knew what I was doing I was shoving clothes into an overnight bag.

Taden always wanted me around, and that was what I needed right then. Because the only other thing I could think of was getting high, which made me feel a righteous kind of anger.

It was complete bullshit that I had the mindset of an addict when I'd never even gotten high before. An *awesome* side effect of time travel. I got to remember things from a timeline that didn't even exist anymore. My hands trembled at the memory of the drug surging through my body, replacing negative emotions with a numbness I craved.

The next thing I knew, I was sitting on the floor of my closet, sobbing, once again blindsided with grief. I'd lost plenty of people to other timelines— my mom, Maria, Trey, Jade. My past demons were powerful adversaries in moments fueled by loneliness.

The next few decisions I made were driven by the addict memories that still resided in my brain—kicking into autopilot. Without ever making a conscious decision, as though I was sleepwalking, the rote memory of getting into my car and selecting the route to my destination needed none of my executive function. I knew where to go. It didn't matter that I'd never gone looking for a high in this timeline.

I sat in my car watching the rough-looking woman exhale a plume of smoke from her lungs. Thick black eyeliner and wine-stained lipstick hid her real face. Leading up to the decision to actively seek her out, I'd driven past her—walking up and down this stretch of pavement—countless times. She didn't know me in this present. But I was one of her favorite customers once upon a timeline.

The sidewalk she claimed fringed an abandoned storefront with blackened windows and a tattered vinyl awning blowing in the wind. A remnant of the past. Three more run-down shops attached to the vacant chain store completed the dump that this forgotten shopping plaza hosted. It was an eyesore in the city, but one that had become host to its unsightly human counterparts.

Steely nerves were all that I had in those moments. My heeled boots wobbled across the crumbling pavement of the parking lot as I made my way to her post.

Still sucking on a cigarette—the second one since I arrived—she watched me approach, sizing me up. The hardened woman stood adjacent, looking me up and down with an angsty, crooked smile.

"A lady like you probably comes at a high price," she said.

I crossed my arms, irritated by her assessment.

"Are you selling or what?" I asked.

"I'll tell you what—my boss over there," she pointed to a car in the lot, "would probably really like having you as a featured customer."

She tapped two forefingers to her forehead in the direction of the car, and on signal a large scruffy man emerged from the driver's seat. As he slowly strolled toward us across the parking lot, my pulse quickened.

Alert to the possible danger I'd stepped into, I considered my sister's habit of putting herself into reckless situations. Although I was terrified, it felt like a level of relief from the loneliness I'd been feeling.

"Hi, sweets," he said through a sleazy smile. I offered no pleasantries in return. "You're new around here?"

"You could say that," I responded.

"What can I do for you, babe?" he asked.

I resisted the urge to pinch my face with disgust. "I'm looking to get high."

The side of his mouth lifted into a smirk. He reached into his colleague's back pocket, extracting her pack of cigarettes. She rolled her eyes but pulled a lighter out of her front pocket and held it to the cigarette dangling from his lips. He closed his eyes and pulled in a long drag before releasing the fumes.

"Anything in particular?"

I shrugged. "I want to feel…" I shook my head. I felt stupid for even having come there. "I just want to forget for a while."

His creepy smirk grew to a smile that didn't reach his eyes. Inside his collared New York-style black leather jacket he retrieved a small baggie, which he discreetly held between his massive fingers.

"This will make you forget everything." He touched my shoulder, and I shuddered at the gesture. "And if you're looking to feel, I got something for that, too."

The woman flicked the remaining butt of her nicotine habit and pressed the ball of her shoe into it. "Man, she ain't into you. Just give her the product." She winked at me and shoved her hands into her oversized hoodie.

I nodded at the clear packet in his hand. "How much?" I just wanted to get the hell out of there.

After an excruciating slow-motion ten minutes, in my hand was a small vial of liquid within a little plastic bag.

"What do I owe you?" I asked.

Driving home, I couldn't believe I'd done that. What was I thinking? I glanced over at my passenger seat where my purse had spilled. I could see the edge of the tiny Ziplock seal. My shame wasn't a match for the feeling I remembered. I couldn't wait to get back home and disappear for the night.

Sitting on my bed, coat still on, I poured the vial into my soda drink and chugged it down in three swallows. I then lay in wait to feel nothing. Before it kicked in, a notification pinged my phone in the living room.

It was Dakotah. She'd responded to my text, much too late. Already having made my choice for the night, I didn't want to answer to anyone. But then she called me.

I considered letting it go to voicemail, but the overriding need to hear another human voice beat my compulsion to wallow.

"Hello," I said. I'd wanted my voice sharp enough to cut through the other end.

A breath. "Hey, lady," Dakotah said.

I slid my tongue to my upper lip, sighing a forced breath.

"Ruth?" she asked.

"Yeah. It's me."

"I didn't think you heard me."

I nodded, my lips now pursed.

"Ruth?" Her voice was alert with concern.

"Mm hm," I responded, feeling the first wave of mellow flood through me.

"I'm calling because I got your text earlier. It looks like Taden's not around this weekend, but you should still come. I'd love to hang out."

Even with the beginnings of my drug-induced calm, I couldn't hold back my surprise.

"You want me to come, still? And hang out with just you?"

"Yeah," she said, stretching out her answer. "That doesn't sound fun?" Her voice was hinting offense.

"It sounds..." A wall of confusion stopped my words. I suddenly felt woozy. My train of thought had been displaced as I sank deep into my couch cushions. I heard Dakotah's voice, but it was like she was in a tunnel. Or maybe I was in the tunnel.

I rolled over to my side, wincing from the stabbing pain in my head, and glanced at the clock. It was close to two in the morning. I rubbed my eyes, squinting harder at the numbers. My blanket was tangled around my legs. I had no memory of coming to bed. My last clear thought was drinking the soda. The sensation still lingered, but I was gaining perspective with each moment.

In the dark, I peered over my shoulder—and there she was, sitting up against my headboard with her arms folded across her chest and her legs beneath her in matching posture. Dakotah was here, and she had drifted off to sleep.

Was she really here? Was I still high? I'd remembered talking to her on the phone earlier, before I'd succumbed. I blinked. It was maddening to figure out reality. I reached for her to confirm my hallucination. She jumped as I touched her arm. She felt real. Sucking in a deep breath, Dakotah turned to me.

"Are you up?" she asked. "I've been worried sick about you."

"I feel like shit," I told her, wrapping my arms around myself. "What are you doing here?"

"You don't remember anything?" She dropped her hands and scooted her body so she was lying next to me on her side. Her face was traced with lines of concern.

"We were on the phone?" I said, not sure if I'd recounted accurately.

"That's the last thing you remember?"

"Yeah, and that's not even very clear."

"I called you back from earlier and invited you to come into town hoping the two of us could go out." She waited for my reaction. When I didn't give her one, she continued. "You sounded bizarre. I've never heard you like that. Sort of withdrawn. Maybe even desperate. But then you stopped talking. You didn't hang up either. It really freaked me out."

"I'm sorry," I told her, still having difficulty following the path of our conversation.

"I panicked, and here I am," she replied.

"Did you drive here?" I asked, bile rising in the back of my throat. "That's an awfully long drive."

"I did. Thank goodness I had the wherewithal to pack a weekend bag." She pointed to her bag at the bottom of the bed. "So, I'm here for the rest of the weekend. Hope you don't mind." A single brow rose as she said this, like it didn't matter if I minded. "You've clearly got something going on, and I'm here to help."

I groaned, putting my hand to my forehead. "Please tell me you didn't mention this to my sister."

"I said nothing, and I plan on saying nothing. This is your business to tell her." She paused. "Besides, I don't even know what I would tell her. I'm not exactly clear myself." She sat back down on the bed. "I can guess this has something to do with drugs."

Inhaling through my nose and wishing I was oblivious to life a while longer, I pulled my blanket over my shoulders. She settled into the silence with me as I drifted in and out of sleep. Hours must've passed before I woke again.

Desperate for water, and with no interest in discussion, I attempted a silent exit.

"Ahem." Dakotah cleared her throat. I froze. "Where ya goin'?"

"To get water. Do you want some?" I asked.

"Nah." She jumped from the bed. "I'll join you."

I pushed out a heavy breath. Her persistence won.

"I'm ashamed to tell you what's going on," I said, finally ready to spill the details.

I'll never forget the look on her face. Her lip a slight upward curl—not quite a smile—and her green eyes soft. My breathing accelerated, preparing for the crash landing a post-truth reveal would undoubtedly bring.

"Nothing you could say would change my perception of you." She handed me my nearly empty glass of water. "You know how amazing you are, don't you?"

She shook her head, like it was a silly notion that I didn't know exactly how amazing she thought I was. I swallowed the rest of the water and set the glass down, pretending I didn't hear her compliment. It was confusing, and I didn't know why she was telling me these things. Or why she was here in my living room at five in the morning following a Friday night after I sort of fell off the wagon in this timeline.

"I guess it's because everyone seems so put together. All the people I love have their lives on a fast track. They're surrounded by people...people who want to be around them." I paused. "And here *I* am."

"What do you mean, 'here I am'?" she asked incredulously. "Step back with me for a minute and just look at your life. You are a hard-working and highly successful party planner. Your name, in certain high-standard social circles, makes people stop and listen. Your parties have a reputation only the upper rung of society can manage to afford. You are fun to be around..." She paused to roll her eyes for effect before continuing her point. "...when you're sober. That's not a feat easily accomplished by most. And have you seen you? You are drop-dead *gorgeous*. Pssh. 'Here I am'? My friend, *there* you are!"

Her point of view about me was shocking. "I thought you were just friends with me because I'm Taden's sister."

"Well, yeah, sure, that's how we *became* friends, but I'm surprised you haven't realized after the last couple of years that I *want* to be around you. I'm not only around you because of situational reasons." She threw her hand in the air, and I knew Dakotah well enough to know she was righteously mad. "Whenever you come into town, I make sure I'm there. Do you think Taden and I *always* go out on the weekend? We only do that when you're around."

"I have to admit, it feels good to know that. I never considered it that way." A shiver ran through me, and I pulled my legs together, reaching for the blanket draped over the arm of the couch. "I'm still kind of surprised you're here, though."

"What can I say? You scared me half to death." She followed my lead and pulled her legs together on the couch, taking the reposition as an opportunity to move closer to me. Her momentary jovial look washed away with a more serious stare. "Are you going to tell me what you took?"

I reached into my pocket and held out the empty baggie. She read the label through close inspection.

"Gamma-hydroxybutyrate!" Her inspecting eyes were now back on me. "Are you kidding me?"

The shame was creeping back into my thoughts. I didn't even know what it was. Clearly she did.

"I'm afraid to ask, but what is it?"

She sucked her lips in and blinked. "It's GHB," she said matter-of-factly.

I lifted my head, understanding the gravity. "I told the guy I wanted to disappear for a while. Relax. Forget. That's what he gave me."

"I bet he did," she said. "Are you planning on doing this—"

"No," I said before she finished her question. "I just, I don't know. I just wanted to feel something else. Not alone."

Instead of getting up, grabbing her weekend bag, and leaving through my door like I expected her to do, she inched even closer to me and pulled me in.

"You can count on me to be around. I don't mind being someone you think of. I actually kind of like it. You know?"

I rested my head on the shoulder she offered. "Yeah, I do."

· · · · · ● ● ● ● ● ● ● ● ● ● ● · · · ·

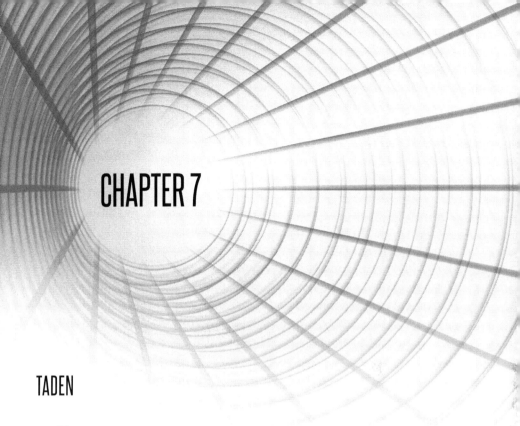

# CHAPTER 7

## TADEN

I stood outside our apartment door, looked through the half-moon window, and knocked. I hadn't seen my mom since the day she died.

So much pain was wrapped up in that day. I was worried facing her in this moment would undo me. But this woman was my mom. She was equipped to handle an emotional breakdown from her daughter. It occurred to me for the first time to wonder how *she* would feel about seeing a version of me that had aged twenty years.

She opened the door and a flood of memories with it. A living memory of the mental snapshots I'd locked away. The way her brown curls bounced at her shoulder drew images of her early in the morning with the rollers in her hair while she cleaned the house. The bright glow of her skin, that was a definite pre-cancer feature that I'd almost forgotten. Her wide smile could power an entire city of its required energy source. This moment quickly became an out-of-body experience. Physically, I stood in proximity of my mother, but it was as though my sense of self was watching the exchange from above. The whole encounter was absolute, and the most real experience I'd felt in a long time, but it was marked with a strangely altered perception. Almost like my brain couldn't process so many neurons firing at once. But then she spoke, and the sound of her voice grounded me from the dissociative state I'd floated into.

"Oh, Taden!" She put her hand to her mouth.

Her face performed postures of recognition and wonder. I couldn't speak, and the sight of her was what home felt like.

"You are magnificent." She was engulfed with pride as she began to understand that her daughter did become a scientist and traveled to her from the future. "How did you...?"

My mom never doubted my intelligence, and she rooted her belief that I could accomplish anything. Still, there in our doorway, I was just realizing the depth of her confidence with the rate she grasped at how I was there.

"Come here," she squealed, holding her arms wide open. My mom danced me around the hallway, jumping with excitement. I couldn't see through my burning eyes, but I could smell her and I could feel the warmth of her skin. There was nothing like being held by the person who was my essence. It was a living dream, a dream I'd often held onto and yet never thought to be attainable.

Eventually she settled and pulled herself from me, still holding my hands. "I need to see you. Your beautiful womanly face, still sprinkled with freckles. Those blue eyes are just as vibrant as the ones I saw on you this morning, before you went off to school."

I looked into hers as well. Every feature, just as I'd remembered—only I hadn't allowed myself to see her in my mind for years. The soft glow of her skin, mirroring the myriad freckles she gave to me. Her brown eyes settling on me with familiar pride. I still hadn't said a word.

"This morning, I was talking to you, the younger you, and couldn't help but think—listening to you ramble about your science project—how amazing your brain is. Now, here you are! Tell me everything! I can't wait to know how you did this."

She led me inside to the couch, where we sat, leaving no space between us. Her every focus poured onto me, waiting to listen to her genius daughter.

"I don't know where to start." I paused, trying to stifle the lump in my throat. I pushed my tongue to the roof of my mouth and took a deep breath through my nose. Once I felt steadied, I tried my voice again. "I've discovered time travel, Mom."

"I knew it!" She beamed. "Tell me more."

"I'm a physicist. I work at the NIST. Dr. Pasterski got me the job."

She was now the speechless one.

I held up my left hand. "I recently got married."

She grabbed my hand, studying the ring. "It's beautiful…it's so…*you*. I want to hear all about him."

"He's kind, and tries really hard to be funny."

We both laughed.

"Tell me about the wedding."

"It was small." I looked down, rubbing my knee. "We went to the courthouse. Only a few people."

"What did I wear?" she asked in a tone of jest.

Silence took me. Unable to hold back, my chin ruptured with quakes. Understanding was in her eyes.

"It was my cancer diagnosis, wasn't it?"

I nodded.

"How's your dad? Your sister?"

"They're good. It was hard to lose you, and it took the three of us a long time to adjust, but we've learned how to deal with the loss. I mean, in the best way we could."

She reached for me, and I fell into her chest.

"I figured out time travel so I could see you again."

"You figured out time travel to see me, and I don't even have anything exciting to tell you," she said, her hand moving in small circles on my back.

For the first time, I realized Abel often offered the same gesture of comfort that my mom always had.

"I'm just happy to be here with you," I said.

"I wish your dad was home to see you."

From her statement, I'd understood that altering the timeline in The Reckoning to save Dad prevented his death *backward* in time, too. I hadn't considered that effect. Because of that time alteration, she didn't lose him. They were still married and living happily.

I sat up, folding my hands together, preparing to tell her why I'd gone through my grief, accepted her loss, and then after all of it, jumped backward in time to see her.

"Mom, I'm here with a request." I bit my lip with hesitation. "I'm not sure how you're going to feel about this."

"Go ahead. Tell me."

I stared at her, considering my words. Finally, I just blurted it out. "I want to bring you into the future." She blinked through squinted eyes. "I've only figured out time travel into the past. I've been working on how to get into the future for a while now, and I think I've got my finger on it. I've come to finalize my testing."

"Honey," she said with a look on her face that reminded me of the time I invited her bungee jumping. She wasn't a big risk-taker.

"It's perfectly safe. I've time traveled plenty of times and it hasn't caused me harm…well, the physics of time travel haven't caused me harm." I adjusted my posture to show her my professionalism. "I'm not just trying to avoid all of this," I said, gesturing to her cancer as if it was something that could be physically identified. "According to my research, I can only bring someone I'm a descendant of."

"Why not your dad?" she asked, still painted with apprehension.

The tension in her eyes didn't give me confidence that she'd agree to do this.

"Look." I sat upright, prepared to convince her. "You're currently in the beginning stages of your cancer. If you come with me to my present, medically, you'd have a much better outcome of surviving this."

"Sweetheart, I…" she trailed off. "It's just an overwhelming idea for me to grasp. All of this is. Seeing you—from the future. Learning I died from the cancer, and then this offer to bypass it by traveling to the future with you to treat it…" She busied her hands straightening the pillows near her. "Does it hurt?"

"Time travel? No, it doesn't hurt. It feels like the rush of a rollercoaster free falling." Her eyes bulged.

"You hate roller coasters," she said.

I nodded. "Indeed, I do."

"Being that you're on a time travel right now, does that mean when you go home you'll go right back to the instant you left?"

"I could return to that moment in time, but it's easier to avoid memory overlaps from rewritten timelines if I return to the actual present and miss what happened while I was time traveling."

"That's a bit confusing." She held a pillow on her lap as she listened.

"It just means I don't go back to the moment I left, although I could. Instead, I program my return time in this," I held up my wrist to show her my Timed Release Band, "to send me home to the present."

"I see," she said. "If you took me with you to the future, then I'd be missing whatever happens here while I'm gone."

"You could think of it like traveling anywhere, really. While you're not here, you miss what's happening without you."

"The question I'm really asking then is how would I explain my absence?"

I nodded. "You could always just stay with me." A nervous laugh left me. Her surprise was evident as it replaced the tension in her eyes.

"Will you consider time travel, Mom?"

I felt selfish allowing my ulterior motive to save her take center stage. My proclaimed need of my mom to achieve future time travel was clearly not my main motive

A tight-lipped smile inched along her normally wide, toothy grin.

"I know it's a lot to think about. I'll let you mull it over," I said.

"I will. I'll think about it," she finally said.

Instead of getting to my feet and leaving my mom to consider my offer, I lowered my head back onto her chest. She reached for my hand and continued to study my wedding band, rubbing the stone under her thumb. I wondered what she was thinking about. I'd imagined she was picturing my wedding day without her.

"You were with me," I told her.

"What, sweetheart?"

"On my wedding day. You were on my mind. I sewed a piece of your favorite blanket into my wedding dress, and your picture was in my bouquet of Forget-Me-Nots."

"I'm sorry I wasn't there."

"Mom, please. You don't have anything to be sorry about. I'm the one who has apologies to make."

"Whatever for?" She lifted me from her and looked at me with tight eyes.

I swear she could see every ounce of shame I'd carried about the way I handled her dying.

"When you got sick, really sick…" She reached for my hand again, this time holding it between both of hers. "I wasn't around. I left a lot. Spent most of my time at Dr. Pasterski's."

She brushed her hand down my cheek, rested it under my chin, then tilted my face to hers. No other person on Earth could console and comfort me the way she did.

"You did the best you could with the hand you were dealt," Mom said. "I wouldn't have wanted you taking care of me in my final days. I would've preferred you to do what you did. You know, your dad and I arranged that mentorship with Dr. Pasterski for a reason. She is a friend of ours that we carefully selected to be a part of your life. You are my shining star, and I love you. Never be sorry about being that little girl. Forgive her."

She didn't know about Dad and Dr. P. I remembered our Sunday dinner together the previous week. The way we felt like family.

Suddenly, I was feeling the reality of bringing my mom to the future. She would have to experience her husband with a new love, and she wouldn't be able to feel the pain of that in honesty because he had done nothing wrong in finding comfort with Dr. Pasterski.

Mom had been gone for so long before he even allowed himself to laugh again. He never betrayed the love he felt for her. What would this do to him? To Dr. Pasterski? They would both be happy to have her back, I assumed, but what of the cost?

"I understand why it's a hard concept for you to consider—coming to the future," I said. "If you decide not to, I get it. I won't force it. But maybe you don't come to stay. Maybe you just come with me to help me test my theory—and see Ruth, possibly Dad," I lifted my ringed hand, "meet Abel—and then we return you here."

She gathered my hair together and twisted it around her fingers. "Maybe," she said. "It does sound like a fascinating invitation. I can't imagine getting to see everyone having aged. Just seeing you has been extraordinary. And I would love to meet the man you married."

I glanced at my wrist, assessing the TRB for how long I had left before it automatically sent me home. The preset hour was almost up; it would never be enough time.

"You know, you can talk it over with Dad," I suggested.

"What do you mean?" She pinched her brows together.

"He already knows I discovered time travel. I visited him like this once before. I actually saved his life, too."

"I cannot believe…" Her words faltered and the baffled expression that took form left me regretting having told her. This was the sort of alteration I shouldn't have interfered with in my past timeline. "…he's never told me about this."

"I don't want to start trouble between the two of you, but," I chuckled, "he doesn't tell you a lot of things."

Instant regret for making light of this revelation left me choking back my laugh. My mom was not entertained. Her eyes narrowed. She slid the pillow off her lap and folded her hands in its place.

"Anything else I should know about?" she asked.

"Just that you picked a good guy there, Mom. You should be proud of him. I am."

The sentiment melted her icy glare. She squeezed my arm. "Can you stay longer? I'm sensing you're getting ready to leave."

"I should get going. If I settle in too long here with you, I'll never leave."

"I bet your husband is waiting for you to get home," she said, brushing her fingers on my wedding band again. I pulled my hand away and stared hard at my knees, hoping she didn't see the guilt sweep across my face.

"What's going on, Taden? I know that look."

She waited expectantly. A long silence lingered. My mom didn't stir.

Finally, I admitted, "He doesn't know I'm here."

She sighed her disapproval. "It's not good practice, that. Just because it seems like your father is all right with keeping secrets from me doesn't mean it is a good way to operate in a marriage."

"I feel terrible about sneaking behind his back, but he didn't think I should come here. And he doesn't think I should bring you to the present."

I hated telling her these truths, because I was afraid she would agree with him. She grimaced, which didn't make me feel any less terrible.

"Would you be able to accept it if I came back to my present afterward?" she asked. It gave me hope she'd entertain the possibility of visiting.

My eyes big, I said, "Yes, you could definitely return if you wanted." I paused, reaching into my bag for a DNA kit. "I need a tissue sample from you. When I go back home, I'll need to create a serum mixed with DNA from both of us that will give you the ability to time travel forward. That's the part I'm testing out, if you agree to it."

She was hesitant, but held out her arm.

I fought the urge to sink into that timeline and spend the rest of my life there with her. While my internal storm brewed between staying and rushing back to the NIST to mix her serum, my only solace was that I could come back to her as soon as the serum was mixed.

"Before you spend too much thought considering whether you want to come into the future with me, I feel like I should tell you something. But I only want to tell you about it if you're honestly going to consider time traveling."

"You should tell me," she said.

"This is hard to say." I bit my bottom lip considering how to say it. "Dad and Dr. Pasterski…"

"… are together?" she inserted, giving me a knowing smile.

"How could you know that?"

"I'm a perceptive person." She placed her hand on top of mine. "You don't need to worry about any of that. Your dad loves me and I love him. In his future, where I'm not, if he's found happiness with the stunning woman that is Dr. Pasterski, I am happy for them."

I don't know if I imagined the sadness I picked up from her, or if it really was there in her posture.

"It's not going to make you feel hurt?" I didn't want to say the word "jealous". It's such an ugly word, but if my mom felt it about Dr. P and Dad, it was completely justifiable.

"I bet this news will be more difficult for your version of your father," she said. "He has no idea what's in store for him."

We grimaced at the thought of him being caught off guard by her presence.

Listening to my mom restate Abel's warnings only added to my guilty conscience. "If you talk to Dad about this now, then my version of Dad will know it's coming. He'll know it all along."

"And Dr. Pasterski? All she's done for my family? I can only imagine how she would feel. She may doubt if he loved her enough to stay with her, or worry that he will leave to be with me. Wondering if *you*," she tilted her head my way, "would still love her the same way you did when she was the mother figure in your life. Maybe she'd even wonder, if these cancer treatments save me, if it would change the outcome in the whole family." She looked at her hands, wringing them in her lap like I've seen Ruth do countless times. "These are human responses," she said. "The truth is, darling, I still have cancer. You might've talked me into coming into the future with you to receive treatment, but even that isn't guaranteed to heal me." Her hands now flat on her knees, she looked me square in the eyes. "If I do agree to this, and it is successful, I already know I will still need to go back to you. To my version of you, here." She gestured toward my bedroom door.

"Considering the things you've said, I don't think it's a good idea." I couldn't believe I'd said anything that might make her reconsider, but Abel's concerns suddenly became clearer in my thoughts. "If you respond positively to the treatment in the future, but then come back to this timeline, it could alter everything we know about our lives."

She folded her hands. I hadn't ever noticed how many of my mom's mannerisms Ruth had. I really didn't want to discuss with my mom all the ways that her surviving cancer in this timeline would be negative. It seemed like insanity to even entertain the butterfly effect of her survival.

I released a heavy sigh and repeated the mantra Ruth had instilled about changing our timeline to see our mom.

"I might not develop time travel if you survive in this timeline. It was born from my drive to see you again. And if I don't develop time travel, the country will be destroyed by a terrorist event. So many awful things happened during that attack."

"A terrorist attack? Here?" She lifted her hand to her lips in dismay.

"Mm-hm. It was hard to believe even as it played out right in front of my eyes." I tilted my head toward her. "I've tried to forget about the terrorist attacks though. Mom, you would have to choose to either remain here," I pointed to the couch cushion beneath me and broke eye contact, "and let cancer defeat you, or come with me permanently and beat it in the future. That way we don't drastically interfere with the timeline."

"This makes my decision a bit more complex," she admitted.

"As a physicist, I'm hoping you will do this to help me move forward with my technology. And as far as the physics of this go, that doesn't mean you *must* receive cancer treatment or even be in the future for very long. The science aspect wouldn't require any amount of time from you that would seem out of context to your present. Mom, we really need future time travel. It could be key to prevent a dangerous person from destroying humanity." I closed my eyes, sensing that I should give her a fair chance to turn the invitation down. "But we aren't without other options if you decide you don't want to participate. I get it. I just really want it to be you."

Her eyes widened. "I have so many questions! Are you in danger?"

I continued before she fully launched into her worried interrogation.

"But the physicist aside, the regular everyday person, Taden, *I* need you to do this." My throat constricted as I forced the words out. "I've become detached. I still don't know how to live without you, and I don't know how to stay open to people."

It was dumbfounding how easily I shared these dark, internal struggles with my mom. These were feelings I had locked away and kept from everyone, and they were just pouring from me to her.

"I know your version of me will survive without you," I said. "I've done that part. But I don't know if *I* will survive without you again." I put my hand on my chest, just to soften the ache. "I feel like I'm slowly disappearing, and I need my mom."

My chin quivered so that I barely forced out my last sentence.

"I understand that you feel like you need me," she said. "And it's nice to be needed. But don't you see what you have become, and what you have accomplished without me?"

"None of that matters," I said.

She chuckled. It was my turn to give her an icy stare for laughing at my expense.

She put her hand to her mouth. "I apologize for laughing. But really, that's the most ridiculous thing you've ever said." She reached out to me and lifted my chin to look her in the eyes. I felt like a little girl. "You listen to me, Taden Barrett. You can manage without me in your life. You have love. You have passion. You have important work. And sweetheart, even if I'm not with you, you have me."

I wanted to beg her to come and stay with me. Like a child, I wanted to kick and scream until I got my way. She expected me to accept—with grace—a life without her, no matter if I talked her into time travel or not. The lump in my throat expanded to the point where I could no longer deny its force.

My mom pulled me to her chest and wrapped her arms around me until my sobbing subsided.

Finally I said, "Even if I don't get to hold on forever, I've finally been vindicated with what I wanted from time travel to begin with—you."

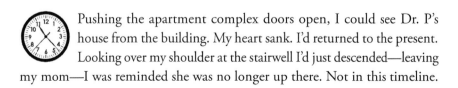 Pushing the apartment complex doors open, I could see Dr. P's house from the building. My heart sank. I'd returned to the present.

Looking over my shoulder at the stairwell I'd just descended—leaving my mom—I was reminded she was no longer up there. Not in this timeline.

If I decided to turn around and make my way back to our apartment, I'd find a new family.

A renewed sense of loss burned in my chest, but it was missing the regret I'd carried with me into adulthood. Grounding myself, I reflected deeper, and I was surprised to find that regret *was* there. This time, my regret felt like betrayal to the living—my dad and Dr. Pasterski in particular. I was going to have to prepare them, at some point, to be ready for the possibility of my mom coming to this point in time with me.

But first, I had to tell Abel and Ruth.

· · · · · · ● ● ● ● ● ● ● ● ● ● · · · · ·

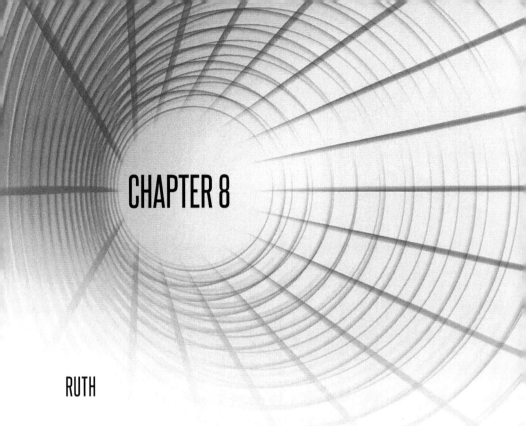

# CHAPTER 8

## RUTH

"I can't tell you how happy it makes me to have you visit without a major 'save the world' angle," I said, reaching for her luggage.

Taden grimaced, a look of guilt flooding her face. "Don't get used to it. I'm sure the world will fall apart before intermission."

I smirked and lifted the suitcase into my trunk. "Geez, what do you have in this thing?"

"Gotta be prepared," she said, shrugging. "Where are we going to eat?"

"I made a reservation right around the corner from our show so we can walk to the theater right after dinner."

"Nice." She clapped her hands together in approval. "But can we pick up something little now? I'm actually starving. Didn't eat at the airport."

"Which do you prefer? Pizza or fries?" I asked, starting the car.

"Both," Taden said, smacking her lips.

Smiling at her, I said, "I'll stop at the pizza joint at the end of my block." She nodded with fervor.

"I have exciting news," I said as I merged into the flow of traffic. "I've been waiting to tell you in person, and I can't wait another minute."

"Tell me," she said, turning her body in earnest. "Tell me!"

I checked my rearview mirror and switched lanes. "I've decided," I started, glancing out of the corner of my eye as I continued to keep my view on the road, "to launch my own PR firm." My eyes big from the announcement.

"Oh my goodness!" she squealed. "That's amazing!"

"Yep. After the Inaugural Ball, business has been pouring in. I just started to think, I could really go anywhere and do this."

"Anywhere?" Her forehead crinkled the way it did when she got worried. "Where are you thinking?"

"Are you ready for this?" I asked.

"I think so…"

"I'm coming home." I slapped her arm. "I've already made an offer on an office space in Baltimore, and I have my eyes on a few apartments halfway between there and Gaithersburg."

"Agh!" She squealed a new pitch this time. "That's incredible news. When do you move?"

"I've already started packing boxes," I said, chuckling. "I can't wait to move home."

"I'm surprised to hear you say that," Taden admitted.

"I've been really busy at work, but as soon as I get home I'm alone. Most of the time I'm okay with it, but some nights I can't shake the loneliness."

"You haven't said anything to me about this." Her brooding expression was on display as she mentally recounted any evidence she might've missed of my sadness.

"Yeah, I know. It's just been some nights that I really feel it. But the next day, I'm fine."

I didn't intend to tell her about the drugs. She continued to furrow her brow, waiting for me to tell her more.

"My lease is up next month, so in a few months I'll be home and this won't be an issue."

She breathed a sigh of relief. "I totally thought you were going to crush me with an announcement that you were headed to a sunnier, much-farther-away location."

"Believe me, I considered it, but ultimately, I just want to be closer to you, Dad, and Dr. P." I glanced over at Taden. "Your face is all red," I said with a little chuckle.

"I'm just excited." Taden pulled the visor down to check herself out in the mirror. "My cheeks always betray me."

"How's married life treating you?" I asked.

"It's actually wonderful. But, you know, I *am* married to Abel, so." She shrugged and gave me a wry smile.

"You guys talking about kids yet?"

"Ruth, I've been married for like, five minutes. Relax."

"I know, I know. Just asking."

Taden looked as though she'd fallen into deep thought about the baby question.

After a long moment, she told me, "You'd be the first we tell, if or when…"

I smiled brightly. "I better be." Inside, I wondered if I really would be. Loneliness occasionally invaded my daytime thoughts, too.

But Taden didn't need to worry about me.

I had this under control.

· · · · · · · · · ● · · · · · · · · ·

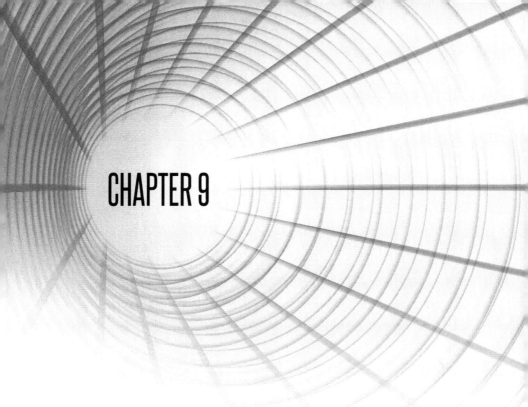

# CHAPTER 9

As intermission crept closer, I noticed Taden's anxious glances.

"You good?" I whispered. "You seem like you're worried about something."

She nodded, sipping her wine, like it was delivering her a sense of peace. I thought she'd probably want more wine after the show, but I knew I didn't have any at my apartment. Being a recovering addict who was recently experiencing bouts of depression and just underwent an embarrassing relapse, I generally didn't keep any drinks on hand.

Throughout most of the last act, I felt her stare. She was more interested in my profile than the show. The theater usually brought me childhood nostalgia that'd leave me gaping with a painted smile throughout the whole show. However, my usual easy distraction was repeatedly interrupted by Taden's watchful eyes.

Then she whispered, "I wish Mom was here."

I was surprised to find her eyes glassy, with a pained tinge in her cheeks.

"Me too," I whispered back, pulling her hand into my lap.

We finished watching the play without further exchanges and walked back to my place in silence. I kept feeling the sense that Taden had more to say, but it wasn't until we were hanging up our coats that she finally found the gumption to speak.

"I've done it," she told me.

"Oh geez," I said, walking to the kitchen for a drink. "When you're vague like that, it never means anything good." I filled my glass with ice, enjoying how the cubes clinked together as each one dropped. "You want some water?"

"I'm good," she said. "Unless you have a bottle of wine around here."

I grimaced. "Sorry, no wine." I sipped my water as I made my way over to the counter that opened from my kitchen into the living room. "All right, tell me what you've done."

"As per usual, what I'm about to tell you is a secret," she said.

"Obviously," I agreed.

"This time it's a secret even from the NIST. Only Abel and I know."

My mouth gaped. "Okay, you're going to need to tell me why that is."

"I'll tell you that part later. The big news first. I think I figured out future time travel."

"Wow. I never doubted—when did you do this?"

"Very recently. Just this past week, actually." She hesitated, like she was second guessing if she should continue, but after a moment of pause she went on. "Do you want to hear the most amazing part about it?"

"Of course," I said, setting my ice water on the counter. I leaned onto my forearms, giving her my full attention.

"The breakthrough to go forward instead of backward might be that the DNA of the genetic match just needs to be from someone born of the traveler's family line—after the traveler's birth."

I furrowed my brow, trying to understand. "You mean, like, your kid?"

"Yes," she said. "Or grandkid. And so on."

"That's a problem then, isn't it?" I paused. "You don't have kids."

She nodded like she was waiting for me to arrive at the point.

"How did you even figure this out?" I regretted asking as soon as it left my lips. There would be no chance that her scientific brain could explain that process to me in a way that I would follow.

"What do you mean?" she asked, instead of diving into her time-travel theories.

"I mean, if you and Abel are keeping this secret and, in order to get to the future, you need a child of your own, who will you use to get into the future?" I gulped down the rest of my water. "You have to tell someone else about this. I mean, I don't have a kid to offer up." I picked my glass up again to pull a broken chunk of ice into my mouth. Crunching it, I said, "Oh! You should have Dad time travel. You're his kid."

Her smile rewarded me for getting to this thought, but then her eyes trained on the swirl of my granite countertop.

"You know, I think I will have a glass of water." She walked around the kitchen island and over to my cupboards for a glass. I didn't move from my position, but I watched her. She looked at me, amused with herself. "You know I'm going to get thirsty after I eat the rest of this leftover pizza," she said, pulling the box from the fridge.

"Do I get to know why this is a secret from the people who usually make you keep all of these secrets in the first place?" I asked.

"So my glass of water distraction didn't really work?" she asked, laughing at herself.

"You're the one who brought this up."

"Touché," she said.

"All right. I can tell this discussion has run its course. Let me know when you've figured it out, okay?"

"You want a piece of pizza?" she asked as she agreed to keep me in the loop.

How could I have known I was only a thought away from arriving at her confession? How could she know I was already having anxiety about the fact she was leaving in the morning, and I would be alone in this apartment again?

· · * * · · ● ● ● ● ● ● ● ● ● ● ● · · ·

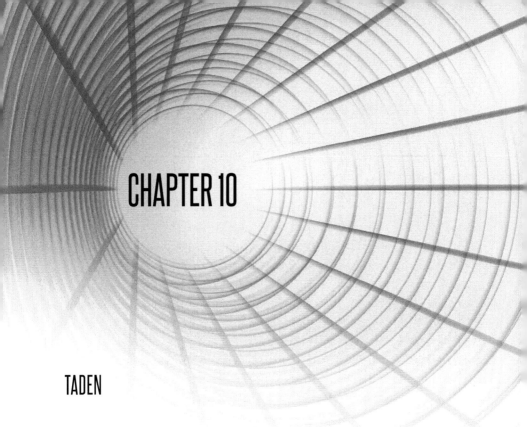

# CHAPTER 10

## TADEN

To keep Dakotah and Quinn safely in the dark, I didn't work on my mom's time-travel serum at the NIST. Instead, I went to Dr. Pasterski's lab.

Since I still hadn't admitted to Abel or Ruth that I'd time traveled again, this secret weighed heavier with each day. And each day, I justified what I had done with the simple fact that time travel existed for the sole reason that I needed to see my mom and make amends. I never got to fulfill that purpose, and they both knew it. Neither of them should be surprised that I went to see her.

"I'm holding on to information," I said, following Dr. P down her hallway. "I've done something, and it's eating me up." I couldn't bring myself to look at her straight, but I felt her watching me as she slid the key into the lock.

"Oh?" She turned to me, the door open behind her. "Would you like to talk about it?"

Her voice was gentle and mothering. I barely nodded.

"Certainly, my girl." Dr. P swiftly glided her hand through a strand of my hair. "Would you like a cup of tea?"

I nodded again.

She had been a stand-in mother to Ruth and me since Mom died, and now she was my dad's companion. We'd become a family. If I owed anyone the truth about time travel, it was Dr. P.

"I don't know how to say this to you."

Admittedly, I was finally feeling the reality of my decision—what Abel had more than once tried to get me to consider. Even my mom had done her best to show me the cons of this plan, and I was only now understanding them.

"Sweetheart, just say it. Once it's out in the open, it will hold no more power over you," she said.

"I went into the past."

Still avoiding eye contact, I traced my finger along the rim of my teacup, peering up for only a quick glance before I admitted the rest.

"I went to see my mom," I finally said, then quickly averted my eyes to my tea—of which I took a long, noisy sip.

"I see." Her tone was still offering me support. "And what happened there?"

I listened harder to her voice for any indication this conversation was painful for her, but all I found was understanding. It was such a relief to talk about this.

"All these years," I said, my voice faltering. After clearing my throat, I sipped more tea before starting again. "All these years, I hadn't been able to make peace with the way things were between my mom and me when she died."

"I've watched you struggle with that as you grew," she said.

I nodded. "I know you have, and you were a great help to me through all of it." My smile was an offer of love to Dr. P. "I was able to address all of that baggage with my mom and... I don't know." I shrugged. "I feel like a weight has been lifted."

"I can see how that would be a good feeling. I'm a little confused, though." Her voice pulled the slightest bit tighter as she smoothed imaginary wrinkles in her tablecloth.

I stopped fidgeting with my cup, looking at her aged hands busy ironing the linen.

"About what?" I asked, not sure why her tone had changed.

"Why do you seem burdened by this?" she said, her hands not yet stilled.

"I haven't told you everything," I admitted.

"Ah." She pressed her lips together, then let them roll slowly apart. "Okay, well, go on."

I took a quick breath before I told her the most difficult part of my admission. "I visited my mom to request that she travel here with me."

Thoughts ran through my mind about how selfish I was. Dr. P needed to know this wasn't just a childish ploy to get my mom back. Her lips parted to ask a question, but I beat her to it.

"You've probably deduced that I think I know how to get into the future." When she didn't respond, I continued. "I mixed my DNA with my mom's in order to test my theory."

In the quiet that pervaded, I resumed tracing the rim of my teacup. It was actually ludicrous, I realized, for me to be sitting at this table, asking the woman who'd essentially raised me to help bring my mom back. I could only imagine, too late, that she must've feared losing all of us—my dad, Ruth, and me—to my mom.

I cleared my throat again. "You and I don't usually talk about this sort of stuff," I said, wondering why everything that came out of my mouth seemed to make the moment worse. "What I mean is, most of our time together has an intended goal and that's the way we get on." I took a sip of my tea, hoping to steady my nerves. "Telling you all of this was difficult for me, but I wanted you to know before anyone else."

"Thank you for telling me," she offered. But the tension I'd carefully searched her voice for registered with her higher pitch and sharper cadence.

"I don't want to hurt you." I reached my hand across the table. "Or have you wondering about your place in our lives."

She rose and retrieved the kettle. She promptly flipped up the faucet and held the kettle beneath the running water. Her eyes were intensely focused on the stream. It wasn't like her to turn her back to me in the middle of me talking to her. I worried that with her abruptness and perceived displeasure that she was upset with me.

"I'm not bringing her here to replace you." I joined her at the sink. "We love you, and would never want that." When she didn't break from the hypnosis of refilling her kettle, I reached for her shoulder. "You should know, my dad is *with* you. He's not going to leave you."

Dr. P's hand momentarily rested on top of mine before she slipped away to place the kettle back on the burner and tap the stovetop controls to heat the water.

I couldn't seem to stop talking. "By my calculations, he already knows she's coming." Her eyes narrowed. "When I left, my mom said she was going to tell him. I'm sure that means she's talking to him about it in the past—probably as we speak."

"Dual timelines," Dr. Pasterksi muttered.

I nodded, relieved she was finally joining the conversation. "That means he entered this relationship with you, he moved into this home *with you*, already knowing she would be back in his life one day. Whatever my mom and dad decided about this reunion, he *chose* to be with you."

Dr. Pasterski's lip quivered while she brushed my cheek with the back of her fingers. "My girl, your words mean so much. I was a friend to your mom, too, you know, and I don't wish to cause her any heartache."

"My mom's a strong woman. If she decides to come with me, this will have been a factor in her decision."

"I'm still curious." Dr. Pasterski said, pouring the steaming water into each of our cups.

"About what?" I asked, feeling a bit of relief that she seemed to be resuming her natural posture.

"You mentioned that you wanted to tell me before anyone else. Does that mean Abel doesn't know you've been to see your mom?"

My face flushed. "I know. I should've been honest with him." The shame pulled my shoulders into a slump. "It's funny."

"What is?"

"My mom clued into the very same detail… and I get the impression you agree with her advice."

"No doubt your mom thought it was a bad choice to keep something this big from your husband as well."

Like an internal warning system had been triggered, powerful nausea took hold of me, turning my skin clammy. Covering my mouth, I ran to the bathroom just in time to be sick. The contents of my stomach emptying into the toilet reminded me of a few months prior, when I found out the truth about Danika—which in turn made me vomit further.

Dr. P followed behind me. "Oh, dear. You look terrible." She retrieved a hand towel from the cupboard and ran it under cool water. "This is too much for your body to handle." Wringing it out, she studied me with worry lines on her face. "Here—put this on your forehead," she said, offering me the cool, damp towel.

With the cloth against my skin, I said, "I think it was the prospect of having to tell Abel where I went that made me sick. He voiced his disapproval, but I went anyway."

"It won't be an easy conversation. But he loves you." The way she said this with such matter-of-factness soothed my anxiety.

# CHAPTER 11

The drive home became a last-minute cramming session for my conversation with Abel. If I was being honest, I hadn't allowed myself to consider this part of the decision. I didn't want to entertain any ideas that might deter me from going home. But what was the alternative? For him to learn about this when he met my dead mom face-to-face?

Another wave of nausea rushed through me, much more intense than the first. I pulled the car off and ran to a roadside ditch just in time to puke again. And again, Danika's face filled my thoughts. Would I forever link that awful woman with vomit? It was satisfying to believe my brain had made that association.

While staggering back to my car and wiping my sleeve across my mouth, another off-the-wall thought popped into my mind. Searching my mobile, I tapped through my apps to check the date.

"Holy crap," I whispered. Was this really possible? I hadn't even visualized myself in this role yet. I had to get home and find out. This would make for an even more intense conversation.

I peeled into the driveway and slammed my foot on the brake, jamming the parking gear in place. In a mad hurry to get out of the car, my forceful exit exacted an equivalent push-back.

"Oh my gosh," I muttered in frustration, having forgotten to release my seatbelt. "Oh my gosh," I repeated.

After pausing to reset and allowing for a measured breath, I pressed my seatbelt release and leaped from the car. I charged through the front door in just a few large strides then screamed wildly.

"Abel?"

No response. He seemed to be nowhere I poked my head. I ran to the garage door, checking for his car.

"Thank God," I muttered, taking in his black Mustang before bolting up the stairs.

"Abel?" My voice was tenuous.

"I'm in the bathroom. I'll be out in a minute," he replied.

While pacing back and forth on our shag carpet, I caught sight of myself in our full-length mirror. I stopped mid-step and turned sideways, studying my profile. I stood as erect as I could, sucked in my belly, and looked over my appearance. Abel walked in, catching my self-inspection.

"Isn't she gorgeous?" he said, as if he was chatting with a buddy.

"I hope you still feel that way after we talk." My guilt was not to be outdone by my excitement.

"Uh-oh. That doesn't sound good," he said, his eyes questioning me.

I took hold of his hand and guided him to our bed. We sat on the edge, facing one another.

"Should I be worried?" he asked, barely audible. "Because I feel worried."

"Do you want the good news, or the bad news?"

He brought his palm to his face. "I don't like this."

"How about the good news first?" I asked. "I don't particularly want to tell you the bad news, so the good news might be a welcome distraction."

He groaned. "Okay. What's the good news?"

"I keep getting super nauseated," I said.

"That's the good news?" He looked at me with big eyes. "Maybe don't tell me the bad news then."

"I thought I was feeling sick from the time travel, but then I got sick again at Dr. P's and…"

"Wait. What time travel?" He stood from the bed.

"I'll address that question when I get to the bad news. Let me finish the good news first."

Abel licked his lips and folded his arms across his chest. "Okay."

"I felt sick again on the way home. I had to pull over. Anyway, as I was walking back to my car, it occurred to me that I hadn't started my period yet this month, and so I checked my period tracker, and I'm two weeks late. Abel, I might be pregnant!"

The pure joy in his blinking eyes left him frozen everywhere else.

"I know! Isn't it exciting?" I screamed. "I got a few pregnancy tests last week, since we'd talked about trying. I'm taking one right now!" I said as I ran into the bathroom and rummaged in the drawer I'd tossed them. Closing the door, I slid my pants down. Peeing on a stick was much more exciting than I'd ever considered it could be.

"We have to wait a few minutes before we know for sure," I said after pulling up my pants and returning to the bedroom. "Why don't you reveal the results? It'll be fun!" I hitched my thumb toward the bathroom where the test sat on the sink, already undergoing its chemical reaction.

"Yeah!" He was on his feet. "Yes!" He nodded. "Absolutely."

He stumbled into the bathroom with me following closely on his heels. Leaning over the bathroom sink, waiting as the indicator soaked up my fluids, Abel grabbed my hand.

"So," he said, "you said there was bad news?"

"One thing at a time," I told him, wishing I didn't have to explain.

I buried my head into his back, waiting for the results.

It struck me that, for the first time since the earth-shattering revelation that Danika Farkas was not the leader I believed her to be, I didn't feel detached. With my head resting on Abel, I felt deeply connected to him. My mom had just held me in her arms for the first time since I was fifteen years old. Her scent lingered on my clothing even then. In the moments I waited to learn if I was pregnant, I wished Ruth was with me. I missed her in my soul. I imagined the way I would tell my best friend, Dakotah, about my baby. I pictured the smile on her face while she'd wag her finger.

And it was like I forgot for a minute, all about isolation. I forgot how, yesterday, the distance I felt from everyone was so overwhelming that I thought I might die of it. Only one day had offered a completely different perspective.

I put my hand on my belly and wished this to be my future. As I did, Abel's knees buckled. He caught himself on the cabinet.

"Whoa!" I said, reaching for him.

"You're pregnant. There's a baby in there," he said pointing to my middle. "You. Are. Pregnant." His hands went to his cheeks in excited disbelief. Tears spilled down my cheeks and he pulled me to his chest. I etched every detail—every feeling, every smell, the way his hands tapped along my shirt, all of it—into my memory.

Bad news had no place here.

"What in the world do we do now?" I asked through laughing tears. "I don't know any babies or anything about babies."

Abel pulled himself away from the hold he had so he could see me clearly. "We are going to be the best parents ever. We'll figure it out together." And then he squeezed me back into his embrace.

"We have to tell someone! I cannot keep this news secret!"

"Agreed!" he said. "Who should we tell?"

In unison we both said, "Ruth."

I whipped my phone from my back pocket and pressed Ruth's contact. While listening to the phone ring on her end, I whispered, "Pick up. Pick up."

"Hello?" she asked into the receiver.

"Agh!" I screamed into her ear. I imagined her pulling the phone away, and I waited a beat to ensure she'd returned it back to her ear. "I'm pregnant!"

Ruth echoed my scream. I, in turn, pulled my phone away. Maniacal laughter ensued.

"When did you find out?" she asked.

"Literally just a minute ago," I said. "Abel is still standing in the bathroom, holding the test in his hand."

"Oh my gosh! This is amazing." She took exaggerated breaths. "I'm going to be Aunt Ruth!" she said, followed by more squealing.

"This little human is going to call me Mom!" I uttered in disbelief, looking down at my stomach—which did not reveal any indication of holding a tiny person. "That doesn't even make sense!" After a fit of giggles, I said, "Okay, I've got to get back to Abel. I just wanted to tell you as soon as I found out," I said, and for good measure, I slipped in, "Oh, listen, I have other big news to tell you later. Are you coming into town this weekend?"

"I am now! We have baby shopping to do!"

"All right. It's a date. See you this weekend."

Abel sat on the edge of the bed, contemplative, while he watched me share the good news. "And, this bad news? You have to tell Ruth, too?"

I cringed.

"I don't want to ruin this beautiful moment," I told him.

"We'll talk about it tomorrow," he said to my relief. "But tomorrow, Taden." His brows rose to make his point.

"I promise," I agreed.

"We have a family," he said, looking at me with his ocean eyes.

# CHAPTER 12

## RUTH

I could usually predict when Taden was keeping something big from me. I saw it on her face the night she first told me about time travel, then again when she told me she saved the boy version of Marius—after the adult version of him killed her—in another timeline.

It's not always easy to tell people you care for about the very difficult decisions you've had to make. I understood the underlying concern that someone you love might take your honesty and walk away from you. Taden couldn't possibly think I'd ever leave her though.

I knew the baby news at Friday dinner with Dad and Dr. P was going to be followed up with a one-on-one about this other big news. I suppose I was preparing myself to be understanding and accepting of whatever she'd been keeping from me, because I had news of my own to reveal to her.

This was how life went as a result of living in different states. I didn't want to be hypocritical. Besides, soon enough I would be living back home, and we would have more daily face time with each other.

· · · · · ● ● ● ● ● ● ● ● ● ● · · · ·

# CHAPTER 13

I pulled into the NIST parking lot with a carry-out order for Dakotah. She'd asked for an extra side of fries, which made me smile. I wasn't eating anything because of Friday dinner. The security guard saw me approaching the doors and buzzed me in.

"Hi, Maxine," I said.

"Hi, honey," she replied. "Dakotah called ahead for ya. You can go on up."

I smiled brightly at Maxine. She'd called ahead for me? That was thoughtful of her.

Did I have butterflies in my stomach? This was silly. Why was I getting nervous? It was just Dakotah.

She was waiting to let me in. I swear she beamed when she saw me. The glass door between us kept it muffled, but it looked very much like an audible noise left her lips. Dakotah pushed the door open with a burst of excited energy.

"I'm glad you're here—and you have fries!" She gave me a quick squeeze and waved me inside with her. I followed to her office, which led right past Taden's. My sister's office was empty, which was a relief, because this was the first time I'd ever been to her workplace when I wasn't there for her.

"Taden already left for your dad's house," Dakotah said. "She seemed jazzed about tonight's dinner. You know anything about that?"

I raised my right brow and pursed my lips. "Actually, she has her own big news to share."

"Whew! Those Barrett sisters, always keeping the secrets!"

"Tell me about it."

"You know you're one of those sisters, right?" Dakotah pointed at me.

"I do."

I locked eyes with her as we walked in step. We walked in silence the rest of the way to her office, and I was conscious of how comfortable and intimate it felt.

Once in her office, I set the food on the counter where she spent so much of her time studying the microscopic world.

"Whatcha working on?" I gestured to her scope.

"Still trying to get your sister into the future," she said, reaching for the fries. "At the moment, it's extremely frustrating. We're right there. I can feel it."

"You guys will figure it out soon."

Not sure what came over me, I brushed my fingers along her arm. It was so out of place, instant regret took hold.

As I pulled my hand away she found my retreating fingers with hers, slowly dragging them along my skin, all while giving me a knowing smile. Dizzying sensations filled my body. I was stunned by her fluidity. Not until later did I recognize she had made the first move.

"Want some?" She held the container in my direction.

"Sure, thanks." I pulled a perfectly salted fry from the container. "Who would turn down a French fry?" I asked.

"That's what I'm saying."

She held my gaze with a quirky smile. A tension built between us, and Dakotah was clearly comfortable orchestrating it.

"Do you and Taden have plans afterward?"

"Other than her big reveal?" I replied. "I don't think so."

"Are you staying at Taden's this weekend?"

Twice I had referred to Taden's news, but Dakotah didn't urge me to reveal anything. This was one of the features Taden loved most about her best friend; the way she respected privacy created a trustworthiness about her.

"I didn't ask her. I thought I might finally try staying at my dad's," I said.

She shoveled in a few fries, coyly peeking at me from beneath her hooded eyes. "You know, you're welcome to come hang out at my house after dinner."

She paused and downed a few more fries, moving her focus on the burger. "You can stay the night, too."

She said this so quickly I barely registered the entirety of her offer before she swiveled her stool around, sinking her teeth into the sandwich.

A nervous laugh escaped before I stifled it. "Yeah…" My voice squeaked two octaves higher than normal. "Are you sure?"

"Totally," she assured me.

Glancing at her giant wall clock I shifted my weight, knowing I needed to leave if I was going to make it to the family dinner on time.

"I'll call you after dinner is done," I said, pausing before adding, "just to make sure."

She turned back around on her stool. "Ruth, I'm sure."

"Okay, then, I'll see you later," I said, raising my brow.

"See you later," she repeated, showing the humor she found in my hesitation.

# CHAPTER 14

"Hello?" I asked, walking through the empty house. "Where is everyone?"

"We're out here," my dad yelled from the backyard.

Stepping outside, I folded my arms to shield myself from the bite of fall weather. My family was gathered at the oversized wooden patio table. A small bonfire crackled in the distance where I wanted to gravitate. A few of the background trees dancing in the breeze already displayed their autumn red.

"It's chilly!" I whined. "Why aren't we eating inside?"

"Come sit down at the table," Dr. P said, waving me over. "We just got this fancy outdoor heater." She pointed to the glowing orbital lamppost arched overhead. "It'll warm you right up. Promise." She leaned over and rubbed my arm as I settled into the chair next to hers. "We're all here!" She beamed at my dad.

"Your sister and Abel have some big news to share," Dad announced.

"Abel, do you want to tell them?" Taden said, looking to him.

A goofy grin spread across his face. "No, you go ahead."

Dad—with growing impatience—inserted a plea into the silly back and forth. "Someone, please tell us."

Bursting with excitement, Taden broke the banter. "Abel and I are going to have a baby! I'm pregnant!"

Dr. P gasped with delight. "That explains the sudden sickness the other day."

"Yeah! That's actually how I figured it out!" Taden chimed in. "We haven't been to the doctor yet, but I took a test a few days ago, and…here we are!"

Dad removed his glasses to rub the gathering liquid from his eyes before replacing them back on his face. "Can I get you anything?" he asked Taden. "How are you feeling right now?"

"Aw, Dad, I'm okay. Thanks, though," Taden responded.

I watched Taden continue to chatter on about all the signals she'd overlooked that should've clued her in to the pregnancy. I'd never really seen Taden so content. I thought the idea that pregnant women glowed was just a ludicrous old wives' tale, but her effervescence was undeniable. She was definitely not the type of person to paint on a smile for the benefit of others, yet she hadn't been able to deny her toothy grin since I arrived.

Being near Taden in this light had a similar effect on me. Despite the chill in the air and the failing attempt of the outdoor heater to provide promised warmth, love radiated through me.

"Brrr. It's brisk out here!" I said. "That furnace could use a couple extra jolts." I got to my feet, seeking a short intermission inside. "I'm going to make coffee, anyone else want a cup?" I asked.

"I'll come with you," Taden responded.

We left the excited baby chatter. Ahead of me, she pulled open the sliding door and peered over her shoulder. "I think I should tell you the other news now."

"Is everything all right?" I asked.

She nodded. "I just know you're not going to be too happy with me in a minute."

"Why does every bit of news you tell me start out like that?" I asked.

"It's a bad habit." She shrugged. "I really should work on my delivery, I guess." Drumming her fingers on the kitchen table, she watched me rummage through the coffee options. "So…"

"Just tell me, Taden," I said.

"Okay," she paused. "I time traveled again."

Surprised—but not stunned—I slowed my search through the variety of coffee options. "I thought you weren't doing that anymore." Upon selecting my favorite, creme brûlée, I bumped the drawer closed with my hip and dropped the pod of coffee grounds into the machine. "Couldn't that be bad for the baby?"

"I didn't know I was pregnant." She put her hand on her stomach. Worry washed away the glow. "I hope it didn't do anything to the baby."

"All right, you went on a time travel. Tell me more about it."

Still holding her belly, Taden closed her eyes. "It's actually a much longer story." She paused. "I technically went on two time travels, both fairly recently." I turned around to face her while my coffee brewed. She was still setting the stage, and I was sensing "time travel" wasn't the actual reveal here.

"Hm," I said, my voice rising to match the prickly sensation traveling up my spine.

"The first time was a few months ago. I was with Abel. We discovered something abhorrent." She put her hand up to stop herself. "But now's not the time to dig into that particular issue." With nervous swiftness, her fingers tucked tufts of her red locks behind each ear. "I don't know why I even brought that part up." Her eyes rolled with self-irritation. "Anyway, because of what we found on that trip, the urgency of getting into the future became more intense."

"You're worrying me," I said.

"I should tell you, this is an extreme secret. No one at the lab knows about this. Not even Dakotah."

My ears were hot at the mention of Dakotah's name. "Why haven't you told her?" My chest burned with concern.

"It's not that I don't trust her—I think. Mostly, I don't want to put her into a compromising position. More importantly, the less she knows about this the safer she'll be."

"Enough, Taden. What the hell is going on?"

"Okay, okay. I'm sorry. I'll tell you about this other thing, but what I really want you to know is that I chose *who* I decided on for my future time travel events." The pause was almost long enough that I knew Taden's next words. "I didn't ask Dad. I went back to see Mom."

The burning-hot worry in my chest instantly became ice. On instinct, my hand located my quickened heart rate, assessing the icy burn. As my chin jutted upward, numbness spread across my face. I had no words.

"I can see you're not happy about this," she said. "And before you say anything, I want to stress that this is a secret, too. Actually, I haven't even really had this discussion with Abel yet."

Shifting her weight between each foot, she peered through the sliding door at her husband's giddiness. I considered that my sister could be insane. I had heard pregnancy hormones could make a person behave irrationally, but this was next-level.

"Are you telling me you went *alone* into the past, and told no one you were going?" I demanded.

The overwhelming desire to smack her or shake some sense into her grabbed hold of me. Had she learned nothing? The precise moment my mind bent over that question, while deeply judging my sister for this weakness in the face of her demons, I simultaneously visualized the moment, almost exactly one month prior, when I held the vial of liquid escape between my fingers.

My inward harshness dulled with the reminder of how capable I was of making poor choices. But I found it difficult to feel much regret for that night, since it led to this new territory for me and Dakotah.

"Firstly, I think it's real shitty that you're telling me this here and now, standing in Dad's kitchen with everyone just outside," I told Taden.

She glanced back through the window of the sliding door, where our family was still happily gabbing away.

"That was a coward move," I added.

Taden's eyes moved steadily to my face. She was hard at first, but then she softened, a wavering in her stand.

"I'm sorry, Ruth." She wrung her hands. "I *am* a coward. I should've told you when I came to visit you a few weeks ago. I just didn't want you to talk me out of it. I was being selfish."

My head bobbed as I looked distantly at her. Taking a deep breath, I matched her swaying with my own. "Okay." I pulled my attention to her and centered myself. "Okay," I repeated. With my hands on my hips, I released a string of barely audible mutterings. "I know how badly you've needed to see Mom for closure. You never got it." My head tilted. "I got to see her. You didn't."

Taden nodded.

"I can't judge you for wanting something I unexpectedly got to have." My arms fell to my sides. "Also, I think I'm falling in love with Dakotah."

Whoa! That just slipped out. Hoping Taden wouldn't register my confession, I kept right on talking.

"It's not like you made any big changes on this visit to the past, right?"

"I'm sorry," Taden said. "What did you just say?" She stepped closer to me.

"It's not like you made any big changes?" I hesitated and lowered my chin, holding her eye contact. "You *didn't* make any big changes, did you, Taden?"

"No. Nope. Back up to what you said before that," she demanded.

"I know. It's not fair for me to get upset with you for wanting to see Mom when you never got that experience. Especially when I accidentally got to be in the room with her again."

"Um, still no," Taden asserted. "The thing you said right after that. The thing you said about Dakotah." Her eyes grew wide with surprise. "There's no way I heard that right."

My arms spread wide as I shrugged. "I don't know. Okay. I think I might have feelings for Dakotah." I looked down at my shoes.

"I did hear you right! This is incredible news! Does *she* know?" She threw her arms around my neck, not waiting for my response.

"You're not mad?"

She pulled back like she'd been stung. "What? Why would I be mad?"

"Your best friend. Your sister. I dunno. People get weird about that sort of thing," I said through winces.

She clicked her tongue in disappointment. "People. You just chalked me up to 'people'. It's *you*. It's *me*. All I want is for you to be happy."

A slow smile grew on my lips. "Same. I want your happiness, too." I pulled her hands to my chest. "And for you to stop messing with time. Your happiness, and no more time manipulation." I playfully slapped her on the arm.

"We'd better get back out there," Taden said, backing toward the door. "But clearly we have more to discuss tonight after dinner."

"Not tonight…I have a date," I said sheepishly.

A grin spread on her face and she didn't even try to prevent the silly giggle that followed. "Shut. Up!"

"I know," I said, eyes wide. "I'm kind of nervous."

We both walked back onto the patio.

"I'll be counting the minutes until you come over tomorrow. We are going to be off-limits to everyone else until we get this all caught up," Taden said, her head confirming the plans.

Abel raised his eyes. "Uh-oh," he groaned. "The Barrett sisters are up to something."

"Aren't they always?" my dad chimed in.

I interrupted the flow. "I come bearing good news, too!" Everyone paused and looked up at me expectantly. I reached into my jacket and pulled a set of keys out of the pocket, dangling them on my index finger. "Guess who's a brand-new small-business owner?"

Dad's eyes twinkled at me, and Dr. P leaped from her chair to embrace me.

"To Ruth," Abel said as he held up his glass. I beamed, lifting my shoulders like it was no big deal.

"Ahem. I think you might've left out a very important detail surrounding this new business," Taden inserted.

"What?" I asked sheepishly. Taden widened her eyes. "Oh, you want me to tell them that I'm moving home?" I asked with some drama. "My new small business is here in Maryland!"

Dr. P still hadn't released me from her embrace, and with my additional reveal she squeezed even tighter.

"This evening needs a dance party," Dad said.

"I was just thinking the same thing," Dr. P agreed, turning her attention to the musical backdrop. Once she'd managed to fill the yard with dance music, she slipped inside. "Dancing and dessert. I'll handle the dessert."

Dr. Pasterski was intuitive, and I was well aware that choosing to busy herself with dessert freed up my dad to dance with me.

"My lady," he said, bowing to me with an outstretched hand.

Giggling as if I was the little girl dancing on his toes in our living room, I accepted his hand, and he twirled me toward him.

With my head against my dad's chest, I had a perfect view of Taden and Abel dancing under the twinkling lights over the patio. I could see her mirroring me. She rested against him in complete assurance that the man who held her in his arms was her perfect match.

We met each other's gaze with a knowing smile that this moment would be one we'd cherish for the rest of our lives.

· · · · · · ● ● ● ◉ ● ● ● · · · ·

# CHAPTER 15

"I'm on my way," I texted Dakotah. "Leaving Dad's house now." The text had a dual purpose. First, it was meant at face value to give her a head's up I'd be there soon, but also it was to give her a way out if she'd changed her mind.

I watched the notification show that she read my message, and I held my breath for a response.

I wasn't sure why it was hard for my brain to accept that Dakotah would really want to spend time alone with me, but it was nagging in the back of my most self-conscious thoughts.

"Can't wait," she replied. A smile crept onto my lips.

Dakotah opened her door before I even knocked. Her anticipation calmed my need to disappear.

"Dr. P sent over some leftovers if you want," I said, lifting the bag full of food.

"Thanks." She reached to accept the offering with one swift motion that resulted in a surprising hug. "Where's your stuff?" she asked, looking for my overnight duffle.

"I left it in the car," I said.

"Oh, I see. You're going to play it by ear." Her giggle was infectious. "Well, let's get this party started then. I've just made us strawberry smoothies and a game of Scrabble set up at the table." She cocked an eyebrow to emphasize the exciting night she'd line up.

"Scrabble is my favorite game," I said, wagging my finger. "Did you know that?"

"I might've," she replied. I followed her with my eyes as she disappeared from the room. I stood looking around her spacious living room, her punctual nature on display with the various items of décor related to clocks or time throughout. Above her TV, she had exactly twelve clocks on the wall. I thought about how she must've decided on twelve for each hour in the day. For every shelf in her bookcase she had an array of time pieces dotting the stacks of books. I lifted the hourglass filled with red sand and turned it over. Looking past the quickly falling sand into her dining room, I spotted the game set-up.

"I put the leftovers in the fridge," she said, reappearing, holding two smoothies. "Let me know if you get hungry and I'll pull it out." I nodded. "How'd it go at family dinner?" she asked, gesturing for me to follow her.

"Quite exciting, actually," I said, returning the hourglass. Rubbing my hands together, I joined her at the table. "Get your popcorn ready because I'm about to put on a show." Laughing at my own smack talk, I immediately arranged my letter tiles. Dakotah scoffed and followed suit.

"What was all the excitement about?" she asked, not breaking her focus on the letter tiles.

"What excitement?" I asked, already forgetting about family dinner. Before she clarified, I blurted with excitement having my first word formed, "I'll start." Placing the word 'seek' onto the gameboard. "Oh, dinner. Both Barrett sisters had big news," I said.

Dakotah lifted her gaze to me. "Both sisters?" she asked.

I nodded.

"What was your big news?"

"You're not interested in Taden's?"

"She'll tell me her news when she's ready." Dakotah slid the smoothie she made me across the table and sucked in a swig of hers.

"I updated the family on my new business."

She placed her word on the game board using the 's' from mine.

"Skin. Good one," I said.

"New business? This does sound like good news. Tell me more."

"I'm moving home," I blurted.

Her eyes bulged. "You mean home as in Maryland?"

I nodded.

"Ruth, that is exciting! You're going to be living here? Like, all the time?" She nodded her head, slurping in more of her smoothie. "That has a lot of interesting possibility."

I played my next word and worked up enough courage to ask, "What do you mean? Possibility of what?"

She laughed. "I mean, your business will flourish here. And I bet your personal life will, too."

There was no matching the boldness of Dakotah.

"It'll be a slow build for my business. I won't have the agency booking gigs for me and the clients won't be as active as they are in New York, you know, with the big-city action, but I've looked into the projections and I'll do all right."

"Are you nervous about the move?"

I thought how no one had asked me that. "You know what's funny? I hadn't even thought about if I was nervous. That was a perceptive question," I said.

"I don't think so," she said, placing her next word. "It feels kind of obvious. I mean, you're leaving a hugely successful position at your firm to start your own business. It's a ballsy move. On top of that, you're moving to an entirely new and less bustling city."

I gulped. "Wow. If I wasn't nervous before I truly am now."

"Oh! I wasn't trying to stress you out," she said. "I wanted to validate your feelings."

Looking into her worried stare, I didn't actually feel nervous. Having her in my corner made me feel like I could do anything. "I'm only kidding. You didn't stress me out at all. Truth is, I do that all on my own. It's a driving force in what has motivated me to make this move. I was thinking with a change of scenery and pace maybe I could be more happy."

Dakotah studied me for a moment. "You feel stressed often?"

"I'd say my fair share," I responded. "Work stress with a dash of time-travel-altered memories."

"Well, I don't know if this is some kind of cosmic fate," she said, adding her last three letter tiles to the board to finish with the word 'ohm'.

"Ohm," I said. "Like the electrical measurement, right?"

"That, too, but I meant it like the mantra."

"Ohm," I said dramatically, stretching the syllable as I pushed my hands together in prayer, satisfied with the grin on her lips. "Cosmic fate for you to win with."

"That and I actually do meditate to address my work-related time travel stressors and it relieves those issues for me." She stirred her melting smoothie with the straw. "I can show you how. It might help you, too."

"Sure, I'd be interested. I've tried acupuncture and yoga before but neither are really my thing."

"Let's go into the living room." Dakotah collected the Scrabble pieces and placed them back into the box. "The couch will be more comfortable."

I followed her to the couch as she instructed. "First thing is that you don't have to sit like you see online, just be sure you're upright, not lying down. You don't want to fall asleep while you're trying to transcend."

Sitting with our legs touching, I felt awkward not knowing what would come next. As if she read my mind she said, "Don't worry, there's nothing embarrassing about meditating. I won't watch you or anything." I released a sigh of relief. "In a few minutes you'll close your eyes, and I will too. When you do this you will think of the sound I give you."

"Is that the mantra 'ohm'?" I asked.

"Sort of, yeah. Except it will be a different sound. You won't ever say it aloud. You'll just think it. While your eyes are closed and you're thinking the mantra, pay attention to your thoughts. If you start to drift into other thoughts simply go back to your mantra."

"Do I focus on my breathing at all? Like in my yoga classes?"

"Not with this method of meditation. Just breathe naturally, and focus on your mantra." She made a deep humming noise. It was an odd sound, and I wasn't sure if it would be able to compete with the memories that haunted my mind.

"Okay, so I just hear that sound in my mind." I scooted back into the couch like Dakotah was sitting. "How long will we be doing this for?"

"We'll try it for ten minutes to start."

"That's not how long you mediate?" I asked.

"I meditate twice a day for twenty minutes each time."

"Wow! That's a lot."

"It is," she agreed. "But it's time well spent in keeping me centered and mentally healthy."

I nodded. "All right, let's do it." With my eyes closed I followed Dakotah's soft-spoken directions and drifted into the deepness beyond my thoughts.

"You can stop thinking your mantra now." Her voice pulled me from the ocean of my mind. "Open your eyes slowly."

As I lifted my gaze to Dakotah and her living room, it felt as if I had been transported from a waking dream.

"How was it?" she asked.

I cleared my throat. "Was that really only ten minutes?"

She nodded.

"It felt much longer."

"In a bad way?" she asked.

My eyes widened. "No, in a good way. It was peaceful."

"Do you want to try it again?" she asked.

"Sure. Ten minutes again?"

"Yes. Another ten minutes. And if you want, we can do the full twenty minutes in the morning." She winked.

"Deal," I said, grinning.

· · · · · · ● ● ● ● ● ● ● ● ● · · · · ·

# CHAPTER 16

Time was visibly marked by the growth of Taden's belly. The two and a half weeks since I'd resettled back in Maryland spotlighted the beginning of a baby bump. As excited as I was for every new stage of my future niece or nephew, I was even more excited to finally be settled in enough at my apartment to stop working from home and get my office space squared away.

Looking around the small office, I envisioned filling the blank wall in front of my desk with the framed photographs in the heavy box I was buckling under. I carefully slid it, with the visual contents of my career, onto my new desk.

The desk, left behind from the previous renters, surprised me with its old-school character. Maybe I'd keep it…after giving it a makeover. I pulled out the frame poking through the top of the box. My eyes fell on the image of Mary and me standing together with glowing smiles. Behind us was evidence of the magical evening we'd spent months preparing for her Inaugural Ball.

My pulse quickened, remembering that evening. I was caught by the awareness that I wasn't focused on the loss of Maria. Instead, I was reliving the joy I'd experienced in creating that event for her. And then I realized that this picture reminded me of the joy I'd created for myself.

I glanced back up at the wall, thinking how it would need to be painted a bright color before I'd consider the place *my* office. I spotted a nail remaining, and hung the frame on it. Stepping back, I took in the vision of my future photo gallery.

A gentle tap on the oversized bay window that opened my office up to the passersby in town startled me. A quick glance revealed Dakotah holding up two ice creams and wearing a sparkling grin. She nodded toward the door. I waved her over with excitement and found myself running to let her in.

"It's really empty still, but I have to paint before I start unboxing things," I said, holding the door open for her.

"I brought you a frozen yogurt to celebrate!" She handed me the cone she wasn't busy licking to prevent drips onto her hand. "Lick it fast, though, it's starting to make a mess."

Her giggle moved through my nervous system.

"Thanks!" I replied, following her instructions. "Mm, is this a Dole Whip?" I asked, enjoying the bright yellow treat.

She winked. "I saw it on the list of flavors in the ice cream store down there," she said, her elbow jutting toward the dairy spot on the corner. "Your sister has mentioned before how the two of you used to get that on vacation when you were kids."

The icy treat couldn't chill the warmth that moved through my body. "Would you like a tour?" I asked her.

"I'd be delighted." Her hip delicately bumped mine.

"Okay." I swallowed a huge mouthful of yogurt, wiping my lips with the back of my hand. "Over here will be the reception area." I pointed in the direction of the desk holding my box of framed pictures. "Down this hallway is my office, the tiniest kitchenette ever, and the restroom."

She followed me through the office as I pointed out the spaces. Brimming with excitement, all my energy was directed at the quickly disappearing ice cream cone.

"Mm," I said, licking my lips. "Right there—" I gestured with the elbow bent from holding my cone. "—I'm planning on making a Zen corner to meditate in, like you taught me."

"I love how the light shines in through the window onto that spot," Dakotah said. "How is your meditation going?"

"I'm still doing the 'twice a day' thing, as instructed by my teacher." I winked at her.

"Nice. I'm proud of you." Her compliment wasn't just words. The way she stood taller and more open communicated that she indeed was proud that I'd committed to this. "Are you noticing it eases any anxieties when you're nagged with time travel memories?"

"It is really helping me come to peace with my other timeline memories."

Her proud teacher moment was interrupted with the crunching of our ice cream cones.

"This is my favorite part of ice cream," she said, taking the last bite.

"It's Taden's, too." I pushed my last bite into my mouth and looked over to Dakotah.

"You have a bit of cone right there."

She pointed to my upper lip. Slightly embarrassed, I brought my finger to my mouth to brush it off.

"You can't take me anywhere. I swear I eat like a pig."

"No." She reached for my lip. "Right here," she said, delicately wiping it from my face.

As her hand left my face, she let it fall into mine. Our fingers laced together and instinctively we turned about the room together, as if commencing the future of my business.

"Knock-knock!" a voice echoed from the front of the office.

We exchanged a quizzical glance before I led her from my office into the main entry. There stood Taden, with her barely noticeable baby belly, holding a can of paint in each hand. She immediately looked at our interlocked fingers and flashed a beaming smile.

"I brought the welcome wagon," she said. Trailing behind her were Abel, Quinn, and Jaxson.

"Congratulations!" Quinn said with her bright smile. She ran up to me and gave me a squeeze. Thinking about how awkward she was when we first met in Taden's office as we discovered her brother was Marius, it felt like a lifetime ago.

"Thank you!" I replied. She stepped back as Abel gave me a fist bump with one hand and placed two gallons of paint on the floor with his other. As I attempted to greet Jaxson with a welcoming grin, he returned a stony stare my way. I felt like he might not even remember who I was, even though we'd met on several occasions.

"I'm Taden's sister, Ruth," I said, offering my hand.

"I know who you are," he returned dryly.

*What a strange dude*, I thought to myself. But it was too exciting a moment to get stuck on Jaxon Duncan's weird demeanor.

"Did you know about this?" I turned to Dakotah.

She nodded, blinking with anticipation as she reached into the bag I hadn't even noticed over her shoulder until that moment. Pulling out a stack of paint rollers, she handed one to each person.

"You guys! I'm overwhelmed. You're the best," I said with a lump in my throat.

Taden squeezed my shoulder. "Proud of you, sis."

"I don't think you're supposed to be painting," I said, pointing to her pregnant belly.

"I got the anti-fume paint—and I can paint. I'm not injured." She was already busy prying the lid from the paint can.

Acknowledging my disapproval, she added, "I got the okay from my doctor." Her brows shot up in challenge. Dipping her roller into the paint tray she'd already filled, she gave one last, "Try to stop me."

I looked around to see each person already busy rolling the brightest turquoise and soft gray paints on the different walls in my brand new PR office, and my heart was full.

. . . . . . . . . ● . . . . . . . .

# CHAPTER 17

## TADEN

Time travel seemed like it would never become any less disorienting. Along with going into the past, it was becoming a kind of religious experience to stand outside the door of my childhood home and peer through the window, knowing that on the other side of that door were living memories.

This time, I used the key I'd kept in my memory box to our apartment and let myself in. According to the current time, younger Ruth and I wouldn't be home from school for another hour. Dad was working; he was always working back then. I checked the calendar on the fridge to find out where Mom was. Old habits easily resurfaced.

"Oh, that's right," I muttered. "Wednesdays are grocery shopping days."

She'd be home any minute to unpack the food in time to get dinner started before she left for her evening shift.

I had the place to myself. I pondered whether to dig into this open memory box of my home or resist the nostalgia. The distinct fragrance that each room held unlocked enough treasures I'd forgotten.

I found myself sitting on the corner of my bed, twirling my finger about the soft blanket I used to tuck under my chin to sleep with. Some of my best thinking had happened in this exact spot. I'd look out the window, fidgeting with this blanket, and create solutions to the engineering tasks my dad would pose. Regardless of what I'd produce, my mom could never contain her pride.

 "No way. You built that on your own?" Mom asked.

"Yep," I said. "Dad challenged me to put the engine back together."

"Was that the box of parts he brought home last week?"

My nod produced a beaming smile that lit up her eyes. She'd dialed my dad's mobile.

"You aren't going to believe what your daughter did," she told him. "Yep. I'm looking at it right now. She put the entire thing back together."

Mom grinned at me and giggled, unable to contain it.

"When will Dad be home to see for himself?" I asked.

"Okay. Love you, honey," she said into the phone. Her fingers gliding over the mechanics I'd puzzled together, she gushed, "Your dad will be home before you go to bed. He can't wait to see what you've done."

 Hand to my stomach, sitting on my childhood bed, I swelled with the same sense of pride I'd felt on that night.

Startled by a knock on the door, I broke from the memory.

"Sorry, I didn't mean to scare you. I didn't realize you'd be back so soon."

My mom was as stunning as she was three months prior, when I'd first come to visit her. But that made sense since, for her, I'd only been here a few days ago.

The two days that had passed—for her—hadn't really been much time to contemplate whether she would come into the future with me. Wanting to give her the best fighting chance with the treatment I hoped she'd accept, it was necessary to return to her as far out from her cancer growth as possible.

"Have you thought about leaving with me?" I asked.

She leaned against the doorway. The way she stood—allowing her body to be held up by the wall as she studied me—was a subtle habit of hers. It transported me to my youth, so much so I would've believed anyone who attempted to convince me I was still a kid. Scoffing at the notion (all while knowing exactly how possible such a brainwashing was, as Marius had attempted it), I left the bed to greet her properly.

"I missed you," I said, wrapping my arms around her. In her embrace, she planted her lips on the top of my head.

It was storming outside, the slow rumble of thunder occasionally making itself welcome in our reunion.

"Come into the kitchen with me. I've got groceries to unpack. You can help me." She smiled as though she was suggesting something unpleasant.

"I'd love to," I said. The fact that I could help my mom unpack groceries was a gift I would never take for granted. If she asked me to clean the toilet with a Q-tip, I'd be delighted if it meant she was near me.

"Here, unpack this one. It's the freezer bag," she said.

I chuckled. "Get them in there before they melt," I said. "I unpack these items first, as well."

"Like mother, like daughter."

"So, Mom?" I asked.

She nodded, eyes closed. "I have thought about it. It seems like I haven't been able to think of much else."

"And?" I asked.

"I'll give it a go. But remember, you promised if I decide not to get the treatment, if I want to come back home, you won't pressure me otherwise."

"I promise," I said, rushing to her with the TRB and her pre-mixed serum to go into the future.

"Whoa, whoa, whoa," she said. "Slow down. I haven't said any goodbyes. I haven't even unpacked these groceries."

"But Mom, we really need to get you there and get started on treatments, and…"

She lifted her hand to stop me.

"Taden. This can wait. I will be ready to leave with you tomorrow. You can stay here," she gestured to our home, "or you can come back tomorrow."

I'd not been corrected by my mom for more than half my life. It was jarring to find that no matter how "adult" I'd become, when my mom instructed me on something that was the end of it.

The thought of staying there with my family for the next twenty-four hours was tempting, but my fear about the multitude of ripples I might cause if I stayed motivated me to leave.

Setting my TRB to jump to the next day, I looked back to her. "I'll see you tomorrow, then." For me, it would only take a moment. Still, I wrapped my arms around her until I dissolved into the next day.

"All righty," I said, pulling myself together from the time jump. "Your bags are packed? You're ready to go?"

My mom's face was blotchy, and I saw her as a woman, not just my mother, maybe for the first time. I was astonished to view my mom in this light. It was then that I realized she was about the same age as I was. We looked like we could've been sisters.

She wiped her eyes and cleared her throat, the telltale signs of attempting to hide her tears.

"Mom," I said, overtaken with guilt. "If you don't want to do this…"

"No, this is my only chance to survive. You girls are there, in the future. I can't be here for you girls if I stay. So, I want to take the only option I have to be there for you later on."

"We are going to take a short trip to the future site of Abel's and my house. That way, when we time jump we'll arrive there. I'll know right away if we made it into the future."

At the location we would be living, I attached her TRB to her arm.

"This will be uncomfortable," I said, "but it won't last very long."

I pressed the button and held on tight to her hand until it dissolved, ready to meet her in the future.

 "It worked!" I screamed with elation after I confirmed the last name Mihal on the mailbox of our home. "Oh my gosh! It actually worked." I couldn't tell if I was feeling stomach tension from the time travel or the overwhelming experience of finally breaking into the future.

My mom was too distracted recovering from the molecular jolt to join my celebration.

"I promise the nausea will pass soon," I assured her. "It freaking worked!"

She sat on the steps of my porch and leaned into her knees.

"Sorry! Are you okay?" I asked, putting my hand on her shoulder. "Come inside and rest."

She followed me through the front door and a surge of joy rushed me. I had finally accomplished time travel into the future and, more importantly, I had my mom with me.

"Here, drink this. It helps," I said, handing her a bottle of water.

She accepted and took a sip. "Honey, you did it." She reached her hand out for me to grasp. Upon contact, she gave me a gentle squeeze. "I'm so proud of you."

It felt tremendous to hear those words from her again. All the years I'd become accustomed to living without her affirmations really left a hole.

"You should relax," I said, fluffing a pillow behind her on the sofa.

"I don't know how you do this, though," she said, leaning back and closing her eyes. "It feels terrible."

Getting myself a water from the kitchen I yelled, "It's a doozy, that's for sure!"

By the time her drink was emptied, the color had returned to her cheeks and curiosity replaced her desire to rest.

"So," she said, looking around, "this is the future."

I followed her surveying eyes, interested in what she thought of my home.

"It looks kind of like the past, but more modern," she said with a chuckle.

On my mantel she spotted her blue elephant I'd asked Dad if I could have. A small smile crept up the corner of her mouth. "I'm glad you kept that. It's one of my favorites."

"Would you like a tour of my space-age home?" I asked.

We matched each other's grins and I already wanted to keep her there forever.

As we walked through the house and I showed her different technologies, she smiled placidly back at me. She was never one for modern devices.

"That's him," she said, picking up a photo on the nightstand next to my bed.

"Mm-hm, that's Abel," I confirmed. "He should be home any minute."

"How do you think our introduction will go? I assume you've told him I'll be here," she said, her lips clenching together and her nose tweaking to one side.

"Wow," I said. "You have perfected that mom look. Of course he knows you're coming. I told him as soon as I came home from my first visit to you."

"To be clear, he will be expecting me to be here, today, when he walks through that door?" she asked.

I nodded, and thought to myself it was probably why he still wasn't home yet. He'd usually leave work earlier than I did and have dinner ready. "Yep. Any minute now."

She set the picture frame back to its place on the table and suggested we return to the living room. "Your house is beautiful. It reflects your style and even has a bit of boldness weaved in. Is that from Abel, or did your sister help you decorate?"

That comment earned her a hearty chuckle. "It was definitely Ruth. In fact, Abel and I had to tame her while we were putting this place together."

"I'm home," Abel's voice carried down the hall. He met us in the hallway, holding a bouquet of flowers for my mom. Even if he disapproved, he made it a point to show her how honored he was to meet her. The tenderness I felt for Abel—watching him give her flowers and embrace her the way he did—could not be undone by any force or dimension.

"It's truly the greatest privilege to meet you," he said to her. "As long as I have known Taden, she has talked about how fantastic you are and how much you've meant to her life." He smiled wide as she looked through the bouquet to find her favorite flowers mixed together and pulled the bouquet to her chest. "These are gorgeous. Thank you, Abel."

"Can I put them in water for you?" he asked.

"That would be lovely," she said, releasing the bouquet to him.

"Excuse me for a minute and I'll go take care of these."

As soon as he left the room she turned to me wide-eyed, wearing an equally wide grin.

"Honey, he is a looker and he's quite kind!"

"I know! Isn't he?" I said, laughing. "Besides the fact that he needs to eat regularly or he becomes a huge grump, he's pretty much perfect."

"Looks like he's in good company," she jabbed back at me.

"Hey now," I said.

"Unless you've grown out of that issue, you've always needed food to keep your mood in check."

"It's possible."

"What is?" Abel asked, returning with the full vase and setting it on the coffee table in front of us.

"We were just saying how crabby Taden gets if she doesn't eat," my mom said.

Abel stifled his own laugh. "Speaking of, what's the plan this evening? Will we be meeting with any other family or should we have a special dinner out with just the three of us?"

I looked at my mobile, hoping to have a text from Ruth, but saw nothing. "I think it'll just be us tonight. Is that all right, Mom?"

She nodded. "I'm still bouncing back from the time travel adventure. It'll be good for me to take it easy." A look of disappointment crept from her eyes to her wavering grin. "Do you think I'll see Ruth tomorrow, though?"

"I'm sure of it. I bet she just had to work late and probably hasn't even checked her phone."

"My girl is a hard worker. I'm glad she still has that quality."

"She's the hardest-working person I know," I said. "And she's going to be so happy to see you tomorrow."

Even as I said those words, I could taste the doubt. What was Ruth's issue? What could keep her from being here?

· · · · · · ● ● ● ● ● ● ● ● · · · · ·

# CHAPTER 18

## RUTH

I should've been over the moon about my mom's return. I'd gone into the past and saw her fighting her last day like a rerun episode of a canceled show. That experience was hauntingly beautiful. It gave me closure. People don't know that the last time they hang up the phone that they will in fact never receive another text or phone message again, when it's the last time. There's always the chance. But once a final goodbye has been sealed by death, it's the end. Somehow, going back in time didn't feel like an interruption to that finality. But my sister pulling our mom from that timeline and bringing her here? That was a clear disruption. It didn't feel natural, and it took massive energy to tame the chills running along my nervous system.

"Mom?" I said, locking eyes with my memory of her coming alive. We were a perfect symmetry of one another. I could've been looking into a mirror. "How weird is this?" I blurted, reaching toward her with a stiff greeting.

She touched my cheek, and even the warmth of her fingers tracing my skin didn't help keep my goose pimples at bay. "Sweet Ruth." Her focus on me didn't break for an excruciatingly long moment.

"I don't even know what to say," I further word-vomited. "I've missed you." Although my words were forced, they were the truth. But my truth couldn't hide the fact that I was seriously uncomfortable with my dead mom standing in front of me.

"Are we ready to go?" she asked, looking to me and Taden. "Your dad must be getting impatient. We were supposed to meet him fifteen minutes ago."

I felt the heat climb my chest into my cheeks. "Mom, I'm not sure he'll be there. This has been a hard couple of days for him." I caught her deflated look and the slightest part to her lips. My heart pinched. "He wants to see you. He really does. It's just…"

"A lot to process," she said, finishing my sentence. "Believe me, I get it." She slipped her coat on and threaded my arm through hers. "I'm delighted to have lunch with my girls. Let's get going."

I made a conscious effort to loosen the tightening of my body. Why was this so eerie? She looked and felt genuine. I couldn't have painted her more realistic in my dreams. But this was already difficult, I couldn't fathom how painful this lunch would be if Dad decided to join us.

I spotted his car in the parking spot that jutted up to the large bay window of his favorite diner. He was in the booth, waiting. His head was in his hands, coffee steam swirling from his mug. His face was blotted by the sun's glare on the window.

"Is that him?" she asked, squeezing between me and Taden.

"I think so. Are you nervous?" Taden asked.

"I'm really not. I see him every day," she reminded. "I suppose if I feel any nerves, it's for him. I realize this is a much higher-stakes type of meeting for him."

The bell dinged as I pulled the door open. Time slowed to a crawl. I hung back with Taden to let the two of them have a minute. I watched as she approached and his head lifted. The unmistakable quiver to his chin. His eyes welling. He was on his feet in an instant and their embrace only ended when Taden approached them.

"Doesn't she look amazing?" Taden asked Dad. The full-body cringe that her comment triggered made me queasy.

"Absolutely. Elizabeth, you look beautiful," he told her. "Have a seat." He guided her to the bench across from him. I scooted in next to my dad as quickly as I could, hoping to alleviate the pain he was feeling and to give myself some space from my mom. The internal struggle this experience offered would need a long recovery.

"Tell me!" she exclaimed. "How are things?"

Dad blinked and gave Mom a knowing smile, her ability to ease him apparent. We seemed like a normal family having lunch in a greasy spoon. A normal family that was anything but, brought to our awareness when Mal, our waitress, who knew Dad and Dr. P—as they were regulars in her section—asked, "Where's Dr. P today?" Silent tension replaced the soft chuckles of seconds prior.

Mal raised her coffee pot, gesturing the inquiry for any other refills. Mom smiled and lifted her mug. "I don't think I've ever met you before," Mal said to Mom. "I'm Mal, these guys are some of my favorite regulars. Especially this one." She lifted her elbow toward Dad.

"From what I've seen, Mal, they are certainly in good hands here," Mom said, accepting her now-full mug. "I'm Elizabeth, an old family friend." She stuck out her hand to formally greet Mal.

"Mom, don't be weird," I blurted. "Mal, this is our mom. We haven't seen her for a very long time."

Mal's smile faltered, and she blinked rapidly. Taden kicked my foot under the table and trained her eyes on me in dismay. No one had a funny quip or small talk to gloss over my blunder. I shrugged. If my comment was inappropriate, then surely so was the fact that we were sitting at a booth with my deceased mom.

Clearly I was having difficulty processing this situation, and it was making people uncomfortable. Mal had dismissed herself to attend to her other tables and funnily did not return for any more coffee refills. For the remainder of the unpleasant meal I said no more, but my thoughts continued to create uncomfortable commentary.

"And Ruth started her own business right around the corner," Dad bragged, nudging me to join the conversation. I nodded, with my eyes big and a plastered smile to match.

"In fact," I looked at my mobile for the time, "I have a meeting with my first big client, so I'll have to excuse myself." Not waiting for goodbyes, I slid from the booth and gathered my things. Taden was on the outside of the bench Mom sat on, and she made to inch out, signaling to Taden to let her go.

"No, don't get up," I said, lifting my palm. "Finish eating. I'll see everyone later." I produced the most genuine smile I could muster, knowing it wouldn't reach my eyes. I couldn't be sure how my abrupt departure affected my mom because I could hardly direct my gaze at her. But Taden's face told me enough.

Her eyes narrowed and lips pinched. I turned to make my exit, forcing myself to walk slow despite the urge to run.

"Wait!" Taden yelled. "I've gotta get to the lab, too; I almost forgot." She kissed Mom on the cheek and gave Dad a quick squeeze of his hand. "Don't leave yet," she directed my way. Taden quickly gathered her things and slowly jogged the five steps I'd managed from the table. "Dad, can you drop Mom off back at my house after you finish lunch?" Her question was more of a statement.

"Do you really have a client to get to?" she asked me, raising a brow, matching my accelerated pace.

"Mm-hm," was all I could muster.

"It's probably for the best." She took a quick peek at our parents before we pushed the door open, triggering the jingle of the bell. "They could use some time alone."

· · · · · · · ● ● ● ⬤ ● ● ● ● ● · · · · ·

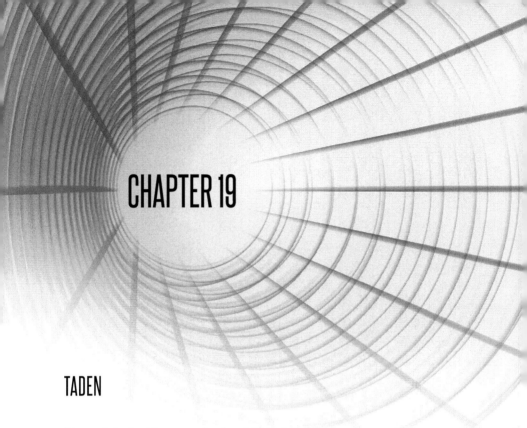

# CHAPTER 19

## TADEN

"Can we talk about the cancer treatments?" I asked.

Mom looked from the photo albums stacked on her lap. She sucked in a breath and bit her bottom lip. "I'm not sure I want to have the treatments," she answered.

Surely she was only responding to the lackluster response from the family surrounding her return. I expected Dr. Pasterksi and Dad to be somewhat distant because it was a deep and more personal blow to their life. And I figured that whatever Dad had to say to her was already said at the diner. But I didn't understand why Ruth and Abel still seemed to be resisting this reunion.

"I get that," I said. "We both knew going into this that you might choose not to have the treatments." I paused, hoping to steady my voice while also refraining from coming across as pushy. "I've secured a medical team through our friend, Mary."

"Mary?"

I chuckled. "Mary Moore. She's the president of our country."

Mom stared blankly. "I'm not sure if you're joking."

"Ruth and I have connections with her and her fiancé. They've arranged for your treatments with their oncologist."

"How will you explain my records? After all, I am deceased and have been for more than a decade."

"It's handled. They won't be asking you about your records," I assured.

Abel cleared his throat, announcing his entrance. "I hope I'm not interrupting," he said, walking up behind me and placing a kiss on the top of my head.

"No, not at all," I said, reaching up to fluff a tuft of his hair. "Come join us, we were just discussing the possibilities of Mom's cancer treatments."

He looked anywhere but at her. I hoped my mom hadn't noticed. I looked to her for a reaction. She was fidgeting with one particular picture in the opened album and I briefly wondered what photograph had captured her attention.

She closed the album with a sudden decisiveness, asking, "Can I help with dinner?"

"We're all set; it's just going to be us and Ruth," I said, reaching for my mobile. "I'm not sure if she is coming for certain yet. I'm still waiting on a text from her."

"I think I'll take a walk in the meantime," she said, unburying herself from the photos of the decade she'd missed.

"I can come with you," I offered.

"No," she said, rubbing my arm. "I need time to think and get some fresh air."

I nodded, worried she'd find her decision on her walk, and that decision would be to go back to her own timeline.

"How will you handle your mom's battle with cancer this time around, already having experienced her first defeat?" Abel asked almost the moment the door closed behind her. Before I could respond to his verbal launch, he continued, "And this time with the added challenge that you're pregnant." I was lost for words. It didn't matter, because he kept on. "Ruth constantly has excuses for not visiting. You two haven't even been talking on the phone."

"What does that have to do with the treatments?" I asked, finally rediscovering my vocabulary.

"Everything, Taden. It has everything to do with her treatments. You won't have Ruth this time around to help go through this battle. She's not dealing very well with this situation. And it's worth noting you won't have your dad in this either. At least not like you did the last time around."

"It's awkward," I muttered. "Ruth and Mom were mostly inseparable."

"Things aren't the same as they were when you were kids," he said.

I retrieved the album my mom had been thumbing through before she left on her walk. Flipping through the pages, attempting to pinpoint the picture she'd paused on, I discovered the pages holding my graduation from UPenn. There was a full-page image of the entire family. Minus mom. With the addition of Dr. P cheek-to-cheek with me. I'd never looked at that photograph through the eyes of my mom before.

Evening arrived along with Ruth. She sat across the room, planting as much distance as humanly possible and staring at Mom as if she was a zombie carrying a contagious disease.

I suggested they watch that show they used to love.

Ruth shot me a sharp look. "I would love to, but I'm swamped at work. Leaving early today has really pushed me behind schedule."

"Early? It's seven o'clock," I scolded.

"Maybe next weekend," Ruth said to Mom, already gathering her things to leave after only staying long enough to make everyone uncomfortable.

"You're leaving? We haven't even eaten yet," I protested.

"It's okay, honey. I understand," Mom told her.

I couldn't believe Ruth was being cold. If she missed her as much as I did all these years, why didn't she want to be with her?

She forced a placid smile. "Thanks, Mom."

Ruth hesitated, not sure how to exit, and reached for a hug. It was that really awful kind of hug that happens when one person pats the other on the back and pulls away in the same motion as the quick-footed exit. I couldn't say I'd ever seen Ruth behave that way to anyone, much less our mom.

"I don't know what has gotten into her. I'm sorry. I'll talk to her later," I said to Mom after she left.

"Taden, I shouldn't be here. Isn't it obvious?" she responded.

"No, it's not obvious, and I don't agree."

"You're only seeing what you want to see. This trip has alienated everyone. It's not right, bringing someone back from the dead," she said.

"I didn't bring you back from the dead. I brought you from the past, where you were alive and well."

She shot me the same irritated expression Ruth had a few moments earlier.

"Well, at least I know where Ruth got her edge from," I said, walking into the kitchen as the oven timer beeped.

Following me, she pleaded, "Honey, I think this was a mistake. I don't feel good about this. You know your science works. I'm here. Everything seems to be working properly. It's time for me to go home."

"You haven't even gotten your treatments yet." I slammed down the bowl of green beans I'd brought to the table with a little more force than intended. "Just give everyone time to adjust."

"I've decided." She paused, making her statement firm. "I don't want the treatments, and I'm not staying. I'll finish out this weekend with you, because I think there's more to address with you—but then I want to go back." She hesitated a quick moment. "Please respect this decision. It's not because I don't love you. It's precisely *because* I love you."

I swallowed the anguish rising in my throat. I'd promised her I wouldn't try to force her to stay here, and it was time for me to ante up.

"Can you show me how you used to season these for us?" I asked, sliding the bowl of green beans in her direction. "The chicken's almost done."

I looked over at the stove, trying desperately to be a grown-up in the face of my mom leaving.

"Of course I can." She squeezed my arm as she passed me on the way to the fridge. Scanning the shelves inside, she muttered under her breath, "Hm, where's the butter?" And then a clear direction for me, "Get the garlic salt."

With a large serving spoon, she dropped butter into the bowl of vegetables. "I usually just put about two tablespoons of butter and a few shakes of the garlic salt," she said, accepting the seasoning from me.

My eyes bulged. "No wonder we loved green beans so much. That's a ton of butter, Mom."

Her laughter filled the kitchen, and I couldn't help but join her. "I never claimed to cook the healthiest things."

The simple exchange lightened the mood. I didn't want to color her last few days with me with fighting her to stay. There was a purpose behind her staying a little longer, and I wanted to receive whatever she was willing to offer me.

"I'm not telling you this to try to get you to stay," I said, "but there's something I want you to know. Actually, I found out after the first visit I made to you a few months ago."

"What do you mean, a few months ago?" she asked, confused.

"Three months passed for me before I came back to you, but I came back to the point in time that was only two days later for you. I did that so your treatments could be started in the early stages of your cancer."

"Ah."

She sat down at the table and reached for my hand. Looking up at me with her liquid-brown eyes, she waited. My own eyes burned with the mix of heartache that she wanted to leave and the joy that I had this moment with her.

"I'm pregnant. Abel and I are going to have a baby."

She tightened her hands around mine with a detectable quiver to her chin, which instinctively beckoned mine to join. She didn't speak. It actually made me laugh. I hadn't ever left my mom speechless before, but for a long moment she sat across from me in utter silence. The quiet we shared in a stolen piece of time took away a fear from my subconscious, as if a life preserver had been offered. It was a long overdue reprieve from the murky waters of grief I'd been treading for the last fifteen years.

Not fitting for the moment, I uttered, "I'm worried."

My mom's forehead pulled tight. "What about?"

Glancing down at the bowl of green beans, I pulled in a long nasal breath. "I've struggled a lot since you died. I mean, who doesn't struggle through grief, right?" With a flippant shrug, I tried to avoid the emotional disaster looming.

She scooted her chair closer to me and placed her arm around my shoulder. "I'm listening," she whispered.

I continued. I told her every bit of my grief before I'd even understood it myself. She had a way of doing that to me. It's probably why I'd felt lost during the long years without her. "I've learned, from my grief, that I need to let people go." Blotchy hot patches spread across my face. "But it seems like I've lost the ability to even connect with the people I love the most. I feel detached, driven by a fear they'll stop loving me, or that they'll see the real me and not like me, or that they'll die…" my voice faded off.

"And this wall you've built around you…is it keeping your heart safe?" she asked.

"What do you mean?" I looked at her, a little shocked by the question.

"I mean, when you close yourself off to your sister and don't tell her your big secrets because you're worried she won't love you anymore…does it help you feel happier?"

"No," I said, insulted that she assumed I was naïve.

"Then why do you keep shutting her out? Or anyone, for that matter. You're right about one thing: you will lose people. To all sorts of things, just like you said. But honey, the pain you feel," she said, gathering a strand of my hair between her fingers, "is proof of the love between you and this other person. If there wasn't love, it wouldn't hurt. And the memories you made together were worth the pain of the loss."

Tears streamed freely down my cheeks. She wiped them away with her thumbs.

"Listen to me," she said, holding my face in her hands. "What is meant for you will remain. If you can't stop looking backward at what you've lost, you will miss the good that's coming. Honey, you'll miss the good right now."

She looked down at my belly.

"Mom, I haven't told anyone this before..." She looked back up at me. "You know how I told you that Dad died in our original timeline?" She nodded solemnly. "I've recently been betrayed in a huge way by someone I held in the highest esteem for a very long time." Her brows pulled together. "The first thought that ran through my mind when I found out she had betrayed me was that it was my penance for interfering with Dad's death."

She closed her eyes, shaking her head. "I suppose that's my fault."

"What?"

"I've always lived with the deepest conviction that the things you do, the choices you make, inevitably come back to you whether bad or good."

I folded my arms and leaned back in my chair. "Okay... I'm not following."

"I raised you to believe that your actions have consequences. And I might have leaned a little too far into the territory of superstition."

"You think it's superstitious of me to believe that I owe the universe for breaking its rules?"

"Honey, you did not bring this recent betrayal you mentioned upon yourself because you changed time. Whoever betrayed you, that was their doing. Not yours." I'd never wanted to believe her more, but deep down I couldn't release the belief that I'd repeated in my head on endless loop for so long that this, all of this, was my own doing.

"That's just not how this works," she said as the second timer went off for the chicken. Rising from her chair to tend to our dinner, she looked back at me. "You have to understand that people in your life don't betray you, or die, because *you've* done something. Especially, my love, when one thing has nothing to do with the other." She slipped the oven mitt on and opened the oven door. Her chin lifted in response to the waft of heat that rushed out to meet her.

I joined her at the counter to gather the serving plates. "I guess I know that," I said. "But what about karma? Isn't that what you raised me to believe?"

She set the chicken on the stovetop and slipped her hands from the oven mitts before cradling my face. "I believe karma is more of a bigger-picture concept. Good things come to good people and vice versa. Taden, the universe isn't out to even a score with you because you understand the science of its core. You are a wonderful person who loves others and strives to do the best and be the best you can be. Karma isn't out to get you."

· · · · · ● ● ● ● ● ⬤ ● ● ● ● ● · · · ·

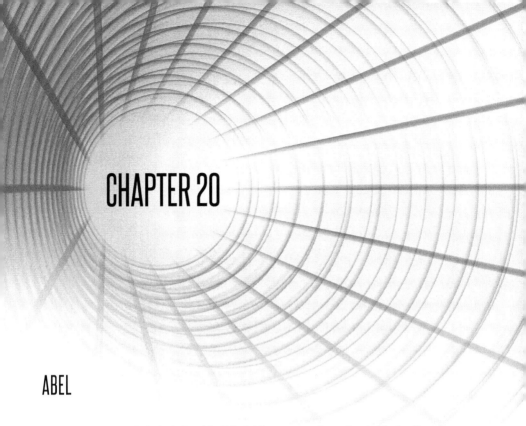

# CHAPTER 20

## ABEL

We were close with Taden's dad and Dr. P. I might even go so far as to say I had gotten closer with Taden's family than my own.

Taden's clan clung to each other and never seemed to have enough time together. It was an adjustment at first, but a welcome one.

Still, the evening her dad called me and asked me to come over to have a drink and talk I have to admit made me nervous. Mrs. Barrett had been in our timeline for a few days already, and tensions were high.

"Son, have a seat," he said, gesturing me toward the leather couch in his study.

He headed over to his matching mahogany liquor cabinet and stood in front of the open doors, pondering which bottle to retrieve. He reached past what looked like his standard fare and selected a bottle. He held the liquor in my direction.

"A prized bottle of American liquid gold," he said, walking toward me and pulling out the cap. Two glasses were waiting on the coffee table between us. He poured one for me. "This is an Elmer T. Lee."

My own top-shelf bourbon knowledge was not much past what his standard fare probably included. Upon recognizing the ignorance on my face, he went on to explain.

"It's aged for many seasons until it's determined to be perfect for consumption." He poured his own glass and held it up to the light streaming in through his window. "Time and patience have worked their magic on this bourbon."

I cleared my throat. The start of this evening hadn't made me feel any less nervous. "Are you sure you want to waste this on me?"

He settled into his sleek armchair across from me and raised his glass. "Considering what I'm about to ask you, you're probably going to need this. Cheers," he said, taking a sip.

I reached forward and tapped my glass to his. "Cheers," I said with hesitation.

"I'm not going to beat around the bush with you." He sipped his bourbon. "Taden bringing her mom here has thrown us all for a loop."

I nodded.

"You don't need to worry, I'm not going to try to get you to talk to my daughter about this. I can see she's working through this on her own. She's a smart woman, and I have every faith she'll figure this one out."

He took a sip. I joined him.

"It's smooth," I said, hoping I didn't sound like an idiot.

He chuckled to himself. "Mm," he agreed. "Elmer Lee would properly boast that it's perfectly balanced and rich." He took another drink.

My blood pressure took a hit. I could see he was right about me needing the effects of the drink for this conversation. It didn't seem like we were headed into any light-hearted chitchat.

"To be clear, I'm not aiming to back you into a corner or force you to choose a side here. That's not why I asked you to come." He crossed his legs. "This is more of a personal request aside from Taden." He cleared his throat. "Having Elizabeth back in the world with me has been a lot to process."

"I can imagine," I offered. Really, I couldn't imagine. Losing Taden and then starting a new life with a new woman, just to have Taden return—through time travel, no less—was impossible to fathom. I stared at the bottle's oval dimples, which were on the side where her dad gripped it to pour. I was already planning on a second glass.

"I love both these women. It's not something I ever thought I'd have to confront. Clearly, I never would have left Elizabeth had she lived. It took decades before I even entertained the idea of intimacy with Sabina."

Speechless, I continued to drain my glass. I'd never heard anyone say Dr. P's first name. I'm not sure I even considered she had one.

"I have so much I want to say to Elizabeth. I want to spend time with her and catch her up. It's all natural. Yet, I feel confined against it. Like it's a mistake. Does this make sense?"

"It does," I confirmed, setting my empty glass on the table.

"Would you like a refill?" he asked, revealing pride in my appreciation of the drink.

I inwardly cringed, unsure of the etiquette of such an expensive bottle. "Should I?"

"Of course." He poured me another and topped off his own glass as well. "Here it is," he plugged the bottle with its cork, signifying our last pour. "I'm imploring you to consider possibly sending me back in time to visit Elizabeth."

I choked on my drink.

"I should get her flowers," he muttered, looking out the window.

"What was that?" I asked, still rebounding from shock.

"How does a man tell his wife that he loves her *and* he loves another woman at the same time? That somehow it's acceptable, since she's dead?"

I took a swallow of my drink, training my eyes on the liquid.

"Flowers don't seem like enough to convey all of that," he said, chuckling. "I attempted this conversation the other day."

He had my undivided attention. "You did?"

"It didn't go well."

"Do you want to tell me about it?" I asked, wishing for the next pour already.

"The girls and I had lunch with Elizabeth."

"Taden mentioned it," I said.

"They left the two of us to finish on our own." He shifted back into his chair. "She and I used to talk about everything, but many parts of who I was, have changed. I didn't even know where to begin."

"What did you say?" I asked.

"I started with the facts. I looked her in the eyes and said, 'Elizabeth, I am flooded with love for you. I spent years resigned to being alone and miserable without you."

"And what did she say?"

"Her eyes welled and she opened her lips as though she had words ready to pour out but she closed them." Mr. Barrett paused and swallowed a sip of his bourbon. "Instead she put her hand on mine and smiled."

"That doesn't sound like it went bad at all," I said, hopeful.

"Son, I haven't even gotten to that part."

"Oh," I said, cringing.

"I'd invited Sabina to meet us, thinking, you know, it would be the big group of us and better to tear the Band-aid off immediately."

I exhaled, seeing where this was going. Also, I couldn't help but still be weirdly uncomfortable with Mr. Barrett's repeated reference to Dr. P as Sabina.

"Sabina approaches the table as Elizabeth's hand is on mine. Mind you, I don't even realize Sabina's there yet."

My eyes squeezed together tight. "Oh no."

"Tell me about it," he said. "She just stood there, unsure if she should sit next to me or Elizabeth." He scratched his head, recounting the lunch. "Did you know that the two of them were friends?"

I nodded. Taden had told me that Dr. Pasterski was an old family friend.

"Anyway, she sat down next to me and Elizabeth withdrew her hand to greet her old friend. The two exchanged pleasantries and then a tense silence fell among us."

"Is that how it ended?"

"Pretty much, after a few more attempts at polite conversation ensued. Sabina seemed fascinated to see Elizabeth. I'd never seen her tongue-tied." He turned to look out his window. "Elizabeth refused a ride home, stating she'd like to walk around a while and call a ride later."

"Oh?" I questioned. "She left without you?"

"She did," he said. A long moment later, he traded his silent meditation out the window back to me.

"Flowers would probably be a nice touch," I wise-cracked, instantly regretting it. To my relief, he granted me a smile for circling back to his original joke.

"How could I explain what grieving her felt like? Or what living alone did to my way of life?"

"From what Taden has told me about Mrs. Barrett," I said, "she'd understand." My unacknowledged agreement to send him into the past lay hidden in my statement.

"I shouldn't want her to hear these things. But I look at her, back from the dead, still in her youth, hurting for her family. She should only be a memory. Having her here is not natural, and we shouldn't be expected to face any of these hardships." He set his drink down on the table and crossed his arms. "But here we are, and we must face them."

I followed his lead and set my drink down, too.

"Before you answer, I want to add the hard part," he said.

"The hard part?" I asked incredulously.

He sounded just like Taden.

"I don't want you to tell Taden. Well, at least not until it's already done. This is between her mother and me. I deeply love Elizabeth." Arms still folded, he turned his back to me. "The only way I can be sure to lessen her pain about my relationship with Sabina is to go back to before the relationship happened and say the words I need to say to Elizabeth now. The words she deserves to hear, in the right context." His speech hit an emotional pitch, and he rose from his seat, avoiding my line of sight.

Was he crying? I panicked. I didn't have any experiences of another man crying in my presence and I wasn't sure how to respond.

"I've come to you for this request because you're a neutral party to this situation." He cleared his throat, returning to his glass for his last bit of golden liquid. "It's not a fair task for me to ask of you, I realize."

He looked out his window again, taking in the last shimmers of evening sunlight. The bold display of his torment moved me. This was bound to be a mistake; my senses were on high alert.

"I'll do it," I said weakly.

He lifted his hopeful eyes. "Well, all right. Cheers to that." He held his now-empty glass to me.

"I should be forthright with you," I said. "I am not one to keep secrets, especially when it comes to your daughter. I'm a firm believer that honesty sets you free."

"I respect your desire to be open with Taden," he said.

"I grew up in a family that loved each other but never risked sharing the hard truths. Because of that, when we're together we feel like strangers." The bourbon was acting as a truth serum. "I don't want that with my own family with Taden. She's my best friend."

"Son, I'm overjoyed that you love her like this. I'm only wanting to protect her as well. She's been so stressed lately. Her mother's death rocked her to her core. I don't want to add my personal entanglements to the issues she's probably reopened having brought her mom back."

I put myself in his shoes and imagined I'd take the same route he was asking me to grant him.

Not only that, but his plan would lessen the pain of the woman who birthed Taden Barrett, the love of my life. How could I not do my part to ease some of Elizabeth's pain?

"I'll keep the launch between you and me. But sir, I'm asking you to tell Taden. I don't want to be in the middle of this issue."

"Agreed," he said, sticking out his hand.

I didn't go right to my car from Mr. Barrett's. I needed to walk off a bit of my charged energy and his bourbon. My mind was already drowning with guilt. After I'd walked several blocks, I pinged my car pilot. Within a few minutes it had located my coordinates and pulled into the closest parking. I crossed the street, pressing the code into my mobile to open the door. Sliding in, I programmed it for home and fastened my safety harness. Staring out the window, I appreciated the fact that I no longer had to drive myself around; the autopilot feature on my car was a new technological luxury I'd never take for granted.

That night, I lay awake, running the plan through my mind. I'd meet her dad for lunch, with the serum prepared at the lab that afternoon. He'd use my TRB and go to the week after Elizabeth's cancer diagnosis. After he returned, I'd come home from work like normal and he promised to tell Taden before the weekend.

· · · · · ● ● ● ● ● ⬤ ● ● ● ● ● · · · ·

# CHAPTER 21

A time-travel trip so inconsequential as this shouldn't have cost me any sleep. Except, it didn't play out that way. After the time travel, Mr. Barrett didn't rematerialize back in my office, renewed with relief. Instead, he rushed through my office doors, having first returned to another location. He was frazzled and unkempt.

"Son, we have a problem," he said, attempting to ignore the harsh physical side effects of time travel.

Exhausted from my lack of sleep, I'd been dozing in my office waiting for him. His intense re-entry rattled my nervous system.

"What happened?" I asked.

"I'm not sure," he muttered, "but when I arrived in this spot, I was greeted by your boss. It almost prevented my entire meeting with Elizabeth."

"Hold on. You were greeted by my boss?"

"Yeah, that tall, stoic lady Taden is always going on about."

"Ms. Farkas?" I asked.

I'd considered the fact that Mr. Barrett would be arriving at a time before any of us were even a consideration in the world of NIST. I had also thought about how his past self's presence at that time could easily be probable, considering his early dealings with the downfall of The Reckoning and his linking up with Dr. Pasterksi. It had dawned on me that this time manipulation could, in fact, have been a factor in initiating Mr. Barrett's part in all of this to happen in the first place. But I hadn't configured any scenario where Danika Farkas would be present.

"Yeah, that's the lady," he agreed. "She was standing there with her hands on her hips, tapping her foot, like she was impatiently waiting. When I appeared, it seemed like I was the very person that she intended to find."

"She was waiting for you?"

"We had words. She threatened my daughter, and a bit of a scuffle ensued with a few of her henchmen. I left in a hurry."

"You returned right after that?" I asked, confused.

"No, I found Elizabeth. After she and I had our talk my time was as good as up, but I still had to get back to the NIST. Bad planning on that bit, friend," he opined. "It's lucky I'm even standing here right now."

He scratched his head. I was slack-jawed. What had I done? What were the pitfalls of this going to be?

"First of all, are you okay?" I asked with concern. He gave me a single, sturdy nod. "Then you waited outside the building until you rematerialized in this time, like we talked about?" Another nod. "Did you have any further encounters with Ms. Farkas?"

"Just as I started to be pulled back from the serum, I noticed her spot me from the main entrance area and move in my direction." He shoved his hands into his back pockets. "Glad she had those heels on. They slowed her down a bit. I faded out of there before she got to me."

"She watched you disappear?"

"I guess she could have. I stepped into the bushes along the building in an attempt to hide myself," he told me.

"Interesting," I said. "This means Ms. Farkas could be aware of time travel before it exists." I folded my arms and leaned into a slight bounce on my heels to ponder the gravity of this. "Can you tell me what she said to you when you first arrived?"

"Her first words were, 'I can't believe it. It's accurate.'"

"Do you know what she was referring to?"

"I assume time travel, because then she went on about my daughter."

"What did she say about Taden?" My chest was filled with icy tension.

"She said something like, 'You better make sure that daughter of yours doesn't stand me up. I'll have to come find her.' Then she motioned to the men behind her and told me I shouldn't be in that building yet, and I had to leave immediately. Her security detail each grabbed an arm and practically dragged me out of the building." Mr. Barrett ran his fingers through his hair, fixing his unkempt appearance. "I bumped into Sabina on my way out." He shoved his hands back into his pockets, glancing out of my office like he was looking for something. "It would figure. I go back in time to talk to my wife and run into my future lover."

I cringed at the idea of Mr. Barrett saying the word lover and relating the word lover to Dr. Pasterski. I cleared my throat, wishing I could clear my mind as easily. He returned his gaze to me.

"She actually took me to see Elizabeth. Can you believe it?"

"No," I said. And honestly, I couldn't believe it. "What did you talk about on the car ride?"

"I tried to remember anything we'd talked about before and rehashed the first conversation that popped into my head."

"How did *that* go?" I began pacing the room.

"She gave me her business card." He fished it from his wallet and handed it to me. "It seemed like a harmless meeting. She didn't even know this old man from the version of me she knows."

He had a point. The man standing in front of me had aged quite a bit since his wife died of brain cancer. There were pictures of her parents together all over their home, and he didn't even look like the same guy he was back then.

"Elizabeth gave me a ride back to the NIST. I think she had a hard time seeing me old like this." He pulled back a chair at my office table and gingerly sat down. "I hadn't even considered my age difference when Taden brought her here to the present. I guess being in my own timeline made me ignorant of that detail. It was a glaring piece going backward, though."

My pulse resettled. Maybe this hadn't gone as haywire as I first feared. In fact, having Danika show up like that—revealing she knows something, and revealing how far back she knew it—gave us our first real piece of intel.

"How did you recognize Ms. Farkas? She must've been in her early twenties then," I asked.

I could easily imagine a younger version of Danika in a bold red pantsuit, digging matching heels into the floor as she marched along, her raven hair tied tightly in a bun. I could even imagine her matching lipstick across a thin-lipped scowl.

"She looked exactly the same as I saw her last," Mr. Barrett said. "Not the kind of person you confuse."

"The same age?" I asked, unable to hide the dismay of what that could mean. He confirmed with a nod.

"Can you think of anything else she may have said?" I asked, walking to my desk to retrieve my mobile. He looked upward, carefully recounting the exchange with her.

"No, that's all she said," he reported.

"'You shouldn't be in this building yet,'" I repeated into my voice memo.

"And she said, 'You better make sure that daughter of yours doesn't stand me up. I'll have to come find her,'" he reminded me.

I nodded and added it to my note. "Do you feel better about things with Mrs. Barrett?" I asked.

A sadness took over his aging eyes. "I think Elizabeth will feel better. It wasn't meant to be about how *I* feel."

I understood what he wanted to accomplish. I'd want to do the same for Taden—although, I couldn't ever imagine loving another woman.

"Let me take you home. You should probably get some rest. Time travel does a hell of a job on the body," I said.

"Son, I feel like I've aged a decade from that event." We both had a good chuckle. "That's the last time I do that."

"Mr. Barrett," I said, "I hope you're right."

"You know," he said as we walked to my car, "I'm thinking back to the first time I met Ms. Farkas, that evening of Taden's first time-travel mission."

"Mm?" I asked with trepidation.

I was not feeling good about the way he was bringing up that memory. As the memory keeper, I was the expert on how rewriting a memory from time travel could tweak the way memory recall occurred. To most time travelers, the new memory doesn't seem unnatural. But one of the tells I've discovered about a rewritten memory is how a rather old and random memory will appear in the mind out of nowhere. To the mind, these are new memories— but to the traveler, they are from deep in the past. Retrieving the memory of Danika from Taden's first launch into time travel was an indicator that Mr. Barrett had just rewritten a memory of his from the night Taden first launched time travel.

This could only mean that on that night, Danika already knew Mr. Barrett. She already knew Taden would discover time travel. She was just waiting for it to be a reality.

What else did Danika know?

"When I met her Taden had just introduced us, and Danika said to me and Taden, 'We've met before.' Taden looked confused and asked me how I knew her boss. Because of the work I did, I had a lot of government connections. But I didn't remember meeting her. I apologized for not remembering and she told me it was okay."

He paused with his arms rested above the car door, perplexed.

"It was a long time ago, and a very brief meeting," he added as we got into the car.

I tapped his address into the car pilot and then further pressed his memory in our short ride to his house.

"Do you remember anything else about that night?" I asked.

"It's fuzzy. I only have fragments," he said, throwing his hands up. "I'm an old man. I'm surprised I remember that meeting at all."

"Danika leaves an impression," I said, noticing how tired Taden's dad appeared. Looking out the windshield, I stayed quiet the rest of the way. Sure enough, Mr. Barrett's snores soon proved his exhaustion.

After I dropped him off, there was only one place for me to go next. Danika had made it a point to show herself. She'd clearly time traveled to that event to meet Mr. Barrett there, but how had she time traveled? There was protocol in place—at least, there was in this present. Did that indicate something to be concerned about in the future? Was Danika controlling time travel? Why was she threatening Taden? Had she discovered we were keeping this intel from her?

It didn't matter. She'd sent a message indicating a threat to Taden. I wouldn't let that go. If Danika knew something we'd been trying to keep from her, I wouldn't let her go after Taden for it. I would step in and stop this threat—and I was on my way to do it.

· · · · · · ● ● ● ◉ ● ● · · · · · ·

# CHAPTER 22

I did not expect to storm into her office with such ease. It was known to be always guarded, so my hunch was that I would have at least two security guards to confront.

I found myself missing the days when I could've addressed Danika Farkas through my own military channel with Bernard Richardson. Still, it was too easy approaching her desk. She sat, hands folded, as if in anticipation of my arrival.

I glanced at her screen displaying the cameras that captured my entrance into the building. She'd watched me move up through each floor in pursuit of her, and allowed it. Why?

"Welcome, Agent Mihal," she said in her classic unwelcoming voice.

"What are you up to, Danika?" I slapped my hands on her desk and leaned far into her personal space.

Unrattled, her eyes narrowed at me. "As always, I am a busy woman. I would appreciate it if you could be more concise with your inquiry."

"Are you digging into time travel behind our backs?" I asked, cutting her off.

Her sneer showed I'd tapped a nerve. Good. I intended to ruffle her, that I might shake out information she'd hoped to keep from me.

"You would be grossly misinformed to think time travel belonged to you." She tapped a single finger on her desk. "You work for me. Time travel is mine."

If possible, she sat a bit more erect in her chair.

"I know you traveled to the past," I said. "You ran into Taden's dad."

The satisfied smile that crept along Danika's red lips truly disgusted me. Through pearly teeth, she told me to sit down. In pursuit of Taden's safety, I agreed. Hands clenching the arm rests, I dragged my chair as close to her desk as possible. Danika was used to dispensing intimidation. It was her turn to receive mine.

"I've always found you to be combative, Agent Mihal." She pursed her lips and squinted, as if she were considering my personality. "It's rather irritating, in a comforting sort of way."

"Mr. Barrett said you threatened Taden." I stood again, with clenched fists. "You will not harm a hair on her head."

"Always the hero," she said, flicking her hand to swipe off the monitor screens that alerted her I'd come. She swiped in the air a few more times until she opened a display she intended to share with me. Pausing when it held projection images of a person, she said, "Please sit," directing me to the chair again.

My head cocked as I realized the man on her screen wasn't really a man at all. I only knew the body rotating on an axis in 360-degree imaging wasn't human because the graphics underneath the body clearly identified it as "Artificial Intelligence DNA Host: First Generation."

Danika twirled her wrist, spinning the screen to me so I'd have better vantage of her plans.

"You're going to love the new role I've developed for you."

"What is this?" I asked, my question unnecessary. There was no doubt she would have continued.

"This is how I will change humanity for the better," she said, her power-hungry eyes flashing.

"Oh?" I asked. "How so?"

"Your wife has played her part in moving us forward with science. Because of her, I've been able to track human evolutions not expected to occur for thousands of years and bring them to us much sooner."

She wasn't making much sense, but the way she claimed grandeur it was clear to me I was still in the dark.

The hairs on the back of my neck stood in salute to my quickened pulse. "Why don't you just tell me your plans for world domination, Danika?"

Her lips pursed with pleasure. "You should feel honored to be at the crossroads of this, Mr. Mihal. Your son will benefit from this advancement. In his lifetime, he may never know of cancer or disease. He will not know pain, or the deterioration of old age."

"You sound a little cuckoo, if I'm being honest."

"Do I?" she asked, her voice seeping with irritation. Danika pushed her chair back and crossed her legs. "You're the keeper of memories. You've borne the weight of that job well."

"Thank you," I said, sarcasm in my voice.

"I've felt badly for you since Dr. Barrett discovered time travel and you—by default— ended up being the only time traveler to have gone on every mission."

"I don't know what nonsense you're talking about, but it doesn't matter. Stay away from Taden." I pointed my finger in her face.

"Once we figured out that the only people who remembered the original timeline, before a time-travel-alteration, were the people on the time jump, it became clear you were the chosen one. An unfortunate destiny." She clicked her tongue, simpering.

"Just say what you're trying to say," I demanded.

"It is a hardship, I'm sure, having to be responsible for all of these memories. No one else knows the history of our world as you do." She sauntered closer to me. I certainly wasn't intimidating her. "It got me thinking, what happens when you die? Or what if you live a long life but you start to forget?"

It was a serious concern we'd discussed among our team. "Are you going to tell me your plan anytime soon?" I asked, becoming more irritated by the minute.

"I'm promoting you to the role of Keeper of Destiny," she said, folding her hands together on her knee. "Mm. I like the sound of that, don't you?"

"Listen, I came here to warn you." I leaned forward in my chair. "Back off of Taden. Stay away from us."

Her eyes fixed past me.

"I can make you disappear," I added, hoping to catch her attention.

She ignored my threat. I wondered if she'd even heard me.

"You will be keeping all the technologies meant for our future," she said, pulling her gaze onto me. "Housed in that brain already full of our memories." She tapped her own temple. "You will be kept alive," she paused, "but will be given an upgrade as the mainframe access to all of Earth's past, present, and future."

I rose from the chair, not daring to break eye contact with her.

"Abel Mihal will be gone." Her lips parted into the same wicked smile she'd greeted me with earlier. "Passed on," she said, flicking her hand and pulling up the next image of her AI plans. "But your memory-keeper brain will have an even higher function to hold all of the records of what we have and will have accomplished as a species."

"I decline the offer."

"It's not really an offer, Mr. Mihal. You hold records of everything that has happened before a time event disruption. That is invaluable information, and it would be irresponsible not to preserve them. Besides, we need a human participant for this next stage of my technology and you are the only one I want for this task." She batted her lashes, mocking me.

"I will neither participate in this experiment nor support your notions. I feel a responsibility to see to it you don't continue with these sinister plans you've conjured." I reached into my jacket holster and slid my fingers onto my gun.

"Mr. Mihal, I'm surprised at you. I thought you were a man of science. Of onward and upward." She flipped her hand. "What would Dr. Barrett think?"

"You have literally proposed to kill me in order to preserve my brain in a robot. Are you hearing yourself?"

"Well, yes. I can see how you might take that personally. But think of the bigger picture. You will be donating yourself to science, to the evolution of man into robot."

"Absolutely not."

"I don't want to risk the chance that your lovely wife or future son find you along a timeline somewhere." Her face twisted into a dark, menacing stare as she mentioned Taden. My fingers twitched on the cold metal of my gun. She followed my movement with her eyes. "...your physique will change as well." She held her palm open. "Essentially, Abel, you'll become the host of our first human time travel artificial intelligence. You will carry the DNA of every living being within your programming."

My chin dropped. "What the hell are you talking about?"

"No need to be injected with any serum ever again. Using the access of all human DNA within your structure, you will be able to target any date into the past or future and travel there."

I pulled the gun on her, aimed it at her chest. She didn't so much as flinch. Why didn't she flinch?

"It will be as if *you* are a time travel vessel. We are one step closer to creating a vessel that can host a passenger. No more injections or mixing of serums. All of these complicated steps will be programmed into the vessel. We can eliminate the turbulence of the trip. It's all such an exciting prospect, don't you think?"

"You're really going to harvest people and turn them into AI time-travel vessels? Then what do you want with Taden?" Again, she ignored my questioning.

"Your wife has shown little to no interest in actually getting into the future, but I've been nosing about in past time travels, lining up dates, bumping into travelers, tagging them without their knowledge. From all the puzzle pieces I've gathered from my informers throughout various timelines, I've captured enough intel to know she's solved it. And shame on the two of you for running around behind my back."

Danika stood from her chair to match me. She folded her arms with indifference to the gun trained on her. I cocked the hammer, only waiting to be certain there weren't loose ends regarding her details with Taden. My anticipation was heightened for the moment I'd release an easy trigger to end her.

"I even know how she solved it, and that you're in on it. I know your son plays an important role in getting to the future. Those bits of intelligence were the launching points for me to begin the Artificial Intelligence Time Travel Program." Her calculated step closer to me left us almost nose to nose. "You need not worry, your family will think you're dead."

I recoiled. My body betrayed the message of having the upper hand that I intended to send to her.

"And here's the best part. Your son," she whispered as she pushed the gun away from her chest with her forefinger, "*designs your AI prototype*—the body you will live in for the rest of eternity."

She cackled at the irony, like a mad person.

"Of course, he doesn't know this." She crossed her arms again. "Could you imagine what that would do to the poor child?"

I remained slack-jawed.

"He's designing all of this for me in the future, and my future self is bringing all of this here to our present. And I have to tell you, my future self is very fond of your boy, Jay. She talks about him non-stop."

Danika took a few steps back until she leaned against her desk. The reprieve this offered gave me much-needed room to breathe.

"I've been busy outfitting your new body for you so we can zip-zip on our way." Danika wagged her finger. "The thing is, I know you don't want to be a part of this. I know you're scrambling through that memory-heavy brain, trying to outsmart me, considering if you should just kill me."

She glanced at the gun now dangling in my hand.

"But you need to know, I've considered who I wanted this AI prototype to be for a long time. And Mr. Mihal, you are really the best candidate. Your brain not only holds all of the original memories from before time travel began, but it is one of the most highly efficient brains I've found among my potentials. Getting you out of Taden's life turns her into a much more focused scientist, and that just really benefits my goals. You asked what I want from her. I only want her to be focused and cooperative. And Abel, according to my future self, the relationship I form with your son can only happen if you're gone. Plus, I cannot overstate how important you become to me as the AI life form you're meant to be. Future Danika has made that crystal clear."

I wasn't sure what to say. Her words left me frozen. I never respond with inaction. What was I waiting for? I directed the gun to her heart.

Her eyes widened. I had heard all I needed to finish her.

"Abel, you should know before you shoot me, my future self has already placed smoke signals throughout every route of time that, if triggered, will tell her to destroy your wife and son."

Folding her fingers to her lips, she delivered her final words. The words that would seal my service to her whims.

"The only way they will be able to survive this destiny is for you to cooperate. And for your family to cooperate. We both know that means Dr. Barrett will know nothing of this endeavor. She can be a thorn when her morals are threatened."

She sauntered behind her desk and wiggled herself back in the chair, seemingly to emphasize her lack of concern for her own safety. My throat was so dry a cough spasm took hold. Danika opened her hand toward my chair, indicating I should sit back down. I followed her command.

"Get your affairs in order. I'm giving you time to see your son, to say goodbye without actually saying goodbye." Her eyes bulged to emphasize the entertained smile she wore. "You know, make your peace with this."

"How long?" was all I could manage to say.

"I'll give you time to meet your son while I finish the details on my end, but in the meantime you will report to me daily, and we'll begin preparing your host body to acclimate to your human self." She stood again. "Thank you for stopping by today. It did save me the visit. I look forward to working more closely with you in the future."

I blinked. I couldn't even remember a time when I'd been so flummoxed. I didn't even quite remember what'd brought me to her in the first place. Her heels clicked against the floor and snapped me from my shock.

"Good day, Abel. You can see yourself out." And like a switch she turned from me, already busy with another pressing matter.

I stumbled away and, although I wished to be consumed with a solution out of this mess, all I could manage to think through was that my son knew his father and that my wife never stepped on any of Danika's land mines in time.

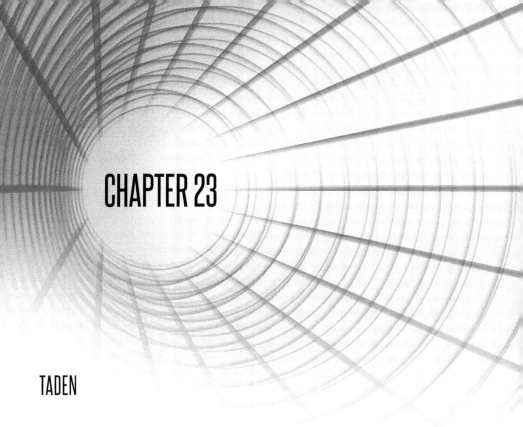

# CHAPTER 23

## TADEN

Dakotah still didn't know my mom was here, and it was becoming a lie of omission. It's just that I had trusted in Danika Farkas. Finding out she was a terrorist hit almost harder than when I found out the same about Marius.

I couldn't help but feel skeptical about almost everyone these days. I'd even caught myself wondering about Dr. P at times. It was enough to make me remember my visit to the mental ward. But, with the smallest of doubt swirling, I didn't want to bring this to Dakotah until I was damn sure there was no way I would be betrayed a third time. Abel agreed. Although he was becoming jumpy about *every* move I made.

"I don't want anyone else to know anything about our time-travel-related life," he said, closing his office door. "At this point, we don't know who we can trust."

"You're starting to sound like me." Folding my arms, I hoped to counteract the chill that ran up my spine. "Did something happen?"

"Nothing beyond the fact that our boss is an egocentric, entitled sociopath."

"Mm-hm. Okay." Something definitely happened. This wasn't normal Abel commentary. "You'll tell me when you're ready. Should I be worried?" I asked.

"I've got it under control," he said.

*Interesting*, I thought. He didn't attempt to convince me there wasn't an issue.

"I'm going to head out to get home and spend some time with my mom. Let me know if you need anything." Before leaving, I pressed a gentle kiss to his cheek and squeezed his arm. "I'll see you at home." *And I'll try not to worry about whatever is stressing you,* I thought to myself.

$\bullet \bullet \bullet \bullet \bullet \bullet \bullet \bullet \bullet \bullet \bullet \bullet \bullet \bullet \bullet$

# CHAPTER 24

"Honey, sit down," my mom said.

"What's on your mind?"

"How do you think Sabina is doing with my presence here?"

I stared blankly at her. "Who?"

"Oh, come on! You know Dr. Pasterski's first name!"

I shook my head like I'd just sucked on a lemon. "I don't call her by her first name. Like, ever. And neither does anyone else."

"Not even your father?" she asked.

"No one."

"I think that's rather odd."

"Maybe so. But to answer your question, I think she's dealing with the change appropriately." I paused thoughtfully. "I'm sure it's an adjustment, but you have a lot to adjust to as well. After all, she is the one who actually gets to have a relationship with Dad in this scenario." I shrugged. "I think that makes your feelings more of a concern at this point. Even for 'Sabina'." My face twisted again. "Nope, still can't call her by her first name."

"Sweetheart, I'm really at peace with this. I've told you your dad came to visit me and told me he'd moved in with Dr. Pasterski."

"No. You definitely didn't tell me that. I would've remembered."

"I'm sure we talked about it. You have a lot going on, and a minor detail like that would be easy to forget."

"Are you saying he came to the house and talked to you? Where was I? Or do you mean this was what the two of you discussed at the diner the other day?"

"I mean he came to tell me long ago in the past. I've always known I would lose my cancer battle and he would eventually end up with Dr. Pasterksi."

Prickly sensations spread up my arms. "You certainly did not know all of that when I brought you here."

"I did, though," she asserted.

"Dad time-traveled?" I muttered to myself. I'd wondered how he'd gotten the clearance, and why he and I hadn't discussed it. It was clear to me that Mom's memories had been rewritten just since our last conversation. The question that haunted me was why didn't I just ask him. Did I doubt him, too?

I concluded that by having my mom tell me about the encounter, my dad had primed me to discuss this with him and arrange for him to make the trip back to do so. It made most sense that it was me that sent him on that trip. I wondered when this awkward conversation was going to happen with him. These loops of time travel into the past to set up events in my present made me dizzy. I might've been suffering from what has been referred to as the butterfly effect.

I should've been discussing these events in the memory collection process with Dakotah, but the only way to make that happen was to come clean to her and hope that it didn't bring danger to her door, or mine. Abel held all of our memories, but Dakotah was the one who deciphered them for inconsistencies and analyzed the patterns to establish the rules of how memories were affected by time travel.

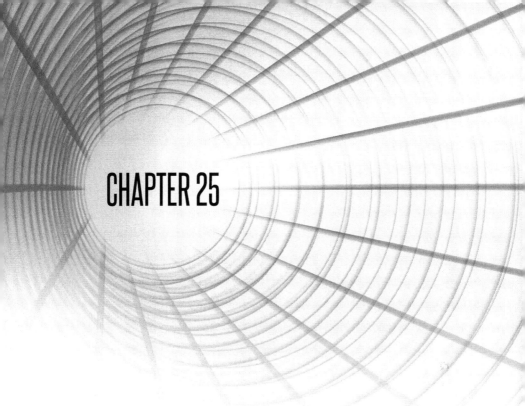

# CHAPTER 25

I inhaled and pushed open the door to Dakotah's office. "I have something important to talk to you about," I said, barging in. "I want to be completely honest with you, though."

Dakotah startled from her task. Blinking, she said, "I would hope so."

"No, Dakotah, this is going to be the hardest conversation I've ever had with you. And after we're done, I'm going to need you to convince me I can trust you."

Her face showed surprise. "Haven't I always done so?"

"I mean, I *should* just believe you have. I'm sure it feels shitty that I'm questioning your integrity. I'm really sorry about this. I'm in a dark place right now, and I haven't always made the best choices in people." I paused, swallowing my nerves. "Marius, for example. As you well know, he really caught me off guard."

"Taden, what is this about? The Marius thing is in the past."

I looked hard at her. Maybe if I looked thoroughly enough, I'd be able to see if she was really, truly my friend or not. In her returned gaze, all I could see was honesty. It's all I wanted to see.

"I've been betrayed within the NIST again." My throat constricted as I spoke. "Actually, we all have."

Her brows pinched. "What happened?"

I didn't know how to tell her. I thought I could just blurt it out, but when push came to shove, I froze. I suddenly worried someone might be listening.

"Let's go," I said.

"Go? Go where?" she asked, her alarm growing.

"We need to get off the grid for this," I said, pointing to the ceiling.

"Um, Taden, you're kind of scaring me."

"That's actually a good sign," I said. "Give me your phone."

"You're crazy," she said.

"I know. Just give it to me." She pulled her phone out of her coat pocket and reluctantly handed it over. I set it on her desk and pulled her from the office. In complete silence, we walked to my car and drove to the nearest park. She remained in a state of apprehension, staring wildly at me. I hoped she didn't think I was the dangerous one in this situation.

"We can talk here. It'll be safer than the lab." I said, pulling into the parking lot.

We each got out of the car and sat on the swings. My growing belly was making the situation uncomfortable.

"I really cannot figure out how to tell you any of this. One, because after you know it, your world is going to change. And two, I'm still scared of the ridiculous possibility you might be a part of it." I felt instant guilt over this accusation, and looked to her with apology. "Not because I don't trust *you,* but because I'm now having a hard time with trust in general."

"Taden, I get it. And I know telling you that you can trust me isn't going to help. But you can."

"There's only one way to find out." I sucked in a deep breath. "Here goes nothing...the night that Berthold was killed, Abel and I time traveled to undo his fake assassination and make sure he was really assassinated."

She stopped moving on her swing.

Blinking, she asked, "Are you telling me you guys killed Berthold?"

I nodded. "But that's not what I'm trying to tell you." I breathed deeply, looking around for proof that we hadn't been followed. "Dakotah, it's Danika."

"What's Danika?" she asked, visibly frustrated.

"Abel and I arrived at the location of his fake assassination, and we saw that Danika was working with him. She had orchestrated his disappearance, which means she was a part of an entire attack on our country that Abel and I undid with the actual assassination of him. But she still has the means to execute the very same attack if she decides to. Plus, who knows what else she's intending."

Dakotah's face dropped. She began to pump her legs, getting the swing going. I joined her. We continued to swing side by side in silence, contemplating our future.

I wished I could say I left any doubts I could have had about Dakotah there on the swings, but I wasn't sure I was capable of fully trusting anyone anymore. It did do a lot for my faith in her to watch her struggle with coming to terms over Danika's betrayal. More than I could ever doubt Dakotah, I felt connected to her pain and shock in that moment. I don't know how long we swayed back and forth, but at some point, a natural ending brought us back to stationary on the long plastic seats.

"There's more, isn't there?" she asked me.

I nodded. She nodded in return.

"This is the part that is going to require me to test my faith in you," I said. "Only six people in the world, including myself, know what I'm going to tell you next."

"Hold on." She lifted her palm. "You've told five other people about this NIST breach and I'm not one of them?" She smoothed her hands down her ponytail. "That must mean you're either worried about me because I'm in danger or because you think *I am* the danger." Her eyes were blinking too fast for the coolness she maintained otherwise.

"I can only be one hundred percent certain about Abel, since we found all of this out together."

"But if you hadn't found out, whatever this is, *with* Abel you'd suspect him as well?" Her voice gained volume.

"Yeah, I think so. I mean, Dr. Pasterski knows—and I'm even finding myself wondering about her, if that tells you anything about my state of mind." I paced in a circle. "But you deserve to know this, and that's why I brought you here."

I looked her dead in the eyes, pleading with her on a subconscious level to be my true friend.

"I've figured out how to travel into the future. And I proved it: I went back, and I brought my mom here."

Her mouth gaped open. She shook her head in disbelief, then pushed herself off the swing and immediately broke into pacing. I dangled in my swing while she circled around me, following her with my eyes. I was just considering I'd told her too much when she halted.

Then she lunged and slapped my arm.

"I cannot believe you kept that from me."

"Ouch." I winced, rubbing my arm. "That hurt."

"Good," she said fervently, her hands on her hips.

With my focus on the fact that I didn't fully trust her, I didn't expect the *actual* secret would hurt Dakotah's feelings.

"I deserved that, I guess," I said. "I was really trying to protect you from whatever danger Danika might be, if you weren't a part of her ploy."

"Well, I'm *not* a part of her ploy. And I *am* a part of your team. I am your best damn friend, and this secrecy stops right here." She pointed at me. "You will not keep shit like this to yourself for another minute. I don't know if I should be furious at you or allow myself to start geeking out with excitement that you figured it out."

My lips curled upward. The stormy emotions swirling about started to dissipate at the mention of her excitement.

"Do you want to know the details?" I asked, hoping the enticing question would distract her from the pain I'd caused.

Dakotah couldn't possibly be anything other than her true self. How I became muddled enough to doubt her was suddenly unfathomable. With childlike enthusiasm she plopped down on the wood chips below my swing, looking up at me in earnest, ready for me to explain.

"My mom had a new memory. One she didn't tell me about when I brought her here. My dad went back in time to meet with her."

"You're saying she didn't realize she hadn't told you about this before?"

"Exactly. It was my red flag that it was a rewritten memory." I tucked my hair behind my ears. "But the strange part was that the new memory didn't re-write my memory. I knew she hadn't told me my dad went to visit her before. This is the first time I've encountered someone's rewritten memory and have been able to identify it."

"Mm, that is interesting," Dakotah muttered.

"Unless I went on that time travel with my dad. But if I had done that, wouldn't that memory be written into this timeline for me?" I continued to pace. "Unless I didn't go on that time travel with him. And if not, who did?"

# CHAPTER 26

"I'm ready to go home," my mom told me. She was lying next to me on the floor of my baby's nursery. We were staring at the ceiling where I had sponge-painted big fluffy white clouds onto the bright blue.

"I know you are," I said, rolling on my side to look at her. "Thank you for coming here and spending this time with me. I really needed it."

She stroked my hair, her eyes smiling at me. "I needed this, too. You gave me a precious gift. I wouldn't have gotten to see how you girls turned out. To meet your husband. Learn about my grandchild. Know your dad is happy. This has been…"

"Karma. It's all because of how good you are, Mom. All the greatness in our lives you were a factor of is leading us to these outcomes."

She kissed my forehead. "Thank you for letting me go. I need to get back home to you and your sister and make the days I have left—with you there—count."

"I love you, Mom."

"I love you, too, sweetheart."

Ruth finally faced the fact that this was her very last chance to say goodbye. I stood outside the room, listening to the two of them sob. Leaning against the wall, feeling sad but not empty, my baby kicked around inside my belly. He could hear his grandma, and he was saying goodbye, too.

She left on a Tuesday. It was an ordinary day. I went to work after she left. The time we had together left nothing unsaid. I would certainly always miss her, but for the first time, with joy, I was moving forward.

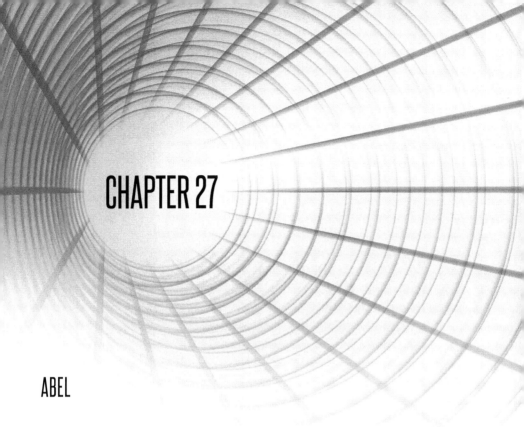

# CHAPTER 27

## ABEL

"Whatcha working on?" Taden asked, leaning over me.

I tapped the icon to enlarge it for her to see. "I'm making the baby an album." I swiped past the initial video I posted of Taden peeking at her stomach in the mirror.

Her cheeks pinkened. "I didn't even know you took that video."

"I'm already glad I did," I said. "Look how sweet it is." I looked up at her. She wasn't yet convinced. "This virtual album will host a series of video diaries for him."

"Or her," she added with a jab. "We don't know what it is yet, so be prepared for either."

"Or her," I agreed.

"It's funny that Dr. Mihal, who hated uploading video reflections of time-travel events into his TRB, is willingly creating a video series for his unborn child." She ruffled my hair, softening her teasing.

"It's just that, considering my work, it's not too far of a reach to think something could happen to me, and I want our child to know how much I already love him…or her."

This made her nudge the back of my head. "Abel, I don't like you talking like that. Or even thinking like that."

"It's just my way of covering all the bases."

"Mr. Prepared," she said. "Prepare for our child to never need these videos." Her face was crimson then.

"Aw, Taden, don't get upset. Nothing is going to happen to me. I'm just inspired to do something special for our baby. Besides the video series what else should be posted here, you think?"

I was surprised she was responding emotionally, but I had noticed her pregnancy hormones triggered responses I wasn't expecting. Maybe I'd gone too heavy. I'd been trying to be normal with her. Not let her in on what Danika had planned for me, for our family.

"It would be nice to post pictures of big events throughout *her* life," she said, chuckling. "With a caption about it so that when the baby graduates high school we can send an invitation for him or her to view all of this content. Wouldn't that be fun? To keep it a surprise?"

I pulled her onto my lap. "I love that idea."

She pressed her lips to mine. Her eyes stayed closed, but I kept mine open. I often did at the start of a kiss with her. I loved the way her head always tilted ever so slightly to the right, and the instant her lips were close enough to sense mine tension lines on her forehead would dissipate.

She pulled back, opening her eyes to meet mine, still open.

"How about this?" I said. "I'll do the video segments and you just post every important event that ever happens in our child's life."

She scoffed as she climbed from my lap, sliding her hands to her hips with her feet planted back on the floor. "Sounds like a fair distribution."

Chuckling, I sent her the link with our password. "Okay, we vow to keep this secret. Till he…or she graduates."

Taden flashed her hooked little finger. "I pinky swear."

The day we officially found out we were having a boy, I recorded the doctor's visit and posted it to his memory album.

"You see that right there?" the technician said, pointing to a shape protruding from the baby's image.

Taden nodded. My camera moved in tandem.

The tech looked at us with the anticipation one often has before sharing big news. Her eyes grew double their size. Her brows practically disappeared in her hairline, and she spread her lips so wide the camera even picked up the hints of pink lipstick on her teeth.

"That means you're having a boy."

In the video, you can hear the moment that news sinks in for me. My breath hitched so loudly I originally intended to edit it out, but after watching, I changed my mind, thinking our son would love to hear my excitement.

"Do you have names picked out yet?" the tech asked.

"We have a few on the docket." I winked at Taden.

 We'd already picked out names for each possibility, but instead of keeping the gender reveal a secret from everyone we decided not to share the baby's name until after Taden delivered.

"Will we name her Elizabeth after your mom?" I asked.

"Aww, that's sweet. I'd love to name her after my mom. But it's funny, growing up, my mom asked me to name my daughter, if I ever had one, after *her* mom, my Grandma Patricia."

I smiled. "Patricia. I like it."

"Oh!" she exclaimed. "What about Patricia Elizabeth Mihal? And we can call her Patty for short?"

My cheeks were beginning to hurt from the overwhelming joy.

"What do you think for a boy?" she asked.

"I've actually been thinking about that one." I quickly jaunted from our room and grabbed a book from Taden's bookshelf, holding it up for display when I returned. Her eyes lit up. She looked expectantly at me, then the book, then back at me.

"Francis or Scott? she asked.

"I was thinking Jay."

"We've done it then, Patricia if it's a girl and Jay if it's a boy."

 The technician pinged both of our mobiles with the 3-D sonograms. I closed the recording and tapped her message. Staring at it, I could barely make out the black and white from the gray.

"Swipe to the next few images," the tech instructed.

As I did, a lump formed in my throat. The sonogram technology projected a virtual age progression of my son and what he was going to look like on the day of his birth. The shape of his tiny mouth looked exactly like Taden's.

My videos from that day on were much more specific to a son. A son that I knew would grow up without his dad. I wanted him to know the truth about why I had to leave, but I couldn't risk Danika finding out that Jay or Taden had knowledge she'd harm them for possessing.

· · · · · ● ● ● ● ● ● ● ● ● ● ● ● · · ·

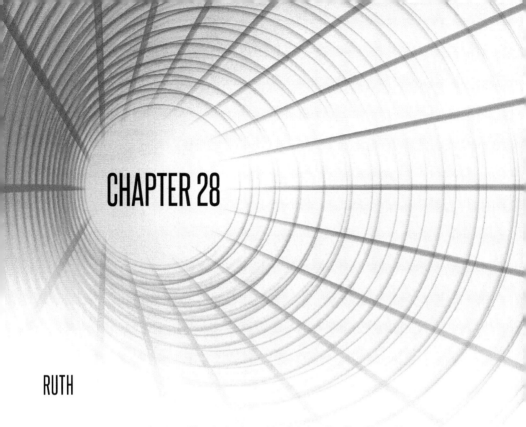

# CHAPTER 28

## RUTH

It'd been many long weeks since Mom had returned back to her timeline. The entire experience complicated how I thought about her, the way I grieved her.

"How are you doing with Mom gone?" I asked Taden. She'd come over for a quick lunch before a doctor's appointment.

She shrugged. "How about you?"

"About the same," I agreed. I sat down next to her at the island in my kitchen. "In one way, my brain no longer files her away as dead."

"What do you mean?" she asked.

"I mean, I had a very real experience with her being alive, here in the present. And even though my intelligence can explain how that happened, my soul felt her alive and it's all so confusing for me to grapple with."

"I'm sorry." She scraped her fork along the rice and beans on her plate. "I didn't mean for this to cause you pain. I thought it would be good for both of us to have her back."

"I know you did. But also, Taden, some part of you knew this was a problem. You kept it secret, you did this behind my back. It didn't feel like you were too concerned with considering how this would affect me, not really."

She stared at me, her chin quivering.

"I want to move on from this," I said. "I don't think I can take any more secrets from you. I love you. You're my best friend." I paused. "Taden, look at me." She stopped moving rice back and forth. "Eventually, you're going to have to trust me and consider how your choices affect me, too."

"I hear what you're saying. I see how I withhold information. It's not because I don't love you, and it's not because I don't care about what happens to you. Quite the contrary."

"Before you brought Mom here, you fessed up about visiting her in the past." She nodded earnestly. "I didn't judge you for that choice. I got it. I was upset you did all that and didn't even talk to me about it."

She nodded again. "Yeah, I should've told you before I went."

"That night you told me about how you'd gone to the past…"

"Yeah?" she asked.

"…there was another thought you wanted to tell me. Something about the NIST and a time travel you and Abel made. Something you hadn't even told Dakotah about?"

She grimaced. "I'm worried that if I tell you, it'll put you in danger."

"Actually, that's not usually how this works with us," I reminded her. "Typically, the things you *don't* tell me for the sake of your work end up being the most life-threatening." My face pinched with the harsh reality.

"Touché." She sucked in a contemplative breath. "I learned unnerving details about Danika Farkas."

As she said her name, I visually watched my sister come undone. She brought her fingers to her mouth and absentmindedly began chewing on her cuticles. I swatted at her hand.

"That's not good for your teeth. Don't do that," I said. "What'd she do? And have you told Dakotah yet?"

"I've talked to Dakotah about it," she said, nodding.

"What did she say?" My curiosity was piqued. Dakotah and I were getting serious in our relationship, and she hadn't mentioned anything like this to me.

"Let's just say, I thought Danika was a totally different person than she is."

"Is it possible you could be projecting unhealed Marius trauma onto her?" As soon as I posed the question, I regretted it. It was a sensitive topic that I hadn't trod into very lightly.

"Are you serious?" she curtly asked, with slitted eyes.

She leaned forward with her hands over her baby bump. The closed-off posture alerted me I'd already hurt her.

"I'm sorry," I quickly uttered. "That was insensitive of me." I put my hand on her knee. "I'm listening."

With her eyes closed, she shook her head. "Nah, don't worry about it. I just think I misread her is all."

Obviously there was more for her to divulge, but I understood how poorly I'd handled the topic. It wasn't the right time to press her.

After that evening, she seemed to be over her issue with Danika.

In hindsight, I'd completely misread that observation.

* * * * * * * * * ● ● ● ● ● ● ● ● ● · · · ·

# CHAPTER 29

## TADEN

I took the bottle out of the fridge and set it on the counter. Pressing the controller to set the temperature of the milk, Abel rubbed my shoulders.

"Are you sure you want to do this?" he asked me one last time.

"Yes, Abel. I'll be safe." I set the bottle in the warmer and turned around to face him. "I won't speak to a single person. I'll go, find out what kind of damage Danika can accomplish in six months, and come back."

"You have to promise me you won't go poking about. Stay away from her," he said.

Doe-eyed, I asked him, "You think I would intentionally approach Danika?"

Abel laced his fingers around my lower back. I swear, my insides still flip-flopped every time he touched me, even in the middle of the night, exhausted from the late-night feeding sessions. Forehead to forehead, he made me give him my word.

"Abel, I promise you. I'm not going to put myself in danger. What trouble could I actually get into, traveling a mere six months forward in time? We now know future time travel works, but this is going to be the first trip past the present into the future. This is huge, and I've spent years leading up to this breakthrough. I really want to be the one to go first. I'll go. I'll look around, try to not touch anything, and then when I return you can go—and dig in—all you want."

"This could be dangerous," he warned. "I don't want anything to happen to you. It's really important that you interact with no one. Pop in and pop out." He tenderly kissed the top of my head. "I love you," he whispered.

He was still giving me notes of concern that I never usually picked up from him. I was about to press him further about it, when sudden fits of shrieking from the next room interrupted my response.

"That's his hungry cry," I said, retrieving the bottle. "I'll go."

"How can you tell?" Abel scratched his head. "Sounds like all his other cries to me."

"Ha!" I stretched my ear toward the nursery. "Sixth months of around the clock bottle feeding and you really can't hear him yelling, 'Come feed me. Feed me now?'" I teased as I headed into Jay's nursery.

I meant to tell him how he and little Jay were my whole world, and how I had zero intention of being gone long enough to miss them.

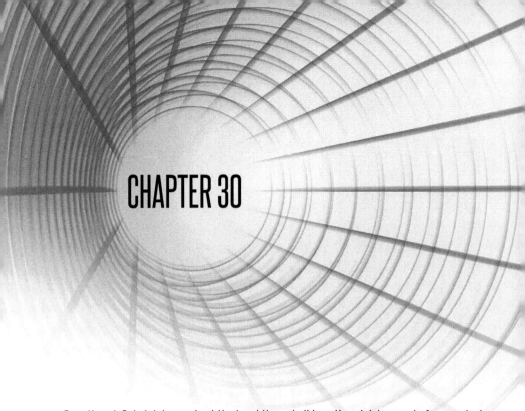

# CHAPTER 30

Even though Dakotah knew about the breakthrough, I'd continued doing most of my work at Dr. P's to keep the NIST—namely Danika—in the dark. I'd left Abel and Jay home. I couldn't pull the trigger with both of my guys there. It would've been impossible to leave them.

The last thing Abel said to me was, "Don't talk to anyone, don't go anywhere. Got it?"

I scrunched my face. The way he was overdoing his protective orders made me want to explore a little.

"I told you, I'll be totally safe," I said.

Maybe I should've listened to him.

Dr. Pasterski was my mentor all these years, so it was fitting that she'd see me off to the future and be here for me when I returned. With my Timed Release Band attached to my forearm already set to six months in the future— the furthest I could go with baby Jay's DNA—I returned a confident smile to my mentor.

"You know," she said, brushing my cheek with the back of her aging hand, "I always think I couldn't be more proud of you, and then you do the next thing that shatters the glass ceiling."

My hand settled on hers, and I squeezed tight. "Having a child of my own has opened my eyes, in a way."

"Oh? How so?"

"I've come to understand the love you have for me. The pride that I've seen in your eyes over the years, but never fully appreciated." She bit her bottom lip. "I want you to know that I love you, and I appreciate everything you've ever done for me."

"Sweet girl," she said, wrapping me in a motherly embrace.

# CHAPTER 31

 An unforeseen great deal can happen in six months. It doesn't seem like that much time in the grand scheme of things but knock down one domino and in an instant they all topple.

I'd time traveled to Dr. Pasterski's lab six months into the future. Other than her absence in the room, nothing appeared noticeably different—but it wasn't the changes of her home laboratory I was there to discover.

My first plan of action was to locate the whereabouts of Danika Farkas, head of the shadow government, The Patriot Party. She was our mole, and I wanted to figure out what type of threat she might pose if we left her unchecked.

I peered at my TRB. Just over an hour. I hopped into my dad's car and programmed it for the NIST. During the short drive, I had time to contemplate Abel's warnings about not interacting with anyone—specifically Danika.

My employee badge worked. That was a good sign. Maxine met me at security without batting an eye.

"How you doing today, Dr. Barrett?" she asked.

"I'm good. And you?"

"Can't complain. You have plans for the big birthday coming?"

"Whose? Dr. Mihal's?" I asked, hoping I hadn't forgotten a milestone he was celebrating this year. I was sure his big birthday was the next year.

Gathering my purse and keys from the x-ray scanner, I glanced up to find Maxine's face painted with concern. Her brow was furrowed in confusion.

"Oh, no. Whose did I forget?" I asked.

"Jay's! Lordy, you better get planning. First birthdays don't plan themselves."

She was still watching me with worry. The concern I saw on her didn't typically cloud her easy nature. Did she notice something odd about me?

I quickened my pace to the lab. I wasn't supposed to be talking to anyone here. I was fairly confident that the future version of me wasn't already here, because Maxine would've been suspicious running me through security a second time. Still, I entered the lab with caution. I preferred not to run into anyone. However, if I did happen to encounter someone, most likely Quinn, my plan was to play it cool. I would not say anything that would come back in conversation with the Taden who belonged in this timeline. I didn't want to throw Quinn off with something odd I might say.

"Hey, Taden! Can you check this calculation?" Quinn yelled.

I hadn't even gotten five steps into the office and she'd already found me. "Sure," I told her, trying to act casual. I looked over the responses to the genetic coding we were working on. I was surprised to learn that in the next six months I'd apparently still not revealed to her the need for a descendant's DNA to make future time travel work.

I shook off the nudge of guilt I felt for allowing my team to keep chasing their tails.

"Hm. It looks like you've got everything recorded accurately. Still just going backward, though, eh?" She pouted and slumped away. "Hey, Quinn? Is Abel here yet?"

Quinn froze mid-stride. She didn't turn around at first, but sort of tilted her head like maybe she didn't hear me. When she looked at me over her shoulder, the mortification was written all over her face.

"What?" I asked. She didn't move but her eyes widened even further, if it was possible. "What's the matter?"

As if standing on a rickety bridge crumbling beneath her feet, she carefully turned full on to face me.

"I'm sorry." She paused, glancing down. "I think I heard you wrong."

"I asked if Abel was here yet." Her face paled, and she stared at her shoes. "Quinn, are you all right? You look like you're going to be sick."

"I'm okay. I, uh…" She kept her eyes trained on the floor.

"I'll go check his office," I said, taking a few steps in his direction. "You sure you're gonna be okay?"

Quinn slid her fingers through her hair and watched me walk away. I peeked back as I left, to make sure she wasn't puking in the middle of the lab. I probably should've handed her the garbage can, but I was still trying to be inconspicuous. Though I considered that having to clean her stomach contents from the floor would be a conspicuous event.

The light was off in Abel's office, and the door was locked. Glancing through the window I noticed his laptop wasn't on his desk, which was a clear sign he wasn't in yet, either. My plan was to snoop around my office, check my planner, skim through a few files, and find out as much as I could in as quickly a manner as possible regarding the state of things here.

If I didn't find anything notable, I supposed I could chat with Quinn a few more minutes, to discover why she was behaving oddly, before I returned home. She'd already seen me anyway.

My planner for the past six months was mostly normal; however, there was a day about four weeks prior that was completely blacked out. No appointments. No plans. Completely shaded in with black. I'd never used this for any plans, ever, not even if I was to go on vacation. It was strange. And I *was* here to find anything unusual. What could I have intended for this? It wasn't like I could come out and ask Quinn what happened four weeks ago. I really wanted to peek at Abel's planner at that point. I was sure whatever I had going on that day, he was aware of it. This thought gave me the idea to get a look at Quinn's planner. Maybe hers would have answers.

I walked back into the lab to find her stationary on a stool. She was just sort of dazed. I was struck by how uncharacteristic it was to find her like this.

"I'm actually kind of worried about you," I told her. "You really don't seem like you feel well."

"Ahem." She began fumbling with the pipette next to her. "I thought you were..." she trailed off again.

"Maybe you should go lie down," I said.

"No, I'm okay, really."

"Do you mind if I check out your calendar for a minute? I had a glitch in mine, and I just want to cross-reference a few dates."

"Yeah, no problem. My tablet's over there." She pointed to the counter across the room.

"Thanks," I said, heading back to my office with her tablet. Scrolling back to the previous month, I tapped on the date I had blacked out on mine.

I blinked. My brain would not register what I read. It was as if my abilities to read and understand my native language were no longer active. I rubbed my eyes and squinted in an attempt to read it again. Two words. I shouldn't have such a hard time logically piecing them together. Just two words.

I returned to Quinn and thrust the tablet in her face.

"What does this mean?" I demanded.

She looked startled. "I don't know what to say."

The horror on her face was enough for me to understand. I fell back and caught myself on the counter.

"Tell me, Quinn. Just tell me." My face was already buried in my hands, bracing myself for the news.

"It was Abel's funeral that day," she said.

For a moment, I thought the time-travel serum had been released as my body came undone at a molecular level. My face was hot and sticky.

Six months. A hell of a lot can change in six months.

Without question, I knew why this happened. My mom wasn't right about everything. It was my fault. I was to pay a cosmic fee for bringing my mom into the future in an attempt to bypass her death. We must have altered an event that the universe determined I owed payment for.

⋅ ⋅ ⋅ ⋅ ⋅ ● ● ● ● ● ⬤ ● ● ● ● ● ⋅ ⋅ ⋅ ⋅

# CHAPTER 32

*Abel—dead.*

The thought circled my brain. I had to get out of the NIST before anyone else saw me.

"Okay. It's okay. I'm fine," I said, one hand holding my mouth, the other pledging to Quinn my well-being. "Please don't tell anyone about this. I just woke up today and, I don't know, needed to believe it wasn't true. I'm back to reality, though, and I just don't want anyone else to know about my momentary break from reality."

"I promise." She gingerly stepped toward me. "I'll keep it to myself. I'm sure it's a normal part of grieving. It's still fresh. You're processing." As she patted my back, I resisted the need to break down.

There wasn't time for an emotional release. I had to get out of there and figure this out. Wiping my eyes as I walked past Maxine on the way out, I forced a smile.

She knew about him, I thought to myself. That's why she was out of character.

I got back in my dad's car and drove to Dr. P's. I wanted nothing more than to be home with my boys, but I was in this timeline—a mere six months into the future—grieving Abel.

Back in Dr. Pasterski's lab, I heard her and my dad come home.

"I'm in the lab!" I shouted.

Minutes passed before they both poked their heads in the doorway.

"Hi, honey. How are you?" Their faces conveyed that they were gauging how broken I was about my husband. The worry was enough for me to crumble.

"I'm fine. Really," I said, clearly not fine. "Dr. P, I have a thing. Can you help me?"

My dad took that as his cue to exit. "I'll go make you two lunch." Dr. P kissed him on the cheek and closed the door behind her.

"How are you, really?" she asked.

I breathed in, maybe the first deep breath since I understood what the blacked-out day was.

"I'm time traveling right now."

"Oh." She blinked. "I wouldn't have guessed."

"I know. It's only six months out," I said.

"I see."

"I *should* be excited." I held the serum mixture toward the light. "This is a first time for me."

She held her gaze, the realization settling. She quickly came to see that I was here from the past.

"My girl, there's something you need to know," she said.

"I already know." I couldn't fathom having to hear it aloud again.

She pulled me into her embrace, smoothing my hair as I wept.

"How'd it happen?" I asked.

"*You* think it was Farkas. There's no solid evidence, but he was tracking her."

"Okay." I pulled away, my brain on fire. "I wasn't supposed to be here this long." My soul ached to return to Abel.

"I wish you hadn't found out like this," she said.

I checked my TRB, willing it to send me home that instant. "How am I going to tell Abel about this? We have to stop it."

"Taden, you might want…" Dr. P said as I pulled from that moment to the one I'd left from, where my husband was still alive. Time travel would never take it easy on me.

 Standing in the same lab six short months before, Dr. P was hunched over a petri dish. I breathed in the present.

"How'd it go, dear?" she asked, looking from her specimen.

"I'm going to have to get further into the future," I said in a huff.

"Jay's DNA is only six months old. You can't go forward more than six months until he's older," she reminded.

"You're right. But I don't plan on waiting a decade to do this."

"To do what? What's happened?" she asked.

"Abel's dead." My voice hitched and I felt dizzy producing those words with my tongue and allowing them to spill from my lips.

She winced as her hand covered her mouth. "Taden…"

"I know. Don't worry. I'm going to stop it from happening. I'll send another traveler using older DNA."

Her silence accompanied the mortified look she wore.

On a gut level, I'd accepted that upon returning to my present I shouldn't tell Abel about his impending death. I'd already interfered with timelines enough, and already paid severely for the changes made. I supposed I could also argue that the cost of most of our time manipulations were worth the change made.

Standing there in Dr. Pasterki's lab, where I'd fathomed so many of my scientific theories, I'd contrived that his death might be avoidable since I knew of it beforehand.

My dad hadn't found any jarring information about Danika from his trip into the future. She was still at the NIST, and I still worked for her. His report was disappointing—lacking the fuel I needed to take her down. And if she was responsible for Abel's death, I *would* take her down.

After all, I knew when Abel was going to die. I had his funeral blacked out in my planner. If I made the right changes in the present, it could rewrite the future to a different outcome. That's always been my hope for future time travel. Find out what could be and make informed decisions in the present to avoid the things we don't want to happen. Unlike changing the past, the opportunities to avoid painful future events didn't present a ripple outward in any negative way.

In hindsight, I'd been foolish.

"But this isn't just about Abel," I said, breaking the terrible silence. "I have to see what Danika is capable of."

"Do you think she killed him?" Dr. Pasterski asked.

I nodded, swallowing with a dry throat.

"I think you know enough, my girl. You should stay here and stop this, stop *her* here."

"We will. I will. But I need to know what she's planning. What the consequences are if we don't stop her."

"Who do you plan to send that far into the future?" She looked at me as though she already knew my answer. Still, I fidgeted, wanting to avoid telling her. She deserved my honesty.

"As you know, we need a descendant's DNA to go forward." I looked to her, wide-eyed. "And we need to keep this discovery tight-lipped."

"Mm-hm," she muttered.

"My DNA is old enough to send someone I'm a descendent of as far forward as I'll need them to go, to get what I need." I paused. "It's gotta be Dad."

She shut her lids tight. "He's not going to like this."

"I know. I think I can talk him into it. I just want to make sure you're okay with it before I ask him."

She put both hands on my shoulders and looked at me square on. "This is between you and him." She squeezed me into a quick hug. While I waited for her to send him in, I resumed spinning in the chair. Each second dragged as my desperation grew to get back home into Abel's arms.

"I was paged," Dad said, peering into the room. I stopped spinning and greeted him with a placid smile. The gesture was inadequate to address him. I replaced it with stern courage.

"Dad," I said, getting to my feet, "I need you to go into the future."

He stared at me with blank eyes. "I thought we decided when we returned your mom to her timeline that this wasn't the right action to take."

"Mom wasn't supposed to cheat her death and live in a timeline that she didn't belong in. We did reconcile that." My insides felt like they were close to waging war. "Dad, I need to get far enough in the future to find out what we need to fix here."

"And you want *me* to make the trip?"

"I can't get far enough with Jay's DNA." I shrugged. "But I can inject you with mine and you'd be able to go."

"What would I be doing?"

"Kind of like what you did when you went to visit Mom. I think you should meet with Jay, see how things are going at my home, collect important samples. You know, that sort of thing."

"What samples? You don't want me to…"

"You could get his much older DNA for me and return with it. From there, I'd be able to get far enough into the future to discover what we need to know."

"I don't think I particularly like this scenario," he told me. "Those DNA extractions aren't as simple as taking a hair sample. Your samples require invasive collection methods."

"It's not ideal. But if I don't have a way to get further into the future, I won't know how to defeat Danika."

"Honey, is this about Abel?"

"Yes, it's about Abel," I snapped. I wondered how Dr. P filled him in so quickly before she sent him to have this conversation with me. "It's about Abel, and it's about you, me, and Jay, too. If we don't know what Danika is really capable of, and why she's been leading a secret government agency through the discovery of time travel, who knows what could happen to our country? To our world, even?"

"Besides collecting Jay's genetic material, what would you propose I do while I'm there?" he asked.

"Well, now that I'm thinking about it, if you sent him back here I could get the DNA from him myself." I folded my arms and jumped, my new idea sparking my nervous system. "…and I would love to see him grown." I began pacing as the thoughts poured out. "I assume he already knows time travel exists. I can't imagine he wouldn't."

"You want your son to time travel?" He folded his hands behind his neck. "This doesn't seem like something you'd want Jay to do."

I turned my back to him. "That's because this Jay is a baby, Dad." My voice was stern but pleading. "I need your help."

"I can see you're emotional, and it's understandable. But I have a bad feeling that if you rush into this without a solid plan in place, it is not going to end well."

I grasped the optic lens on the counter and threw it against the wall, only to startle as the mirror shattered. Thousands of tiny shards spread across the floor. The broken pieces mirrored my heart.

He put his hand on my arm. "I'll go. I'll bring him here." Sobs broke free as I gathered the pieces.

"Thank you. We just need to know."

· · · · · · ● ● ● ● ● ● ● ● · · · ·

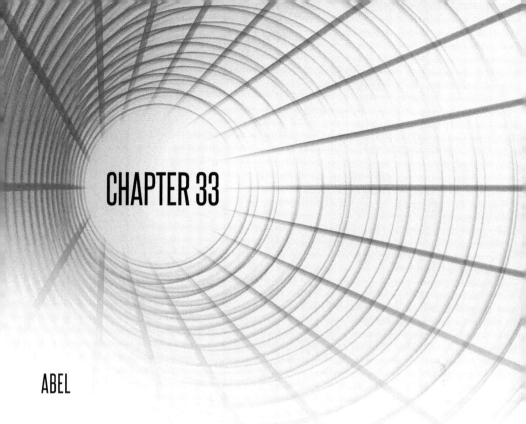

# CHAPTER 33

## ABEL

On my last morning I stood at the top of the stairs, listening to Taden's attempts to get Jay out the door. It would be the last time I'd ever see them. My face burned with hot tears, my memory full of my son's highlight reel—I'd spent the entire night watching. At least Danika gave me these final moments.

"It's time," Danika said, viewing the specs. As she swiped through the images, I stared at her, numb to the decision. "The AI is finally completed, ready for your merge. You've had enough time to know your boy and be at peace with leaving." Her icy compassion heated my soul with rage. "This is your last night with your family."

The moment Taden drifted off to sleep I slipped out of bed, inspired by Jay. The craziest part about time travel is that she didn't even know I was gone and I'd covered a lifetime.

My inspiration after returning home was a series of how-to videos that I had to create. I sat for a moment, making a mental list including how to throw a tight spiral—he'd definitely need that one, I thought, chuckling. How to land a second date, and how to shave were among the lessons I couldn't sleep without Jay knowing. But the morning came as it always does, and sleep never would again. I uploaded the videos and followed the noise of a normal day.

Pulling my cap further down my forehead, I hoped Taden's position at the bottom of the stairs prevented her from seeing my swollen eyes.

I glanced at little Jay, crawling like lightning around her, pulling himself up on whatever he could reach, all the while singing nonsense to himself. It felt like just yesterday we were bringing a baby home, and now here he was barely ten months old. In a blink, he would be a man. Choking back the sobs welling in my chest proved to be more difficult with each passing second.

I'd never get to experience being a part of his life. I could find comfort in the fact that he would know me through the video diaries I'd made these past months.

Still, standing there, I was stunned at how I'd failed. As the time progressed, and I was forced to assist Ms. Farkas in moving her plan forward, I was sure I'd find a loophole or an exit strategy. But that never came.

I could only hope Jay would find the clues I'd embedded in those last recordings. Maybe one day he could undo this. Maybe he would use the keys and take Danika down. My hatred for Danika Farkas was deep and wide, but as I stood there watching him bounce around his mom's legs, I couldn't help but feel grateful to Danika for the gift of my son's future.

 Danika coolly walked over to the wall and slid her oversized oil painting aside. She tapped in a code, which opened a hidden safe and revealed a vial of serum.

I instantly recognized the time-travel vial resting between her perfectly groomed blood-red nails, which sharply contrasted against the silver casing of the vial.

"For your service," she said, lifting the vial to me.

I accepted it, not sure yet what she was offering besides a time-travel trip.

"What you hold in your hands will take you as far into your son's future as you'd like to go."

My face jerked, and I fought the instinct to put my hands around her neck. She read my body language, unflinching.

"Now Abel, you're going to want to stay calm." Her condescension ripped through me. "That serum was made from the very last DNA sample your son gave before he died." Her thin red lips pulled into a tight smile. My throat constricted. "Don't worry. Thanks to your commitment and his genius, he lived a long and healthy life."

She blinked coyly.

My hand tightened around the vial as I pulled it from her grasp.

"Use that to go have a look at the wonderful life you set up for your boy. Don't do anything stupid, Abel. Remember, I have people in place and protocol ready to destroy everyone you love, if you do." She blinked once. "When you're done, I'll be here. Ready for you. We launch tomorrow."

She winked at me and my blood went cold. I stumbled backward out of her office, staring at the serum. I needed to go forward and access Jay's virtual album. Far enough into the future, I'd have access to all of the dates that meant the most in my son's life.

# CHAPTER 34

## TADEN

Our car's autopilot feature allowed me to answer my mobile, which was buzzing incessantly in my purse. I reached to the passenger seat to retrieve it and peeked over the seat at Jay buckled into his car seat singing to himself as he pressed lights on the musical toy on his lap.

It was Danika. I'd just left work. In fact, I was finally home for the day. Ready to shut down my brain.

I selected 'accept call' and uttered a pointed, "Hello."

"Taden, I have terrible news."

My stomach flipped. Immediately my thoughts flooded with all of the possibilities for which Danika Farkas could be calling me to reveal bad news. I didn't guess the dreadful delivery that awaited. But I suppose I should've known.

"Go ahead," I simply said.

"It's Abel."

And then I knew. My mind jumped to the date. The blacked-out date on the planner. That was this weekend. Abel's funeral was this weekend. No. It couldn't be.

"Abel?" I asked, my head spinning. "Is he all right?"

"Taden, he was on a mission today." Danika paused. "I don't know how to tell you. Things didn't go as planned."

"What are you saying?" My voice became insistent.

"He's gone, Taden."

I looked back at Jay, still pressing buttons on his toy.

"He didn't make it," she said.

Words continued to stream from her end of the phone call, but I no longer understood English. I pressed disconnect and gingerly slipped my phone back into my purse and noticed for the first moment that the car was in park. In a blur, I managed to get myself and Jay out of the car and walked to our porch.

Staring at our front door with Jay's little body in arms, my feet were cement blocks. I couldn't fathom how to lift them in order to move forward.

"Mommy," he said, tugging on my fingers.

The entirety of his hand could only manage to grasp three of my fingers. I peered down at him, not sure when I had set him down, and hoping I could muster enough willpower to be a mom.

I forced a smile to acknowledge my sweet little boy, and he took his cue.

"Mama." He reached his arms to me.

My smile no longer forced, I crouched down to Jay. "You want back up, sweet boy?"

I scooped him back into my arms and looked to the front door again. Abel was there in my memory, painting it yellow.

*"Babe, I'm proud of you for picking this bold color for our front door. 'Bye, boring beige!" Abel winked, and continued brushing the bright paint in the grooves of the wood.*

I shook my head, not letting memories yank me out of reality, refocusing on the door. That color made my heart happy even now, with its fractured presence. Abel wasn't there. He wasn't inside, either. I was about to open that bright, happy door for the first time, knowing that he would never be there again. Jay was bouncing in my arms then, fidgeting to get free.

I chewed the inside of my cheek, and the familiar iron taste spread across my tongue.

"Okay, sweetie, come on."

We walked through the door, and were greeted by Abel's boots. I blinked. How was it possible that his shoes were still sitting here, but he was gone? They remained casual, like they were just waiting for him to slip his feet inside and lace them up to head out. One was leaning on the other, sort of haphazard.

Jay toddled off along the furniture, pausing to clap and sing. I recognized the nonsense jingle as our diaper-changing song.

Still, I couldn't tear myself away from Abel's shoes. I wondered, if I tried to climb inside them, would I feel him?

"I'm losing it," I muttered to myself. "Come on, let's change your diaper."

I scooped up Jay, pretending to tickle-monster him, and he shrieked with delight. I brought him to the center of the living room floor and laid him on his back. I pulled off his shoes and instinctively looked back at Abel's shoes, waiting by the front door. *I'll never be able to move his shoes from that spot,* I thought to myself, which triggered another frantic thought that I would have to attend to *all* of his things.

Almost without effort, his scent—which I was sure lingered on his shirts, patiently waiting for me—filled my mind.

My chest was a vacuum, and there was a distant awareness that I was on autopilot. I'd changed Jay's diaper and he was off, crawling across the floor to his toys.

For a moment I sat with my legs crossed, considering how I should go about living my life now that Abel was dead. And then, the next thing I knew I was falling into despair, lying in our bed, buried in his pillow, searching for a trace of him. What would I do when his smell was gone? My body trembled, and there was no use attempting to bury it.

After the passing of what seemed like a great length of time, I returned to the awareness that I had to get up and go be a mom. My son was in the other room. I just needed to sit up. After that, I could stand. Then, I could go to him. But I couldn't. I just lay there. Maybe for hours longer. Maybe for only ten minutes. Time had warped into something that would never end or begin. And all I could do was grieve.

Jay tumbled into my bedside, drinking a sippy-cup. I hadn't filled a cup for him. I wondered where it came from.

"Mama." He continuously pulled himself up into a stand, using the side of the mattress, and then tumbled back onto his bottom. "Mama. Up."

I couldn't even answer my tiny boy. I shook my head and tried my damnedest to stop crying for him.

"Mama. Up." His words more clear.

If it was possible, my heart broke into another fractured piece. This was the first time he actually said the word 'up'. Until now he would just reach for me. But we'd been working on that one really hard the past few weeks. I almost ignored it.

"Yes, sweet boy, Mama will pick you up."

I reached down and pulled him onto the bed with me. He nuzzled into my body like I was his blanky, and he began twirling my hair through his itty-bitty fingers.

With my eyes closed, all I focused on was his innocent voice singing to me a melody that sounded something like 'baa baa black sheep', until we both fell asleep. If I didn't have Jay to anchor me, I would've drifted into the dark that night and never returned.

The first eyelid flutter in the morning following Abel's death was one full of possibility.

It was just a bad dream. I remembered it wrong. I must have made a mistake; misunderstood. He'd be brewing coffee any minute, and the house would fill with the scent of a fresh new day.

And then a tidal wave of reality pummeled me. Hope was replaced by the renewal of this new normal: the one where he was gone, and I'd never wake to his coffee brewing again.

My phone pinged. The screen was flooded with missed calls and message notifications. My initial scrolling landed on Danika's last message.

"I'm sorry, I wanted to say this to you in person but you aren't answering. You are ordered against any time-travel activity." My eyes burned. "It could tear the seams of time. You must leave his death unaltered. What he did was his job and it was meant for the betterment of our world. I've restricted your access to time serum until I've assessed your decision-making skills. My condolences."

I understood, then, that I'd need to operate on autopilot for a good long time. I rolled over and took in the simple magic of my son sleeping in Abel's spot. His cheeks were pink and his lips were pressed together. Delicate lashes adorned his eyelids. I barely rose onto the side of the bed when he awoke, raring to go.

"Up. Mama up!" he yelled as he used my mattress as a makeshift trampoline. I put my arms out to catch him and get day one of the rest of my life without Abel started.

"You're such a big boy. Let's go eat some big-boy breakfast."

As the days blurred, I finally found myself back in my office. Sitting at my desk, completing regular tasks that a time-travel physicist might. The outside narration was constantly running, reminding me that I was a functioning person. Except, I was donned in black, and I'd be leaving my office any minute to attend Abel's funeral. That wasn't normal at all. I opened the calendar application in my planner, fully unaware what day it even was.

"Oh, it's Sunday," I muttered as I clicked on the date. "I shouldn't even be here." But I'd come to gain some sense of myself before I left behind the physicality of Abel. I blacked out the date and closed the application. The white walls of the lab seemed to be my only source of comfort in the darkness that had clouded me. My phone pinged.

"Hello?"

"I'm worried about you," Ruth said.

"I'm on my way. Is Jay dressed?"

"He's dressed and playing with his toys. I just fed him. We're all set," Ruth said gently. "Can I do anything for you?"

"I'm okay. I'll be home in a few minutes. Thanks for staying with Jay while I came in. It felt good to be here."

"I'm glad." She paused. "Drive safe."

"Will do," I said.

And for a second I imagined not driving safe. Driving insanely unsafe. The mind of a grieving person is really unpredictable. I'd almost forgotten how dark a thought can turn in an instant. I shook my head.

"I'm a mom to an incredible baby boy," I reminded myself as I buckled my seatbelt and pressed the home screen to go into autopilot mode.

· · · · · · ●●●● ● ●●●●● · · · ·

# CHAPTER 35

"Mama sad?" Jay asked. It was a phrase that he was repeating often once the days compounded into months.

"Yes, sweetie. Mama is sad. It's okay."

It was devastating that among my baby's finite vocabulary, he learned that his mom was sad. *How many times had I told him I was sad?* I worried he'd learn that crying was bad—but I couldn't find an in-between for him. I couldn't show him how to cry and then how to move on. I didn't know how to do that myself.

I ran my fingers along his baby-fine hairline, wishing his morning greeting wasn't to check if I was still sad.

I'm not sure I did it right, grieving the love of my life in front of my little boy. But starting that morning, he wouldn't see me cry again. I didn't want to be perpetually sad for him, and I was terrified that if I couldn't find a way to box up my pain it would never get out of the way for me to be a good mom.

· · · · · · · ● · · · · · · ·

# CHAPTER 36

I'd moved Jay's crib into my room, unable to fall asleep alone. During the daytime, the joy trailing behind a toddler shrieking through the house was undeniable. But at night, all bets were off. I listened carefully to the rise and fall of his chest and hoped the rhythm would give me the sleep I'd become desperate for. It didn't come.

One night, sneaking from my room so as not to wake the baby, I tiptoed down the hallway. As I did, I let myself drift toward the photographs hanging on the wall: Abel sleeping on the couch with newborn Jay draped over his chest; Abel and me on the hiking trip he talked me into. I swore to never go hiking again after that trip. I'd give anything to be on that trail now.

Pushing myself further down the hall, I opened Jay's nursery door. It would be safe in there. Probably the least amount of Abel was to be found in our son's room.

Flopping onto the cushioned rocking chair, I lulled myself for a slow moment. To my right, I gazed upon his bookshelf. Each title was carefully selected to assist in rearing my boy into a gentle, brave, intelligent, sensitive, well-rounded child. Both my feet boldly flattened as soon as my eyes landed on it: *The Great Gatsby.*

When had Abel put my book in Jay's room? I hadn't thumbed through these pages since well before I even found out I was pregnant. Abel had to be the one to place it here. *But why?*

I took the book in my hands and pressed it to my face. It had saved me once before when I longed to be near him. Maybe it still could. Flipping through the pages, a pleasant torture filled me.

Then I noticed a page bent at the corner. I couldn't help but think Abel wouldn't fold a page of this book. He knew how strongly I disapproved of damaging the pages of any book with such a careless method of bookmarking. He wouldn't dare do this to the most precious of my entire book collection. Would he?

I scolded myself. Was I really this pompous? This would be the exact move he'd make if he wanted me to read something important. Startled by my own laugh—I'd thought it had died with Abel—I flipped to the bent page with anticipation. The chapter ended mid-page, leaving the other half blank for him to write his note, which was dated the morning he died.

*Dear Taden,*

*Things are about to change for you and Jay, but it won't change that my love for you is undying. Please do not try to alter the outcome of what must be. It would be known, and the consequence would be too great. Wherever I am, whatever time, I'm loving you.*

*In all my timelines,*
*Abel*

*Dear Jay,*

*As you become a young man, I hope you read these words I once wrote to your mother and find the beauty in waiting for the right kind of love to meet you where you are in life. I hope you find that love and, together, choose to grow forward.*

*Love,*
*Dad*

I read and re-read his words. They blurred together until I couldn't process the meaning of them separately. *Was I reading this right? Did Abel know he was going to die?* I'd tried to warn him about what I saw. He wouldn't hear of it.

"Listen, I'm telling you it happened," I asserted, folding my arms. "I don't understand why you don't believe me."

"It's not that I don't believe you, Taden." He pulled Jay out of his jumper and set him in the bouncy seat. "It's just that we don't know very much, if anything, at all about the things we see in a future time travel. How many events could've changed since that trip that have now led us to a new outcome?"

I shrugged. My eyes pleaded with him to take this warning more seriously.

"What I'm saying is, on the day you saw my funeral in our future, okay, sure, maybe that would've been the outcome. But since that day, and you having this knowledge, how many different choices have been made that put us on an entirely different course?"

He made sense. His logic was actually calming. After all, this was exactly why I was pushing to stop time traveling to the past and focus on only future time travel.

"You think the future is an unstable chain of events? We shouldn't put much weight on anything we see there?" I asked.

He shrugged this time. "I don't think we know enough about the future to make any certain claims."

"Fair enough," I agreed. But I couldn't shake the doom I felt, knowing a life without him alive. Even if it was brief. Even if it was in an untold future. It was hell.

I replayed that conversation with Abel again and again. He'd really convinced me that his death wasn't imminent. But reading this note, it made me question. Did he know that I was right? What did he mean, 'the consequence would be too great'?

The only consequence that I could think would be too great, would be if something were to happen to Jay.

Precisely as I thought my son's name, my chest constricted. I read between the lines of what he was telling me in his warning. Danika. She would take Jay from me if I tried to undo Abel's death.

Paranoid, I searched Jay's nursery for evidence that she was watching or listening. If Abel had to make it a point to write a cryptic message in our book, he must be warning me. I closed the book, resting it upon my chest. For the first time since Abel was gone, I felt something besides grief.

This new feeling prickled along my spine and laced its icy grip throughout my veins. I tiptoed back to my room, needing Jay within my sight. Leaning over his crib, I rested my chin on the bar.

I knew this feeling almost as well as I knew grief. This anticipation of danger. The painful agitation rising within. Fear had paid me a visit. While watching Jay's chest rise and fall, in my gut I was certain Danika already knew I'd figured out how to get into the future.

She wouldn't respond kindly to this undisclosed information. Was it enough to harm us?

I'd only gone into the future once, and for only about an hour's time. But I witnessed enough to see how much one day can alter everything.

· · · · · · · · ● ●●●●● · · · · ·

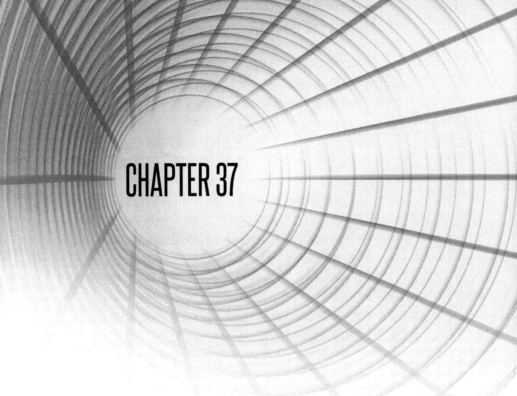

# CHAPTER 37

**"Taden!" he yelled from the bedroom.**

"I'm running late!" I yelled back up the stairs. "Have you seen Jay's pacifier? I can't take him to my dad's without it."

Searching under the couch cushions, I was busy calculating how many minutes this would cost me before heading into the NIST for the day.

"Bbuh, Mama?" Jay said.

"I'm looking for it, honey." I raised my brows at Jay and poked my finger in his belly to make him giggle. "Abel!" I yelled again toward the staircase.

It was actually Abel's turn to take Jay to my dad's, but lying in bed before we fell asleep he asked me if I could. He hadn't given me a reason, and I didn't even think to ask why. Clearly that was an oversight on my part.

"Ah! Found it!" I said, holding the pacifier to Jay, who took it with glee and popped it into his mouth.

"Yeah?" I heard Abel respond from upstairs. I hooked Jay on my hip and met him at the bottom of the staircase.

"I found his pacifier, and I'm on my way out the door. Did you need me?"

He stood at the top of the stairs, taking me in as if he'd not seen me in years. He descended each step with a heavy breath.

"I just wanted to say goodbye," he said, removing the baseball hat as he got to the bottom stair.

I screwed my face together. He was behaving too weirdly for a hectic morning.

"Okay. 'Bye," I said, lifting onto my toes and puckering my lips together.

I waited a beat for the rushed peck goodbye, but instead opened my eyes to find him still searching my face.

"What's going on? You're acting strange," I said.

"What? Can't a guy be in love with his wife?"

I scoffed and again he caught me off guard, pressing his lips to mine. He could still simultaneously ease desire from its dungeon while streaming in light. I was left both whole and dizzy from his kiss. I sighed into his mouth, and he echoed the desire into mine.

"Whoa," I said with a seductive smirk. "I'll see you later, then."

I added a double wink to promise more later that evening. His lips curled back at me, but it wasn't the smile I expected. It wasn't playful. Something was bothering him. Something twisted his smile with worry.

I was definitely late at that point, and resolved to follow up with him at work—when I finally got there, after dropping Jay off with my dad. But he never made it to work that morning. Or that afternoon. This was to be the last time I would see him. And upon replaying the exchange, I'm betting Abel knew that was our last kiss.

# CHAPTER 38

To hell with it. Abel warning me with a scribbled note in our book. Danika banning me from time travel. Neither offering me any sort of forthcoming solace about what happened to my husband or why his life had to be sacrificed. And to be honest, I didn't really give a damn about the greater good at that point. All I knew was that the person I'd believed I'd spend the rest of my life with, and the father of my child, was gone.

I didn't need access to time-travel serum. I had a lab; I had the ability to create my own. For weeks, I'd become alive with the purpose of getting to see him again.

"It's really nice to see you back to work," Dr. P said, coming into her home lab to find I had been up all night working.

"Yeah, thanks for watching little Jay. I feel good."

"Do you want to talk about your project?" she asked, eyeing my serum.

"Nah. I'm just working on a new sequence."

Her brows rose in a curious way, but she didn't question any further.

With the serum in that vial, I'd travel back to see him. It was the only thing I could manage to think about for the rest of that day. I'd go back from our home so that I'd arrive in the same location on a day I'd know he was home.

That last night we'd laid in bed, discussing how he needed me to take Jay to my dad's the next morning. That he had something he needed to do for work. I'd agreed and then drifted off to sleep.

I waited until Jay was in his crib asleep, and padded from my bedroom where he still slept and down the stairs. Initiating my TRB loaded with my homemade serum, I braced myself for the complexity of my physical undoing.

 I'd arrived. I breathed in the air from our home, in the timeline that Abel still very much lived. Could I actually sense him in the air? Did his scent always permeate the atmosphere like this, or was I willing the smell to exist?

Without hesitation, my hand was on the banister as I made my way up the stairs to find him in our bed. My heart raced with excitement and terror. I was certain he wouldn't have good news for me, afraid I wouldn't be able to convince him to avoid the scenario that ended in his death, worried that I'd be thwarted. My stride increased as I leaped two steps at a time.

At the top of the landing, she was waiting.

"What are you doing here?" I asked, the knot in my stomach growing heavy with concern.

"You can't do this. You can't go in there and prevent him from dying."

I looked hard at my future self. I wondered if the ripple that would come from harming myself from another timeline would be too drastic.

"I'm going to see him. Please move out of my way," I said.

"Just listen." She lifted her palm. "You wouldn't listen to reason from Abel, but maybe hearing it from your own mouth will stop you."

I paused just long enough that she saw an opening.

"You did this before and it messed up everything. If you want to stop Danika, leave this be. It has to happen this way."

My throat tightened so that I was momentarily distracted from going to Abel in order to attend to the need to breathe.

"You want me to just leave? Go back to my life of misery and not do whatever I can to save Abel?"

She nodded, her eyes glassy. I continued to stare her down for what felt like hours. A tear trickled down her cheek, but she didn't waver. I swallowed and took a step back. Had I just admitted defeat? Was I going to let my future self win that easily?

"Reset your TRB," she instructed.

I did as she said. I was actually going to leave, not see Abel, and continue on my slow crawl forward with grief.

She'd confirmed I would take down Danika. That was something.

* * * * * * * * ● * * * * * * * * *

# CHAPTER 39

I'd considered quitting my job. Starting anew elsewhere, with no more giant government secrets to hold. My grief therapist, though, suggested I try to make new memories in this building. It figured. She was paid by the same money that I was.

"If you run from this place now, deep in your loss, you'll forever see it only as the place where he was with you. Use this time to make new memories there," she said.

My therapist might have had a better understanding of grief than I did, but every single morning I'd park my car and stare up at the immensity of the building, scanning it for Abel's window and feeling the pinch of knowing it wasn't his anymore.

This particular morning I was running behind, and I didn't have time to linger on the windows. I had a private meeting scheduled with the ever important Danika Farkas. Danika no longer made me nervous—at least, not in the traditional way. I used to care deeply what she thought of me, and if I was meeting her approval. Since I'd learned the truth, the overwhelming emotions now attached to her were a mixture of fear and disgust.

"I have to be honest, Dr. Barrett, I thought you and your team would have a grasp on this by now," she said, clicking her tongue with disappointment.

My face tightened. Screaming internally, I resisted the desire to torch her with my words. Considering the ways I wished to cause her pain, it was possible my decency died with Abel.

She pinched her lips with obvious disapproval. I didn't attempt to make excuses or grovel for her forgiveness. Falling back on her most basic power move to claim the authority, she stood. The shred of respect I held for her was uncanny when compared to how I used to gape at her. Hands flat on the table she leaned in, as if she were trying to siphon time travel from my brain.

"I don't know what to tell you." I shrugged. "I'm working on it."

The tension she exuded was thick. Unaffected, I glanced at the time. I'd wasted enough of it sitting in this conference room pretending like Danika didn't already know I'd solved it.

"Don't you have more pressing matters to be concerned with?" I asked Danika.

Her face contorted, but she quickly resumed her poker face. She didn't look at me; rather, she returned complacently to her seat, crossing her legs and settling deeply into the back of her chair.

"I know," I said with boldness.

"I'm sorry, Dr. Barrett, what does that mean?"

"I know everything about you."

"I doubt that to be true, even if you believe it."

"You must already know that I have insights," I said, leaning forward and waiting for her to continue.

She pulled out a tablet and tapped a few screens. Sliding the device to me, she revealed the eyes that motivated the beating in my chest. Why would she be showing me a picture of my son?

"Your son is beautiful. I haven't seen Jay since he was born," Danika said in an icy tone. "He's having a lovely time at your dad's this morning."

"What do you want?" I asked. "Are you threatening my son?" Panic growing, I scanned the play area where Jay spent most of his time at my dad's. Danika had a camera on him! How long had she been watching him?

"I want you to figure out how to get into the future," she said. A long pause allowed me to fixate on Jay's eyes. "I'm done pretending I don't know you've already solved this," she said with a sharpness in her tone. "It's a shame Abel isn't here to help you along with the fine-tuning."

Her move was meant to rattle me. I had only one counter-move.

"President Berthold," I spat out. "President Moore." This time it was my turn to stand. "I know about both of them. I know what you did." Putting my hands on my hips, I added, "I'm not afraid of you, and I'm going to take you down."

She cackled mockingly. My stance shifted in preparation to walk away.

"Sit down, Dr. Barrett." I paused, weighing my options. "I'm a powerful woman," she reminded me.

Danika's reminder, along with the subtle nod in the direction of my son's image on her device, spoke loud to the threat she insinuated.

Flushed with a fiery vengeance, I said, "Don't you touch a hair on that boy's head."

A pleased smirk revealed her satisfaction at provoking me. "As long as you give me what I require and do not cause me problems, Jay will be safe." Her smirk disappeared. "But this is your only warning, Dr. Barrett. Time travel belongs to me, and so do you. I'll be talking to you soon."

In classic Danika fashion she left the room with haste, leaving me fixed to my chair, reeling at how quickly I'd lost that hand to her. Familiar sensations seeped through my nervous system.

The war waged between fear and vengeance, anger and doubt. It lasted for the next decade and kept me compliant.

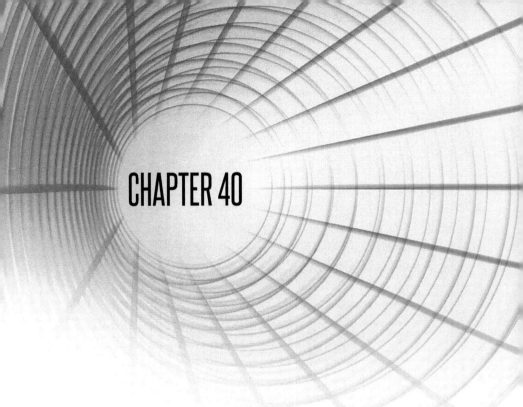

# CHAPTER 40

Jay was the same age Abel was when I met him in college. I hadn't considered he would be the spitting image of his father until I was looking into his young adult eyes. If I tried to speak to him, I was sure I wouldn't be able to finish a sentence. The lump in my throat could not be ignored.

I'd just lost Abel, and the grief stalked my every thought. The way Jay sat, the way his facial features settled into waiting for my response, those similar brown eyes. It was uncanny. If the universe took Abel from me as penance for my time travel faux pas, clearly Jay was my gift of solace for how I would get through the darkness of losing Abel.

"You look exactly like your father did when I first met him."

He smiled. "I know. You tell me all the time."

I took a sip of my coffee in an effort to break my trance. "I'm certainly right. But my other self watched you grow every day in slow, tiny steps. Looking at you now, this is on fast forward for me."

"Yeah," he said, nodding. "It's weird for me, too. You look different."

"Oh?" I sat upright and fluffed my hair. "Who wore it better?"

He groaned. "Ugh. Don't be weird."

It was amazing. The little boy I'd dropped off with Dr. Pasterski today was the same boy sitting across from me. He was my son. They were both my son. Grief had its hold of me in that moment, but pride stepped in for a fighting chance.

"Are you ready to talk seriously?" I asked him.

"Ready as I'll ever be," he told me, his demeanor calm and steady. Even his answer was something Abel would've said.

"I brought you here to this time because I've recently figured out how to get into the future." I took another sip of my coffee.

"That's how Gramps came to visit me."

Nodding, I set my mug back on the table. "I made a serum for Gramps that included my DNA so he could jump that far forward."

"How did the serum, 'know'—" He used his fingers as air quotes. "—not to send him into the past?"

I couldn't help it. A giant smile lit up my face. He was an intelligent boy. "Good question! The DNA automatically sends a traveler into the past, unless…" I trailed off. If he was as smart as I gathered, my answer would logically lead him to why he was here.

"Say what you have to say. I'm not a little kid. Just tell me."

I tapped my coffee cup, considering my words. "If the DNA is from a relative that was born after the time traveler, then that traveler is automatically sent to the future." I watched Abel's son, my son, digest the information I'd delivered.

It was a slow realization, but one that he grasped. His eyes darted from the table to mine. "That's why *you* didn't come visit me in the future?"

I nodded. "I've actually already visited you 'in the future', but only as far as you are old—in my timeline."

"Oh. I get it," he said. "Because I'm older, you need *my* DNA to go farther?"

"You got it," I said.

He looked disappointed. "That's why I'm here?"

I felt a twinge in my chest. "No. I mean, yes, that's why Gramps went to the future. But I wanted you to come here instead of having him ask you for your DNA. That way I could visit with you and tell you these things myself. I had no idea how amazing you would turn out. I could sit here and look at you all day."

He smiled, and gave me a typical teenage response: "You're being weird again."

I couldn't help but think of my own mom and how she felt when I turned up at her door with a visit from the future. I didn't feel as calm and collected as she'd appeared.

"Are you all right with giving me a DNA sample to make a serum that would allow me to time travel into the future?" I asked.

He nodded. "Is this going to hurt? I mean, I'm not a wimp or anything, but I'd like to know ahead of time."

"It's not pleasant, but you'll be fine," I assured him.

He looked at the fridge and laughed. "I'm glad that's not our fridge anymore."

I smirked at him. "An upgrade, eh?"

"Oh, believe me, we have a state-of-the-art model now," he said, laughing.

As I took his sample, scraping a section of his skin above his shoulder blade, I asked, "Anything exciting going on in my eighteen-year-old son's life, besides a new fridge?

"I have a job with you at the NIST," he told me.

"With me?"

"Don't sound so surprised. And no, actually, it's with Aunt Danika."

*Aunt* Danika? How in the hell did that come about? Why would I let that happen?

"Are you close with...*Aunt* Danika?" I asked, trying to hide my disdain.

He nodded. "It's okay, Mom."

The phrase caught me by surprise. Little Jay is still too young to call me Mom. This was the first time I'd heard him call me Mom.

"Have you always been close?"

Again, he nodded. If nothing came of this visit, I'd learned I'd have to allow this relationship to play out for whatever I have in place in the future. Good thing I had this warning and time to adjust to the idea of Danika being in Jay's life. The thought made me queasy.

"Your time is almost up," I said, checking his TRB. "Is there anything you'd like to talk about or see before you leave?"

He thought for a minute and then said, "Can I have his sweatshirt?"

"What?" I asked.

"I bet it still smells like him right now. Can I take it with me?"

I broke into a mad dash up the stairs, ripped Abel's favorite sweatshirt from his closet, and leaped back down in a series of hurdles, hoping to get to Jay before he dissolved.

Jay slipped it over his head and inhaled his dad just as he disappeared from my timeline.

• • • • • • • • • ● • • • • • • • • •

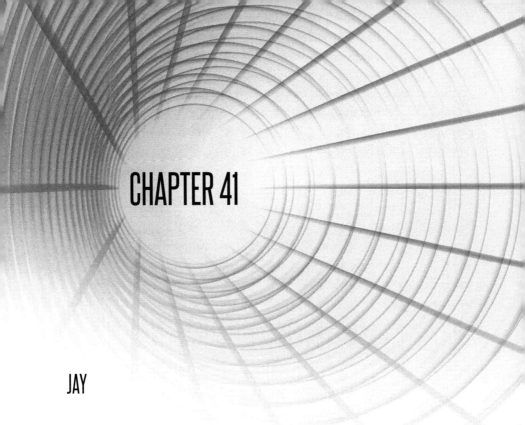

# CHAPTER 41

## JAY

Growing up without a dad wasn't the same for me as most fatherless kids. It was like my dad had an inclination he wouldn't be around. After he died, his Timed-Release Band that he used when on time-travel missions was passed on to me. Any other TRBs had been recalled by the NIST and dismantled. Time travel was no longer sanctioned unless specifically approved by the powers that be.

His TRB had been disabled, but it did have many other notable attributes.

I wore it around my arm and pretended it sent me through space when I was a little boy. As I got older and into sports I used it to track my heart rate, how many steps I took each day, and my speed on morning runs.

When I was about eight, though, my mom held out the watch. She said, "I was supposed to wait and give this to you when you were much older."

"My watch?" I said.

She sucked in a breath. "…but since he's gone, and I think you're plenty old enough now, you should have them. I want you to know your dad. He'd want that, too." She placed the watch in my hand. "Here. Aunt Dakotah helped me upload the videos he made for you."

From then on I often spent hours watching them, desperate to know my dad.

At some point, as the videos progressed, he explained he'd worked the technology so I could project his image like he was there in the room talking to me.

My dad made many short videos on every topic imaginable. Although I grew up without my dad, in this way it was like I still had him.

He filmed an entire series of "How To" segments. When I went on my first date with Jenny, I watched the one he made showing me how to tie a necktie. There's something to be said about having my dad show me how to do that.

As he threaded the wide end of the tie through the front of the knot, he looked straight into the camera and said, "Son, if you really like this person, ask for the second date before the end of this first date." Then he exaggerated his blinking. "That's how your date will know you're serious about spending time together, without being too forward." He winked at the camera as though his secret dating tips were invaluable. He added, "And son, that's how you find out if your date is interested in the same."

My dad was obviously old-fashioned, but I couldn't imagine not having his advice. Even though I have no memories of seeing them together, I knew my parents loved each other in the deepest ways. It's in the air surrounding my mom whenever she says his name, or tells me one of their stories. It's on their faces in every photograph I've ever seen of the two of them. In the videos, his demeanor changes when he mentions her. I hope to have a love like that. Having first-hand advice from my dad was like getting love advice from the expert.

Of course, it was still crushing not having him around. Like at my sporting events. I'd constantly wish he was sitting in the stands, cheering me on, but I knew he would've been if he was alive.

My first big freshman year football game, I remember looking up into the stands at my mom waving at me. Aunt Ruth and Aunt Dakotah sat next to her, relentless in their chants of support. Then I glanced down at the gated area that ran underneath the stands, and I could've sworn I saw my dad standing there, in the same baseball cap he'd worn in several videos. I closed my eyes tight then refocused on that spot, only to find it empty.

Having watched his recordings often (maybe too often), I found myself conjuring him at times. Especially for big moments. I'd always think I could see him in the background, always in that same cap. I never told anyone, though. My mom was sad enough that he was gone. She didn't need to know my desperation to see my dad was causing me hallucinations.

# CHAPTER 42

"Mom, can I get a ride with you to work tomorrow?"

She looked up from the ground beef flattened between her palms with a questioning look.

"Aunt Danika offered me a summer internship at the NIST doing lab equipment checks on the first floor."

I smiled big to share my excitement. I thought she'd be happy, but her pinched forehead confused me.

"When did this happen?" she asked, setting the formed burger patty on the grill sheet.

"What?" I asked. "You don't want your son showing you up at work?"

She couldn't contain the deep laugh that belied her furrowed brow.

"Good luck catching up to your mom, son. Don't you know she's a genius?" She scooped up a new handful of ground beef. "But seriously, I love that you got a job at the NIST." She paused, rolling meat between her hands. "When did Aunt Danika offer this job to you? She didn't mention it to me."

Her voice was strained, like she wanted to be happy about the job but couldn't manage to pull it off.

"She called me last week. I was trying to keep it a surprise. Maybe that's why she didn't say anything,"

My Aunt Danika wasn't really my aunt. She was my mom's boss, but my mom had worked for her for, like, twenty years, and she just eventually became a part of the family. Aunt Danika had always been around. She attended all my birthday parties. Sometimes she would send me gifts for no reason, and my mom would shake her head and mutter that she wished Aunt Danika wouldn't do that. Under the surface, it irritated me when my mom disparaged Aunt Danika for spoiling me.

I looked up to Aunt Danika. She was the most notable person I knew. Her job was to oversee the National Institute of Science and Technology, and she was accompanied by bodyguards everywhere she went. I can't deny that having someone that important who wanted to pull some strings to get my foot in the door at the NIST made me feel special.

I wasn't a genius physicist like my mom, but Aunt Danika made sure every opportunity I needed to further my career in the areas of science and technology that I might want to follow had been afforded to me. Not that my mom hadn't also done so, but Aunt Danika had *connections*.

Naturally, I grew up with science in my DNA—and of course, my mom made sure that I was fluent in all areas of the scientific world—though physics wasn't my strong suit.

I much preferred biology, and my natural inclinations leaned into computer science. No matter. There were plenty of opportunities housed under the umbrella of the NIST for me to know that my "foot in the door" would lead me toward the field of science I would have eventually gravitated toward anyway.

Things were perfect in my life. I'd just secured the internship, Jenny and I had been dating for a while, and my eighteenth birthday was right around the corner.

· · · · · · · · ● ○ ● · · · · · · · ·

# CHAPTER 43

"I cannot believe you did this!" my mom said after I told her what I'd just done. She was livid; I couldn't recall ever feeling her so angry with me. "You really risked your high-functioning brain to have a computer live in your head?!"

She was raging, cleaning the living room as I sat motionless on the couch. Not wanting to antagonize her, I hid my excessive joy about finally having the implant.

"It's not alive," I said, pointing to the tiny knob in the back of my neck. "This is the computer interface. I have to power it on in order for the iCerebrum to work. And it's easy enough to pull the interface portion out," I said, demonstrating.

She shook her head, clenching her jaw. "That thing is not allowed in my house." She folded the last towel and stomped up the stairs with the stack of them.

All my friends had gotten their iCerebrums when they first came out almost five years earlier, but my mom had overreacted about the implant sending electrodes to my brain.

I was the only one my age who still didn't have one. In all that time, the technology had not caused any of the issues my mom was certain they would.

Having an iCerebrum implant wasn't any more dangerous than riding a bike during autopilot rush hour.

Because my mom was overprotective, I was stuck devolving as I witnessed technology pass me by. Aunt Danika came to the rescue and gave me the implant as a "welcome to the NIST" gift.

She said to my mom, "If Jay is ever going to become a successful scientist, he needs to stay up to date with the latest technology," staring hard at my disapproving mother when they discussed the gift a few days earlier.

And since I was of age, I didn't need my mom to sign the waiver for the implant. It was easy enough. My last vaccine caused me more discomfort than the implant. The robot injections were available at every major pharmacy; right next to the blood pressure machine was the iCerebrum implant. Sitting in the reclining chair with the cap strapped under my chin, I felt an uncomfortable pinch at the base of my skull. The computer program reminded me to stay still, and then I felt a flash sensation, like when I suck down a frozen drink too fast, as the electrodes traveled to the different areas of my brain.

In my opinion, my mom's feelings about modern technology were a tad ironic, considering she'd developed time travel. It was sort of hypocritical. But the time-travel argument was clearly off limits with my mom, it being our best-kept secret. After two decades, still, the world was unaware.

 I was, however, keenly aware I shouldn't be in Aunt Danika's office snooping around, but I couldn't resist the opportunity. Plus, I needed to practice with my iCerebrum. When would I get another chance like this? Glancing at the expanse of the entire top floor of the NIST, I found my reflection in the glass-windowed walls surrounding the entire perimeter of the room.

Nothing would hide me from spying eyes, but Aunt Danika told me she wouldn't be coming in due to an important meeting.

Reaching behind my neck, I switched on my iCerebrum and scanned the room. It was still an awkward device for me to use, since I wasn't allowed—on direct orders of my mother—to use the device outside of the NIST.

I scanned her office with my interface. Images of the layout fluttered before my eyes. Every object or structure that was live on the data grid lit up in my line of vision. I tapped on each object that pulled my attention, as if I was using a touch screen but in the open air.

For each object selected, pertinent links of its background information appeared. If I spoke aloud the name of an item, my implant automatically zoomed in for closer analysis.

"Sofa," I said.

My field of vision filled with microscopic images of the couch's fabric contents. Aunt Danika needed to deal with the dust mites in here. It occurred to me that, for all my high school years, my peers had access to this unlimited amount of information and I hadn't. *Did everyone view me as naive?*

The device was overwhelming and cumbersome for the first half-hour, but I was beginning to grasp the search capabilities. I figured if Aunt Danika happened to find me here, snooping, I could easily use the excuse of getting better at the iCerebrum without my mom's judgment. And to be fair, that was *mostly* what I was doing.

So far, I'd discovered that Aunt D's chair had an AI device in it that was developed by Woodside Comforts to simulate a warm hug when lonely. Finding that detail felt like a very personal breach into her privacy, almost like reading her diary.

Was Aunt Danika lonely? I'd never really considered it before. She possessed such a strong, independent persona that the thought of her needing someone else to provide her comfort didn't really seem natural.

With awkward haste I moved away from the chair, feeling embarrassed to learn of it. I tapped at the next hyperlink that popped up in the direction of her wall. My iCerebrum device tagged it as AI. I paused the screen and blinked into the actual reality of the room. I stared at the spot on the wall. There was nothing there. Not a picture or control panel, nothing. I walked over to that part of the room, intrigued why my iCerebrum device tagged it as AI.

The lighting in the room followed my steps. Again that was something that, although it was familiar technology to the rest of the world, my mom refused to allow into our home. Would my mom ever leave the past behind? I could literally walk into a public school building, famous for being technologically outdated, and the lights would follow me. Just about every building in the country had been on the live grid for the last decade; a much more energy-efficient method than the old ways of oil and gas. But my mom would not comply.

Once I had my brain-computer interface, I could enter the NIST without badge-swiping or locked doors. The building's sensors interacted with the electrodes from my implant. The building had also gathered enough data about my movement within that the coffee machine in the kitchenette of my floor had my morning coffee ready-made, exactly to my specifications, at the exact time I'd drink it each day. It was brilliant.

It made me nervous, knowing that the building was tracking me. I'd hacked the system beforehand so the building couldn't read me. It was like I'd found an invisibility cloak in the AI software.

I didn't know what I was looking for or if I would find anything, but my instincts were on high alert that this wall space was more than met the eye.

Again, I switched off my external device. Laying my hand flat against the wall, I studied for traces of activity. With my ear pressed against it, I listened for buzzing or whirring—for any signs that this space was online. Nothing.

I pressed the back of my neck, turning the iCerebrum back on, and continued scanning the room. No surprise: her digital catalog was locked with passcodes. Even with my invisibility cloak, her security was sophisticated enough to block me. Why did I think a teenage kid could sneak into anything top secret that Danika Farkas might have to hide?

Although I was certain the most skilled of hackers wouldn't even be able to pull off something like this, I did feel smug that I was successfully inside her office, so I continued my hacking attempts. On a whim, I'd entered the birth month of my dad, my mom, and myself in order…and the damn thing worked.

Even if my mom wasn't always keen on Aunt Danika, this confirmed what I already knew: she loved my family. But still, using our birth dates as her passcode was surprising.

To my chagrin, I found each of her files held their own locked code. Retyping the birthdate password on the files was unsuccessful. Flipping the order of the dates failed. Perspiration gathered at my temples as I glanced up in the corner of my device to note the time. I'd already been in her office over an hour, and was expected home for dinner soon with Mom and Jenny.

If I was too much later, there'd be a lot of explaining—and I hated lying. Disappointed at finding nothing of interest, I took one last look at the empty wall blinking with the blue hypertext. I tapped in the air, hoping to at least scan the reading it traced. Finally, something worthwhile. In my viewfinder, a link to a wall safe appeared—but there was physically nothing in the space. I searched it.

Just as I started back toward the wall for another careful investigation, a ding sounded from the direction of the elevator. Frantic, I hid behind a bookshelf that filled the wall from floor to ceiling. Hand to my neck, I powered down my brain-computer interface in case whoever stepped off the elevator had theirs on. I wasn't completely sure the invisibility cloak could hide my implant from another iCerebrum.

"We needed his specs yesterday," Aunt Danika said. From what I could see, she was talking on her own iCerebrum. "I don't want to hear any excuses. Deadlines have already been extended." Her heels clicked hard against the ceramic floor. "This is my last warning."

She swiped her hand wildly in the air, disconnecting the call. Behind her followed two agents. They were busy scanning the room with their brain-computer interfaces, as I predicted someone might. Thank God I'd turned mine off.

I peered past the shelf to catch a glimpse of her. Was she tapping that spot on the wall? I couldn't watch long enough to be sure. How would I slip out of here? Checking over my shoulder, desperate for a plan, I considered the restroom to my left.

I edged inside and triggered the toilet sensor to flush. From there, I followed normal bathroom protocol, waving my hand under the faucet to run the water and washing my hands. Creating as much noise as possible I opened the door, humming to myself, appearing distracted. Certain I'd collected all three sets of eyes on me, I turned my iCerebrum back on.

One of the agents cleared her throat, taking an intimidating stance and placing her hand on the weapon at her hip.

"Oh, hi," I said, casually waving. Aunt Danika looked me over, revealing no expression. "I came here to practice," I said, pointing to my implant.

The agent was stone. Maybe her face actually hardened a touch more.

The subtle rise of Aunt Danika's brow preceded her response. "It's fine." She gestured for me to come closer. The two agents took position on either side of her, as if I was the one toting a gun. "How did you get up here?"

"The elevator," I said, pointing. "I came up to ask you if you would mind me practicing here. You know Mom doesn't approve of me using it at home."

She pursed her lips, commiserating with me. "I figure if I'm working on the programming of this AI technology, I should also know how to use it."

She softened. "Of course I don't mind. You're family. I just meant that I wondered how you got in." She looked past me at the elevator and then retrained her watch on me. "The elevator is locked when I leave."

I shrugged. In my short life, I'd learned that there were times when it was best to be naive.

"I dunno. I said, 'top floor,' and the elevator let me out here. We could replay the elevator footage to see if there's a glitch in security. Or, if you want me to, I can…"

"No, it's okay," she interrupted my rambling. Aunt Danika didn't have patience for tangents, and I played to distract her. "Practice. I want you to get comfortable with the technology."

She patted my head like I was a puppy. I understood it was a loving gesture. She wasn't as good with affection as the rest of my family.

My smile softened her further. "Cool. Thanks. I'll try not to bother you. If I do, just let me know. My mom is waiting for me to get home for dinner anyway." I resumed swiping at the spaces in the room that were on the grid in my line of sight through the interface. "I just wanted to try a few things here rather than look like an idiot in front of everyone downstairs. Ya know?"

With a curt nod she took a call as if I wasn't even in the room. I practiced with my iCerebrum another ten minutes before dismissing myself through the elevator.

Upon stepping out of her office, the weight of my deceit lifted. I turned to face the closing doors, and was surprised to find my aunt approaching.

"Hold the elevator," she said, jogging in her heels. "No, stay here," she instructed the agents, who were already in step with her. "I'd like a minute with my nephew."

They both nodded and retreated to their post.

She entered the elevator next to me. Until that instant, I'd thought I pulled it off. How did I actually think I could fool someone this smart? There was no scenario in which I would talk my way out of this.

"Jay," she said, keeping her body to the elevator door as it closed us in together. "I have your first independent assignment."

"Really?"

"I've been looking over the formulas you've written for the specs, and I'm impressed."

She procured a microchip from her bold red pantsuit. Between her fingers, she lifted it to my eye-line.

"Solve this riddle, and we'll see if we can get you fast-tracked through your program."

My eyes bulged. The word *nepotism* streamed across my conscious thought, as I was certain there were programmers more qualified than me for this task.

"I won't let you down," I said, fighting the sting of concern about the high probability that I would, indeed, let her down. I didn't even know what was on that chip. "I'll give it my full attention."

"I have no doubt." She dropped the chip into my open palm.

"Door open," she commanded.

The elevator doors spread wide to reveal we hadn't even left her floor. Without so much as a *see you later,* Aunt Danika sauntered across the expanse of her lofty office.

My all-encompassing focus was on the tiny circuit board.

· · · · · · ● ● ● ● ● ● ● ● ● · · · ·

# CHAPTER 44

## RUTH

I never planned to have children of my own, but along Taden's pregnancy I, too, bonded with the baby she brought into our world.

"Hey, Taden, have you returned the car scat yet?" I hollered, coming through the front door. "I'm heading that way and can take it for you."

"My goodness," she said, placing her hand on her belly. "He always does this when you talk."

"What?" I chuckled. "Is my nephew happy I'm here?" I put my hands over hers, gently rubbing the spots I could easily see his body parts protruding. "Hi there, little one. Aunt Ruth's here. How's it going in there? Is your mommy keeping you warm and cozy?" His wiggling form responded with wild approval.

"Okay. Okay. Enough, you two," Taden said. "My stomach happens to have limits of how far this baby can reach out to you."

When he was born, I couldn't fathom how it was possible that I could love another human this much, but Jay quickly became top priority in my life. I found myself squeezing free time that I'd normally fill with work just to be with him.

Owning my own business, it was easy to create flexible time that I could share in his daycare while his parents were at work. Mostly, he spent that time with Dad and Dr. P, but I could usually manage to carve out at least one day a week to spend with Jay.

Our time together morphed into a montage over the years. From cuddling a baby to stacking blocks with a toddler, from reading with a small child to playing hide and seek tag with a young boy, from offering advice to the awkward tween, to now, as he moved onto his first serious girlfriend.

 "I'm inviting Jenny to the family birthday party," Jay said as I tapped the screen, accepting the vehicle's navigation into the shopping-center parking space.

We'd come for our standing biweekly visit to get a soft pretzel and hang out. The world was absorbed in technology, but Jay and I made a pact to have consistent face-to-face connection time.

I placed our regular order on my device, and it was waiting for us in the heated vending machine when we arrived. Jay's stack of soft pretzels had grown with his age. While watching him devour an entire pretzel in two bites, I wondered how my sister kept this boy fed.

"That's exciting. Must be getting serious to have her meet our crazy family."

He snorted, sucking his lemonade before he tore into his second pretzel.

"I really like her," he managed to claim between mouthfuls of bread.

"I can see why. The few times I've met her, she's impressed me."

The corner of his mouth twinged with a shy smile. "What did you like about her?"

"I liked a lot of things. But, actually, I'd like to know what *you* like about her." I reached across the table to get the cheese dip for my single pretzel.

"My favorite thing is that she's always smiling." He looked past me in a dreamy trance. I couldn't help but smile at the memory of young love. "But it's not that she's always smiling," he clarified. "It's that she's always smiling *at me*. It feels like she really likes to be around me."

"I love that," I said. "You deserve to be around someone who wants to be around you. Tell me more about her."

"Well, I mean, you have eyes. She's really cute. Right?"

I nodded, slurping my own drink through the straw and eyeing Jay in agreement. "She's adorable."

"We talk a lot. About dumb stuff, but it's stuff I'm really into, and she likes it, too."

"Like what?"

"Like, when I talk about my new job with Aunt Danika. She gets it; she has her own scientific ideas and questions, too."

"She seems like a perfect match," I said.

A surge of irritation rushed through my nervous system at the mention of Danika. I tried not to be jealous of her relationship with Jay—though I never understood why he called her "aunt" I had no intention of ever asking why. Instead I paid notice that it was a jealousy trigger for me, and dealt with my own surrounding issues. Jay loved her, and she seemed to care a great deal about him, and I tried to be okay with that.

But lately I'd been getting a vibe from Taden about Danika, and like a sixth sense I didn't feel good about her interactions with my nephew.

The fact that he was now working for her was a tally mark in the negative for the pro/con list I had going for Danika. The most Taden ever said about her in any negative light was way back before Jay was born.

It's wild how one year can turn into ten in the blink of an eye. My nephew was at an age many would consider a man. I couldn't help but reflect on how fast the last eighteen years had passed.

"Aunt Ruth," he said, snapping his fingers in front of my eyes. "Earth calling Aunt Ruth."

I blinked hard. "Sorry. I zoned out there for a minute."

"What were you thinking about?" he asked.

"How's working with Danika going?"

"I like it. She's an edgy person, so sometimes it can be weird. But I like it. I think I'm doing a good job."

"I'm certain you are," I said.

He beamed back at me. "You've always been a hard worker, and with two genius parents your brain ain't bad, either."

"I know, I know," he said, holding up his hand. "And I owe the rest to you for being the one to teach me how to read."

"That's right." I pointed back at him. "Don't you forget it either. I'd better be mentioned when you're accepting your Nobel Prize."

Driving home from our pretzel date, I replayed the conversation in my mind. Jay wasn't one to talk badly about people, so for him to mention how edgy Danika could be stood out like a red flag.

* * * * * * * ● ● ● ● ● ● ● ● ● ● ● ● *

# CHAPTER 45

"I'm home," I sang out, dropping my keys onto the counter.

"In here," Dakotah responded from the bathroom. I turned the knob and peeked through the door. "How'd your hangout with Jay go?" she asked, surrounded by bubbles.

Flicking the air, she paused the book she was reading through her iCerebrum and settled her focus on me.

"Good," I said, walking to the bench near the tub. "I can't believe he's eighteen already."

"Time flies," she said.

Pursing my lips, I nodded. "He said he's liking his job at the NIST."

I watched her face for any tell of withheld information. There was nothing.

"Do you see him much—around the building?" I asked.

"I've not seen him but once." She poked at the bubbles. "He came into our offices to have lunch with his mom once, and I joined them, but that's about it." She looked back to me. "Why do you ask?"

"Just wondering how he's fitting in around there."

She waved her hand in the air, her glistening dark skin distracting me. "Psh, Abel and Taden's son fitting in at the National Institute of Science and Technology? He's practically royalty. You don't need to worry about *that*."

I tilted my head. "Is there something I *do* need to worry about?"

Dakotah's forehead pinched. "What's got you wound up?" she asked, her chin jutting into the air, pressing me for the truth.

This is why Dakotah was my person. We talked through shit. If there was a weird vibe, we didn't ignore it. We pressed right into that space with love and care.

I sighed a long, heavy breath. "So…" I shook my head. "I'm not sure if this is driven by jealousy or a legit intuitive concern."

She leaned in, bathwater rippling with her movement. I had her full attention.

"I think this arrangement with Jay and—" I accentuated with air quotes: "'Aunt Danika' is fishy."

"Yeah," she agreed.

"Wait." I pulled my face in surprise. "You think so, too?"

She looked as though she immediately regretted her quick accord. She sank into her bath water, bubbles closing in above her submerged head. I waited for her to come back up for air. Wiping her face as she resurfaced, she stared off toward the faucet.

"Bathtub, reheat," she commanded the auto heater. Her eyes closed, and I imagined that she immediately felt the sensations of warmth travel through the water to her body.

"Ahem?" I cleared my throat.

"I'm choosing my words carefully, here. It's a fine line of breaking confidentiality and keeping secrets from you."

Pulling out her iCerebrum external drive, she looked to me with heaviness.

We'd been together almost two decades now, and it was unnerving to think she withheld information. It stung a little. I was used to the idea and understood the rules—my sister was the scientist who discovered time travel for a secret government. Secrets were part of the job. But I guess I lived under the delusion that Dakotah bent those rules for me.

She double-checked her iCerebrum was off.

"Exhaust fan on," she commanded. The steady hum of the air vent above us filled the room. In a hushed voice—almost like she was paranoid of being overheard—she said, "I don't trust that woman either." Goosebumps erupted on my skin.

"I didn't expect you to say that." I wrung my hands. "Should I be worried about Jay?"

"I'm certain your sister is keeping a close watch on him and his new job situation. She hasn't said anything to either of us about needing to be worried. Short answer? No, I don't think we need to worry about Jay."

Bobbing my head a little too frantically, I asked, "Is there a long answer?" I hoped she was going to say there wasn't, but that's the deal with honesty—it's asked and answered.

"There is," she sighed. Her polite smile made me queasy with anticipation. "The night of President Moore's inauguration…" She paused.

"Twenty years ago?" My confusion was evident.

Her quick nod filled me with a rush of heat. "That night went another way in a different timeline." My stomach flipped. "And let's just say it was bad." I blinked slow, deliberate blinks. "Abel and Taden time traveled to fix it, and when they did they discovered a terrible truth about Danika."

"You've known about this for our entire relationship?" My voice was filled with accusation.

"I have. I've wanted to talk to you about it, but it wasn't my line to cross. Taden is one of my oldest and dearest friends, and I'm compelled not to break confidentiality on the science we do." She rose from the tub, her body dripping. "Bathtub, empty," she commanded.

The water immediately began its furious spin down the drain. She reached for her towel and I watched her dry her body. Tucking the towel into a wrap under her arm, she looked at me again, harder this time.

"Listen," she said, her hands now on my shoulders. "The reason you trust me is that you know that I wouldn't break your confidence. Your sister feels the same way. I have to honor that."

"Yeah, but now you've told me. Your confidence is broken, and you could've done this years ago."

"I get why you're upset. I think I would feel the same as you do in this situation. I hope you can see how this is a difficult spot for me to be in."

And I did. The truth was, Taden had told me plenty of things through the years that I hadn't told Dakotah. She was right. If I told her every secret my sister told me, I'd be undermining my relationship with my sister. But in the same breath, I couldn't deny feeling hurt about this.

"I do. It sucks, but I do." I rose from the bench, meeting her eyes. "Why now, then?"

"It felt like a crossroad. If I didn't tell you in this moment, I was consciously choosing to lie to you and I don't want to do that. Plus, I do feel like—even though we don't have an imminent concern about Jay's safety—we should keep an eye on this. We definitely need to have open communication about what we notice from here on out."

"So my intuition isn't totally off?" I asked.

"It could be something," she gently confirmed.

My face tightened with worry. Dakotah pulled me in and wrapped her arms around my waist.

"We won't let anything happen to him," she promised.

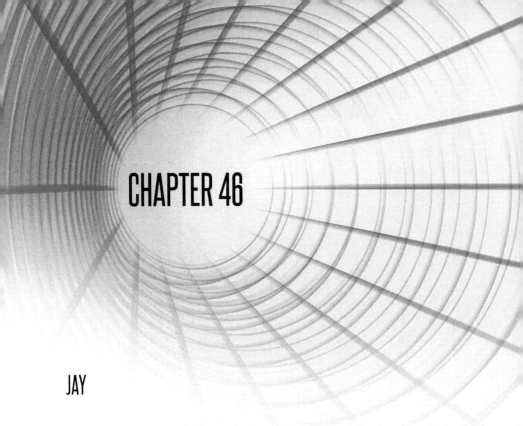

# CHAPTER 46

## JAY

"How was work this week?" Jenny asked, peering at me from beneath my arm. We had been walking through the park, her dog lagging behind us.

"It was great. I thought my aunt brought me in just to do inventory, but she's already given me a small project to work on once I complete the inventory tasks each day."

"That's awesome," she said, rolling up on her toes to kiss my cheek. "I'm proud of you. Hasn't even been a month, and you're already a scientist."

"Well, I wouldn't get too excited. It's just a small project working on AI specs. Nothing too…"

"Scruffy! Come!" she interjected as her dog took off after a squirrel. "I'm sorry! Hang on," she said, holding up her finger and apologizing.

"Scruffy," I commanded in my deepest voice.

Her dog actually stopped and took notice. Jenny clapped her hands together to get his attention and then she gestured to the dog, pointing her index fingers toward each other and rotating them around one another toward her body. Scruffy responded right away. Jenny dug a treat out of her pocket to reward Scruffy for following directions.

"What was that?" I asked her.

"What?" She looked up from petting him.

"The hand gesture."

"I taught him sign language," she said, beaming. "I thought you knew."

I shook my head. "It's amazing." I scratched my cheek. I thought I'd seen that gesture before. "Don't people usually use dog commands?"

She shrugged. "I thought this was way cooler." I loved how she liked to be official. Teaching her dog sign language. "He only knows, like, ten basic signs, though."

It struck me where I'd seen that gesture. "Oh my gosh," I muttered.

My mind replayed the video my dad made about my first job. I was certain a hand gesture he made was just like the one Jenny presented to her dog.

"That's your concentration face." She stood from scratching behind Scruffy's ear.

"Yeah." I furrowed my brow. "I think my dad put sign language at the end of the video I watched the other day."

Jenny linked her hand into mine. Thoughtful about the idea, she asked, "Has he ever done that before?"

"Not that I noticed. But to be honest, I didn't really even see it on a conscious level. Watching you with Scruffy just now triggered it in my mind." I looked down at her and tightened my grasp of her hand. "Weird, right?"

"You have it on you right now?" she asked.

I nodded, lifting my wrist. I stretched my arm out from my sleeve to reveal my dad's TRB. Jenny pulled me over to the nearest bench.

"Let's watch it," she said earnestly.

"Really? It won't make you uncomfortable to watch it with me?"

She shook her head. "I'd like to sort of meet your dad, anyway."

I kissed her forehead. "All right."

I looked around for an open space to simultaneously project his image and keep the video somewhat private from people who might pass. I aimed my wrist at the tree stump to our left and adjusted the brightness of his image.

"Jenny, meet my dad."

She stifled a giggle. It caught me off guard when a surge of emotion flooded me. It was the first time I'd ever watched my dad with another person other than my mom. I peeked at her out of the corner of my eye to find her glued to his image.

"You look exactly like him," she murmured, wide-eyed.

I sat taller. Each time someone said that to me, it made me feel proud. I pressed my nose into her hair and watched a few more minutes until he wrapped up his advice on my first day of work.

"There!" I exclaimed. "Did you see it?" I looked at her excitedly. "That was sign language, wasn't it?"

"It really did look like it," she agreed. "I mean, even if it wasn't sign language, he was definitely signaling to you there. But I'm quite positive it *was* sign language. Can you replay that one part?"

"Hang on, yeah." I backed up the video one tenth of a second and froze the image mid-gesture. "Isn't that the same move you did with your fingers?"

"Sort of," she said. "But he's rotating it slightly differently." Jenny pulled out her mobile and looked up the sign language movements. It was endearing that she refrained from using her iCerebrum around me, knowing how my mom was about the whole thing.

"Hm," she said, sliding her finger down the screen, searching for my dad's gesture. "Got it. It looks like the sign for 'go'. Similar to the sign for 'come', except the way the fingers are rotated."

I scratched my cheek. "Isn't it weird that he used sign language?" I shook my head. "The whole thing is odd."

"We should see if he's ever signed like that before," she suggested. "Let's watch another video. What's the one before this one?"

My face flushed.

"What?" she asked, chuckling as she touched my cheek with a brush of her hand.

"It was one he made for my first date." I felt the heat in my face deepen.

"Oh, I definitely have to see this one," Jenny giggled.

My shoulders shook, joining her amusement. "Thanks, but I'm gonna wait and watch more of these when I get home."

I leaned in and planted a series of kisses across her face. Her laughter encouraged me to continue. It also encouraged her dog to jump onto our laps, not missing the opportunity to swipe his drool-covered tongue over both our faces.

"Ew, Scruffy, get down," she commanded through a fit of giggles.

"Thanks, Jenny." I slid a few loose strands of hair behind her shoulder, and then it was her turn to flush.

"For what?"

"For helping me figure this out. I think we've uncovered something. I'm not going to mention it to anyone just yet, though."

"You mean you're not even going to tell your mom?" She clearly disapproved.

"I will. Just not until I know if it's even anything important."

· · · · · · ● · · · · · · ·

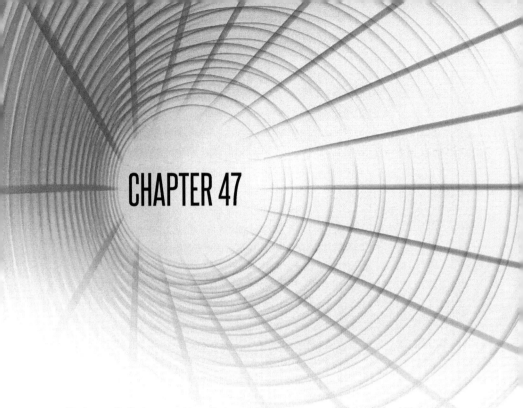

# CHAPTER 47

"And, son, that's how you know if she wants to see you again," my dad said into the screen.

My eyes jerked to his hands, stunned to find he had flashed another gesture. I almost missed it, and I was focused on looking for it this time. His hand was in a fist with his thumb out, and he quickly flicked it on his chin. Replaying the footage, I furiously typed into my mobile, looking up what the gesture meant.

"'Don't'," I muttered to myself.

"What, honey?" my mom asked, walking by my room.

Startled, I tapped the TRB, cutting Dad's video from projecting into the space next to my bed.

"Nothing," I said, hoping it didn't come out as terse as it seemed.

"I thought you said something." She poked into my room, eyebrows raised, waiting for me to respond.

"Nope," I said, shaking my head. "I was just thinking."

"Whatcha thinking about?" She'd fully opened my door and walked in.

"Nothing, really. I was watching Dad," I said, lifting my wrist.

She looked pleased and sat on the end of my bed. "Which one are you watching?"

"I started rewatching the series of how-to's."

Her face brightened. "Those are good ones." She put her hand on my foot.

I sat up straighter. "Mom?"

"Mm-hm?"

"Watch this." I replayed the first-date video and paused on his signing. Then I played the first day of work video right after it and paused on the sign he made at the end of that one.

My mom didn't move. I wasn't even sure if she was breathing.

"Did you see that?" I asked.

Except for her blinking eyes, she remained rigid.

"Play the next video," she ordered in a hoarse whisper.

I obeyed without hesitation. "There's another one," I said. "And look, he blinks three times in slow succession right before the sign."

My mom's imploring look spoke for her.

"I've got the next one," I assured her.

Another sign at the end of the video. This time it was so fast it was almost indecipherable, if not for the three blinks I spotted right before. I replayed it a few times, then finally found it on the sign language site.

"It's an 'I,'" I said, recording it.

"What is he trying to say?" she asked.

"I don't know. Let me look. Earlier in the videos he signed 'go'."

"What else?"

"Go. Don't trust AI," I said.

My mom crossed her arms and stood at the end of my bed. I watched her pace back and forth.

"Mom…"

I heard the weak admission in my voice. So did she. Turning fiercely to me, her arms dropped and she waited for me to come clean.

"Aunt Danika has been letting me work on a side project for her when I'm done with my lab checks."

I paused as the sinking feeling in the pit of my stomach moved up my insides. She clasped her hands behind her neck and stared at my ceiling. After a long moment, she pushed a loud breath from her nose.

"Doing what?"

"I've been coding AI specs for her," I finally admitted.

She returned to the rapid pacing and eventually moved her hands from her neck to her hips.

"Okay," she said, too soft for the tension in the room. "It's okay."

She sat back down.

"We need to re-watch all of his videos and see if your dad has left anything else for us."

Hours passed, and I watched my dad warn us not to trust AI and not to trust Danika. That she was dangerous to us. And the chilling part was that I had done both.

"You'll go to work as normal," my mom said, her hands on my shoulders—a stern posture indicating her direct orders. "We don't know what this means yet. Just keep your head down, do your job, and tell me every detail."

I returned an earnest nod. This whole thing had me freaked out. It was surreal that I'd discovered my dead father was sending me messages from the grave about my aunt. She wasn't really my "aunt", though, was she? Convinced of her love, I had never given that fact much thought. It now pervaded my mind.

My mom leaned over me and kissed my cheek before she hurried to her room, closing the door behind her. I heard her whispering, but couldn't make out what she was saying or to whom. I assumed it was Aunt Ruth. She told her everything. And I was sure she needed to talk about the messages we'd found from my dad.

# CHAPTER 48

I turned on my iCerebrum and glanced around the supply room. Shelves and shelves of glassware carried my vision to the chemical's cupboards. With my implant I could easily—if not monotonously—inventory each item. I robotically placed orders through the direct connection linked up with the suppliers, so that nothing would ever be out of stock.

It was time-consuming, and I found myself working as slowly as I possibly could rather than the frantic pace I'd been working in order to continue with Aunt Danika's side project. The excitement I'd had for my position had been replaced with dread. I once again found myself considering just quitting. It was the easiest way out for someone my age—but my mom assured me Aunt Danika wouldn't hear of it. Still, I felt an eerie chill in the air and a sense that I was being watched—probably through the device synced up to my brain. No wonder my mom didn't want me wearing this crap.

How much did Aunt Danika know?

Tapping the airspace above each graduated cylinder to keep count of how many were on the shelf in front of me, I mentally replayed my dad air-signing, "Go. Don't trust AI. Danika will end us all."

I lost count and had to restart. I grinned, knowing I would have no problem doubling the length of time this task usually took.

Not to be outdone by my own thoughts of distraction, Danika's unmistakable footsteps warned her approach from down the hall.

"I was beginning to think you weren't here today," she said at the doorway.

She was lying, I thought. I could've bet money at that point that she'd been watching me through surveillance, either through the many cameras throughout the building or simply via the iCerebrum connected to me.

She walked closer, crossing her arms as she did. "You're still completing the checklist from this morning?"

Her surprise was evident, yet not completely believable. I offered an apologetic glance, which she didn't accept. Danika's watchful reproach unnerved me. Dammit, I couldn't leave the silence alone.

"I'm almost finished here. I had a slow start, and just haven't been able to catch up."

Pleased with my admission and promise to get busy on a more important task—the one she'd readied for me—she said, "Perfect." Her hands were clasped in front of her waist. "I've actually been waiting for you to check in with me all morning, because I have something exciting to show you about the progress of your specs. That connection you made works seamlessly." As I was still crouched to the lower shelves of glassware, she patted the top of my head somewhat awkwardly, "Your dad would be proud of you."

My knee dropped from its crouched position, causing me to lose my balance enough that she startled. Danika had never mentioned my dad to me before. Not once in my life. Was it a mere coincidence that the day after I found his secret messages, she dropped his name so casually?

I shrugged, standing to meet her face-to-face. Scratching my head I quickly added, "It's my implant; it still throws off my balance sometimes." Her chin jutted to acknowledge my complaint. "Not sure how long it will take me to adjust."

"You'll get the hang of it. Too bad your mom believes it rots your brain." She cackled. "You'd get used to it much faster if you could use it all the time." Waving her hand, she added, "Oh well, finish up here and get to the real work upstairs."

For a long moment I stood with my eyes closed, unsure what move to make. Then I followed my mom's instructions and did my work as normal. Except now, I was paying critical attention to every detail of every word and every move I made.

The elevator dinged open to Danika's office. As I made my way to the opposite end of the room, palms clammy, she called me over.

"It's about time. Look," she said, displaying the function I'd coded. "It's genius. I couldn't see how the machine would constantly move the serum throughout its system, but since you've structured it to behave like the circulatory system it seems obvious."

I watched the animation of her AI pump the liquid from a beating heart in its chest through veins and deliver the serum throughout the body, only to return to the heart where it recycled. Pleased with my coding, I was also wary of what this meant she now held the power to do with her AI.

As soon as my day was over, I couldn't wait to take out my iCerebrum and leave the building. I hopped into a car pilot to Jenny's house, pinging my mom that I would see her at home later.

Jenny couldn't know the entirety of what my dad had said—Mom made that clear. It was for her own safety. But I had to talk to her, and she was most definitely going to want to follow up with the whole thing since she helped me spot it in the first place.

"It seems like he was warning me about technology," I told her. It wasn't exactly a lie. "He made the videos, what, like fifteen years ago? If only he knew how much technology filled our lives today."

Jenny scoffed at the notion that technology could be avoided.

"He wasn't wrong, though." She shrugged. "Look around this place. I'm quite sure the only thing technology hasn't invaded here are my books." Jenny picked up her blanket. "This is filled with nano devices that regulate my temperature while I sleep." She sat on the chair in front of her desk, which provided the exact amount of light needed to see her homework without eye strain, based on the light filtering from her window and the light fixtures in her ceiling. "The chair is connected to the desk, which, as I move—" She spun the chair around. "—weighs my body to judge how much light I need."

Flopping onto the end of her bed, I leaned back on the palms of my hands. "I never really thought a lot about it. It's just how we live."

"Not until you look at it through the eyes of someone fifteen years ago, eh?"

She scooted her chair closer to me. The light on her desk dimmed in response.

"Don't you think his warning was cryptic, though?" I asked.

"It is strange that he signed it. Like, why didn't he just say it outright?"

And why did he embed it into separate parts throughout the series of videos? He could've just stated it. Hell, he could've made an entire video dedicated to his thoughts and distrust of technology. And of Danika.

My ruminating went onto a tangent about my dad, the Keeper of Memorics. A pioneer of time travel was warning his son about the very things he spent his career progressing. Jenny didn't know any of this.

"It's funny," she said. "Why didn't he?"

We remained in a wondering silence. I wanted to tell her what he'd actually said. I needed to share this with someone but I couldn't. Not yet. I didn't know what was about to detonate, and I wouldn't risk her safety. I could meet her where she understood, though, and tell her from that perception.

"Jenny?" Her brows rose. "What if he knew something dangerous? What if that's why he died?"

She thoughtfully took in my question. "Well, then, we should probably figure out what he was trying to tell you."

She put her hand on my knee. In response, I put mine on top of hers.

"Or maybe," she said, "we should do the exact opposite, so neither of us meets the same ending."

Her hand twitched beneath mine. Truthfully, my nerves tightened, thinking about the threat this carried.

Up until last week, I'd lived a normal teenage life. Now I had to worry about Jenny's.

Each day after work, I'd find myself consumed with watching my dad's messages. If he'd embedded secret sign language warning me of danger, what else had he hidden in plain sight? Every detail mattered—where he was making the video, what he said and did, what he didn't say or do, and the topics he chose to share all came under scrutiny.

I had pages of detailed, handwritten notes, all of which I kept off any kind of technology. Almost overnight I'd become a conspiracy theorist, holed up in my room with paper notes plastered to the wall, strung together by my ideas.

It wasn't just my dad's videos that kept me wide-eyed, either. I'd gotten into the habit of carrying one of my mom's old steno pads in my back pocket to write notes on at work. It wasn't like I could take snapshots and store them in my mobile or my iCerebrum.

If Aunt Danika was monitoring anything I did, she'd certainly take notice of me collecting random details about the goings-on of the NIST.

"Here are the specs you requested yesterday," I said, offering them over to her.

"You remind me of your mom when she was younger. Eager and capable."

She accepted the chip and slipped it into her device. Scanning through my codes, the pleased lines creeping on the sides of her face still managed to make me feel an odd sense of pride.

I was conflicted. I was caught between an unclear warning and the high level of respect I'd had for my aunt. I'd grown up to love her as family, regardless of how cold she came across. Assessing her words and actions with caution didn't come as naturally as it probably should have. Aunt Danika tapped each code and dragged it into a locked file on her screen labeled AM/AI.

"Did you know, young Mr. Mihal, that I assigned this very task to one of my mid-level programmers, but he could not successfully execute the parameters you have just made look simple?"

My face flushed. I inherited the stupid embarrassed response from my mom. It was awful. As soon as I felt the heat in my cheeks from Aunt Danika's compliment, the alertness caused me to become even more embarrassed, and in turn even more red. I sighed with the frustration of it.

"I'm quite curious about how this code is coming together, and what the overall project entails," I said, hoping to deflect from my pink cheeks.

"I bet you are."

Danika typed into her keyboard for several silent seconds. She never seemed to have a natural goodbye, and I wasn't ever sure if she was done with me or expected me to remain for further directions. Standing awkwardly, I shifted my weight, hoping to remind her I was still there if she had forgotten.

When she still didn't respond I turned to excuse myself, but she held up her finger. She tapped a few more keys and then used her same finger to swipe a file across her screen before removing the chip I had just given her.

"Let's see if you can do this one."

She beamed, her palm open for me to retrieve it. I guess that meant I was on a need-to-know basis. She just didn't realize how badly I needed to know.

I cocked my head and plucked the chip from her hand. "I'm sure it will be cake."

She stood—a good indicator, I thought, that our meeting was actually ending this time.

"You are my nephew, and I trust you. However, clearance levels on intelligence projects come with experience and expertise."

"I get it. I really just appreciate the experience you're giving me here. One day, I'll be on the inside."

"Son, you're already in. It's just going to take time to work your way up. Keep doing what you're doing."

"Thanks, Aunt Danika," I said, backing out of her office.

"I'll see you when you solve that."

She pointed at the chip between my fingers as she sat back down to her computer. After the elevator doors closed I sighed a discreet breath of relief, fully aware of the camera watching me in the corner of the tiny compartment.

My brisk entrance into the men's restroom echoed among the stalls. I took the one furthest back and pulled the latch to lock the door. The camera inside the bathroom was angled in such a way that a view into that particular stall from the top couldn't be achieved. After removing my jacket, I hung it over the sensors that controlled toilet functioning. I didn't even trust what could be hacked in the toilet sensor.

Yeah, come to think of it, I might have qualified as a full-blown conspiracist at that point.

Once certain I had privacy to write, I produced both the notebook and the chip to identify the serial number of the chip and the most accurate wording that Aunt Danika and I had just exchanged. The file I watched her drag my specs into was labeled "AM/AI", and postulated my first impressions of what I thought it meant.

My stomach twisted while writing the words out: Abel Mihal/Artificial Intelligence? If that was true, I had to unleash the litany of questions I couldn't stifle about why my dad would warn me of AI, and then I had to find a possible connection of him to AI. The question I couldn't ignore was how I would get into her files without her knowing.

I had to learn what she was building—what I feared I was helping her build.

* * * * * * * ● ● ● ● ● ● ● ● * * *

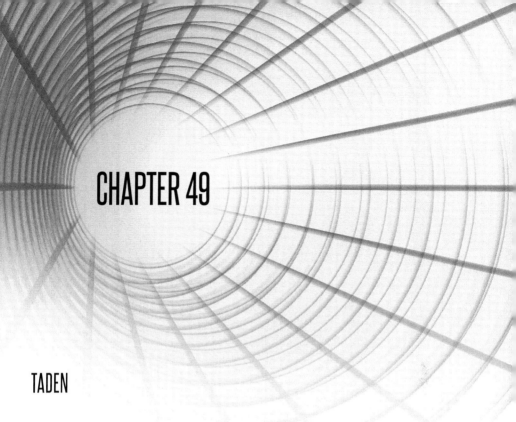

# CHAPTER 49

## TADEN

Everyone but Danika had arrived for Jay's birthday dinner, and several conversations kept the table buzzing with chatter as we waited for our food to arrive.

I hadn't seen Quinn in a few months. Our visits were sporadic since she took a new job a few years back, and life continued to move at a forward pace—but she never missed a birthday of Jay's, and this year was no exception. Quinn had matured into a distinguished woman.

Ruth and Dakotah sat snugly next to one another as if they were a new couple. They'd met each other here after work and were busy catching one another up on their day.

Dr. Pasterski sat comfortably next to the two of them, smiling as she fiddled with her hot water and tea setting just delivered to the table. She listened as she poured the steaming liquid over the bag dangling from her cup.

I was relieved Danika decided not to come to Jay's birthday this year. My nerves were on edge around her, like she might be able to see I'd caught on to her—how she'd ruined me—and that I no longer intended on sitting around and taking it.

Jenny was sharing with Jay and me how her presentation at school had gone that day. She'd been wholly occupied preparing for it that whole week. Jay and I had been her practice audience half a dozen times.

"I volunteered to go first," she said. "That way, I could get it out of the way and the teacher had no one to compare my performance to."

Out of the corner of my eye, I caught my dad squinting at Jaxson as he pressed my dad for stories from his career. "If you're not going to drink your Guinness, I will," Dad said to Jaxson, hinting he back off a bit. Jaxson didn't read the cue. "Of course, go ahead," he said, sliding the pint to my dad.

Dad didn't like to share too many details surrounding his government work. I only knew what I did regarding his role in trying to thwart The Reckoning because of time travel.

In a way, I knew some things about that part of his life even he didn't know. It had been rewritten. But because of that timeline, I was keenly aware that my dad had served the safety of our nation without recognition—or the desire to be public about it.

The way he looked at Jaxson, though, caught me. I turned my attention from Jay and Jenny and gave my dad's conversation a bit more focus. He noticed and found my eyes, throwing me a look of questioning. He seemed put off by Jaxson.

I recalled when I first met him early on for his interview, the methods of his politeness awkward. He would never get whatever joke was shared. Jaxson had a literal quality about him that, while uneasy at first, left an agreeable abandonment of sarcasm.

It took several years for me to attain a level of comfort with Jaxson, but he was a most important asset to the team. His highly professional conduct allowed him to remain cool under pressure. The stress of a deadline or laborious data mining didn't faze him. At the lab, Dakotah and I never tired of having his support, and his meticulous habits were very helpful.

Scanning the table occupied by my NIST family, I did harbor guilt that I was essentially holding them hostage in their positions in my department. We were charged with solving future time travel—which I'd solved yet had let them continue to chase their tail after. At this point we'd redirected to mostly research and theory, testing any new possibilities that bloomed, and I would carefully smother if it got too close to the solution.

My dad only interacted with Jaxson on rare occasions, and never long enough to reach a level of familiarity with his demeanor. After his third one-word response to Jaxson, I knew he needed relief from the intense questioning.

"Jaxson," I said. "Jay and Jenny share a computer science class, and Jenny was just telling us about her presentation on autonomic computing. You helped design the updated systems at work; you should chat with them about it."

Acknowledging the segue, Jaxson produced an exaggerated smile. My dad wasn't off-target labeling Jaxson as void of warmth. The way his lips pulled symmetrically and his raised brows mirrored each other looked mechanical, but I'd long since come to see that Jaxson didn't exhibit social cues like most people. However, he was far from the only person I knew who seemed to function differently. We all had our quirks.

Relieved by the break from Jaxson's attention, my dad moved his chair closer to Dr. P and joined her conversation with Ruth and Dakotah.

Quinn watched me watch everyone else. Her interest in me never seemed to waver. Her bright smile in response to me noticing this transferred to my own face.

"How's the new job at NASA?" I asked.

"Well, it's not really new anymore. I've been there going on five years now," she said, still beaming. "But it's good. I'm enjoying the research project they've got me on."

"I guess I just keep hoping you're not interested and will decide to come back to the lab," I said.

With some exaggeration, I winked. She loved when I made an effort to tell her I missed her. Truth was, I did miss her. Like Jaxson she was exceedingly efficient, but unlike Jaxson she brought a warmth to the place that her absence spotlighted.

I couldn't blame her, though. She'd wanted a serious relationship with Jaxson for a long while. They dated on and off, but he never really could make the commitment with her. She'd constantly struggle with his lack of affection or desire.

"On paper he would be the perfect husband—the dream of a love—but in reality we never seem to be able to connect," she used to tell me. "I talk of a future together, and he physically backs away from me, stiff as a board."

Between her Jaxson troubles and Danika transitioning from The Patriot Party to more of a full-time leadership role over the NIST, the writing was on the wall. Quinn's motivation to leave became accelerated by the distinct tension between her and Danika, related to Quinn's brother, Marius.

Quinn had pinged me an SOS to come save her from a heated conversation Danika had imposed while questioning Quinn about Marius. I walked into the conference room in time to catch Danika on the attack. "I bet if that traitor of a brother of yours," she said, jutting her chin at Quinn, indicating she meant Marius, "hadn't interfered with our time travel, we'd have figured how to get into the future by now." It wasn't too much longer after that incident that Quinn started putting feelers out for different opportunities.

"Jay, tell us about your new job over at the NIST," Quinn interjected into the conversation Jaxson was having with the kids. Her boisterous interruption pulled everyone at the table into the same discussion.

As if on cue the main doors of the restaurant opened, and in walked Danika Farkas.

Jaxson stood from his seat and stiffened with respect. The hush of conversation meant to give way to Jay's response regarding his new job transferred to the dominating presence of Danika.

We'd all grown accustomed to her at these small gatherings, but no one was fond of it. However, we knew she wouldn't stay long—just long enough to put all of us on edge and to show us up with her gift.

"Happy birthday to my favorite scientist," she said, sauntering toward my son.

She set her perfectly wrapped gift in front of him. Jay's delight at being spoiled by Danika never faded, even now that he wasn't sure of her genuineness. He still flashed his teeth in a wide grin, tearing at the wrapping.

It struck me that Jay was the only person I'd ever observed treat Danika with such warmth. I briefly doubted if she truly could ever harm the boy. Even a monster like her needed to feel loved, and I could see—we all could see—that my son truly cared for his *Aunt Danika.*

Ruth pursed her lips, annoyed that Danika had rudely interrupted us with her grand gestures and swept away Jay's attention.

"Oh, man! This is too much!" Jay said. He glanced at Danika with wide eyes. "Is this for real?"

"Of course it is," she said with a sly gleam.

"What'd you get, honey?" I asked, feigning interest. Really, I was already posed to deny whatever ridiculous notion she planned to gift him this year.

"Being that he's officially an adult now, I thought it high time he receive his passport chip so he can travel beyond border patrols," Danika said.

Her voice was dripping with condescension, as though she was daring me to interfere with whatever reasoning she had for caring about my son being able to travel throughout the world. I carefully held my expression, not revealing how appalling the gift came across as. A quick glance at the faces of my family members validated the way I felt. Still standing as if at attention, Danika pulled her arms from behind her back to reveal a second wrapped gift. My mouth gaped.

"Danika, you really didn't have to…"

"Nonsense," she said, waving her hand.

Okay, I thought, he's eighteen. It's a milestone birthday.

This time an almost giddy look took hold of her face, which caught me by more surprise than her gifts had.

Jay looked to me for permission to accept the additional gift. Although I wished to refuse it, at my nod he jumped to his feet and ripped off the wrapping. He was speechless.

"One for you and one for your mom," she said, eyeing me. I still hadn't made out what all the fuss was about.

"Mom," Jay said, breathless. "She got me—us—tickets to Paris!"

"No," I said.

I would not let this woman who I felt positive had destroyed my family, who had blackmailed her way into my son's life, and who'd left me living in fear for the last fifteen years, gift us something this fantastic. There had to be a catch. Why would she do this? Did she want me out of the way? She had a track record of getting people out of the picture to further her agenda.

Although, it then occurred to me that I should accept this as a gift. It was maybe more thoughtful than it initially appeared. This trip could serve as a way to get my son out of harm's way as she exacted her plan.

*Maybe*, I thought, *I shouldn't be so hasty in turning this gift down.* Maybe it was the most humane thing Danika had ever done.

I watched her smile at my son with no trace of accepting my refusal, and it suddenly wasn't too incredible to believe she might actually love him. There was something in her eyes when she looked at him that wasn't there with anyone else.

No, I wouldn't shut this gift down immediately. It might just be what I needed to finish this war with her.

· · · · · ● ● ● ● ● ● ● ● ● ● ● ● · · · ·

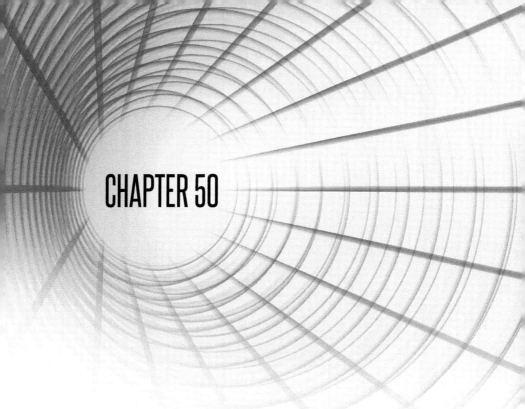

# CHAPTER 50

Washing my hands, I looked in the mirror above me. It was digitally framing my face, grabbing facial recognition sequencing.

"Welcome back, Mrs. Mihal," it said.

I groaned internally. Despite my every effort to remain off the grid, there were always tractions I couldn't avoid.

"Are you feeling ill today?" it asked.

I pulled my face, caught off guard by the computer programming.

"I don't mean to offend," it said, responding to my facial expression.

"Why do you ask?" I asked, hoping it wasn't going to inform me that I looked haggard.

"You were just here four and a half minutes ago, washing your hands. Are you ill?"

The mirror had registered the other version of me. Crap. Now the time-traveling version of me was on this restaurant's database. She wasn't even here that long, and was already leaving evidence of time travel. I shook the water from my hands.

"I'm okay. Spicy food always goes right through me," I said, looking into the mirror.

"The pharmacy on the corner has antacids on sale for fifteen dollars. It will settle your stomach. Side effects include belching and constipation," the mirror said, flashing a product ad for the antacids on sale in the mirror image.

I resisted the urge to roll my eyes, aware that the mirror was still scanning my facial responses. Pulling my mouth into a polite smile I forced a "thank you" and quickly left the restroom to rejoin my son's birthday dinner party.

My mind flooded with the words the time-traveling me had said. "*You'll know everything in a few weeks.*"

I needed to be ready for what she was bringing into our timeline—and I still planned to send Jay into the past tonight. He was ready to go, and I was through with being pushed around by Danika Farkas.

How could I begin to prepare for the multiple off-shoots that would come from this?

If nothing else, my future self-confirmed that I was on the right track. All I needed to do was keep making the next right choice. I couldn't look too far into this plan.

"Mom, look what Jenny got me," Jay said, holding up a stuffed animal. "She must have gotten confused on the invitation, thinking it said my *eighth* birthday, not my *eighteenth*."

His teasing smile that revealed just how funny he found himself to be grew when he looked over at his girlfriend, who was feigning a pout. He reached his arm around her and pulled her close to his side, planting a grateful kiss on her cheek and whispering something in her ear that left her giggling like, well, a schoolgirl. It was delightful to watch.

I found such joy in seeing my son happy with the people he chose to spend his time with. Jenny was a lovely girl who easily matched the beat of our family.

I gathered the gifts from the table and split them between Jay and Jenny to carry to the car. Once they were out of earshot, I turned my attention to Ruth and Dad, who were quietly chatting about her PR business. I pulled up a chair next to them and waited for an opening in their discussion.

"Tonight," I said. They both looked over. "Jay will get my TRB."

They found each other's eyes. They'd known I was planning this. They'd agreed it was a necessary action. But, like me, they were also terrified about what would come of this.

"I ran into a future version of me in the restroom. I got the impression from her…from me…that we are on track. I'm making the right moves related to the Danika takedown."

Ruth let out a sigh. "That's good, right?"

"It's better than nothing," I said.

"Are you sure you don't want me to go instead of Jay?" Dad offered.

He had offered so many times to do this. For some inexplicable reason, his persistence was beginning to bother me.

"Dad, we talked about this. Jay needs to talk to me. I need to hear from my son's mouth what is happening in this timeline. If you went there would be so many more things I'd have to tell you, and it would compromise your safety—and Dr. P's safety."

"I know, honey. I just feel guilty about Abel. It's my fault he's gone. If I hadn't asked him to send me to see your mom that day, none of this would've happened."

I reached over Ruth's lap and pulled my dad's hand to me. "Please stop blaming yourself. It's not your fault." I sucked in a breath. "It's not my fault either, even though I, too, claim blame. I *know* who's responsible for his death, and I'm going to deal with her."

Dr. Pasterski approached the three of us on her return from the restroom. She smiled, walking behind Ruth and draping her arms around the front of my sister. I pulled Ruth's hand to mine and Dad's, and the four of us looked between each other, ready for what tomorrow would bring.

· · · · · · ● ● ● ◉ ● ● ● ● · · · · ·

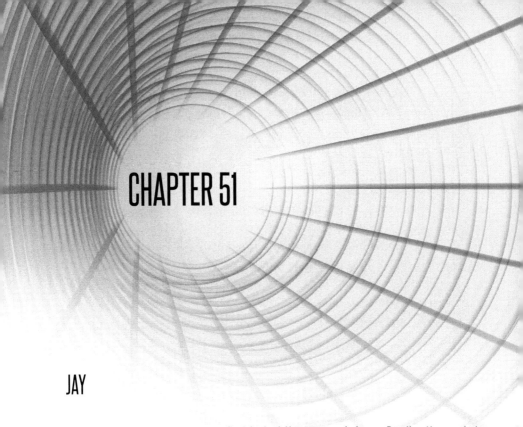

# CHAPTER 51

## JAY

My dad's book to my mom was my first look at the man my dad was. Reading the words he wrote to her in their book saturated me with their love. I was the living evidence of two people who'd found the soulmate connection.

The evening of my eighteenth birthday, alone in my room, while reading one of my favorite pages—a note my dad had written to me—I heard a tap on my bedroom door.

"Yeah?"

"Jay, it's Gramps. Can I come in?"

"Sure," I said, slipping the book under my pillow.

He opened the door, and I was taken aback at how good he looked. His face seemed fuller and his eyes a little brighter. I'd just seen him at dinner and, I couldn't be sure, but he looked a lot healthier now than he did then.

"Happy Birthday, Grandson," he said, handing me a small package.

"You already gave me a gift at dinner," I said to his sly grin. "Do you want me to open it now?"

He sat next to me, gawking. "I think you should."

Tearing off the wrapping, I lifted the lid of the tiny box. From the size, I was guessing he got me jewelry or maybe a pocket watch. I never suspected a Timed-Release Band.

"Wow!"

"I know you have your dad's old one, but this one has a different purpose," he told me.

"Is it real?" I craned my neck toward my bedroom door, wondering if my mom knew Gramps was giving this to me.

"It is. This TRB hasn't been disabled. Your mom sent me here to give it to you."

I wondered if Gramps was losing his mind. He was getting old. "Mm, okay. Does Mom actually know you have this?"

He laughed. "Grandson, listen, your mom sent me here to get this to you."

Aware my mom had discovered time travel and my dad had died in a time-travel event, I was uneasy. What had happened since his death couldn't have been foreseen, but I found it difficult to imagine a scenario where my mom would want me to travel in time. She was averse to even discussing the topic.

"Are you for real?" I asked.

"Look at me. I'm a young, spry guy. Your gramps must be ancient," he said.

It was true; he did look *much* younger now that I looked harder.

"I'm supposed to, what? Put this on and just time travel?"

"Not exactly," he said, pointing toward my hallway. "Your mother has the serum to make it work. Hide this until she gives you the serum."

"She's going to let me time travel?" I asked, bubbling with excitement. This was completely unlike my mom—the same woman who disallowed my iCerebrum.

"She's waiting for you in my present. It's your first birthday today."

This was difficult to believe.

"Has my dad died yet?" I asked.

He looked at me like I'd knocked the wind out of him. "He's gone. It's still fresh, though. You should be prepared for that."

I lifted the TRB from the box. These were thought to all be gone, but now I had two in my possession. My dad's was disabled for time travel, but this was a new one.

"A word of advice when you do travel: brace yourself. It can be a bit tricky on the system."

We both laughed.

I thought, if an old man could handle it I should be all right. Boy did I turn out to be wrong.

"Grandson," he said. "I wish you well. I'm heading back home."

He winked and strode out of my room. I watched my door long after he'd gone, doubting any part of the occurrence actually happened.

* * * * * * ● ● ● ● ● ● ● ● ● * * *

# CHAPTER 52

Studying my dad's videos revealed more I hadn't noticed that was now glaringly obvious: what he wore in more than half the videos.

*He must've made many of these all on the same day,* I thought. Out of the thirty videos he'd left me, he wore the same ensemble—an ageless pair of jeans, a blue-gray plaid button up, and a University of Pennsylvania baseball cap—in seventeen of them.

In an attempt to distract from my growing paranoia, I hyper-focused on any evidence that could support my theory he made all seventeen on the same day. Freeze-framing scene by scene, I'd found enough proof. His facial hair growth was exactly the same in each, his overall mood seemed the same, and—the final factor—the mustard stain near the third button of his flannel was the same as well.

This compilation of evidence drove me closer to what really freaked me out. For the last fifteen years or so, I'd believed I had imagined my dad at various moments of my life.

I hid this manifestation for fear that I was mentally unhealthy—seeing my dead father standing off in the background, watching me through proud eyes, could have been a sign of a mental illness.

But watching him in his videos, I couldn't logic myself out of the fact that he always wore this exact outfit when I thought I saw him in person—down to the hat. The hat had been the most obvious to me throughout the years, but his clothes had gone unnoticed—until now.

I'd watched these videos so regularly it was entirely possible he really was just a vision I'd created, dressed in the clothes I'd subconsciously seen in the many recordings.

However, something told me no. This was reality.

Time travel—while still hidden from the rest of humanity—was a reality that my parents had created together. It wasn't unreasonable to theorize that my dad had time traveled to each of these moments throughout my life on one singular day of his. The same day, in fact, that he made these seventeen videos.

It was time to talk to my mom.

# CHAPTER 53

"Good morning, honey," Mom said as I trudged past her office on my way to the kitchen. "I left cinnamon rolls and orange juice on the table for you."

I rubbed my swollen, sleep-crusted eyes, the heavenly scent bombarding my senses. "Mm, thanks, Mom."

"I'll join you in a minute. I just have to send this off first."

"Okay," I said through mouthfuls of the glorious gooey rolls.

I fully understood the phrase "eating my emotions" as each bite further subdued my inner turmoil. The last bite, meanwhile, left me reeling in my reality.

Searching the fridge for more food to drown my feelings, I tapped the bacon-and-eggs image on the door screen. The door opened, with both items retrieved from the grapnel inside. Marveling at the technology, I smiled about how I'd won the debate with my mom over this fridge.

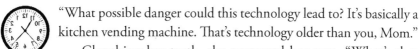 "What possible danger could this technology lead to? It's basically a kitchen vending machine. That's technology older than you, Mom."

Clenching her teeth, she narrowed her eyes. "What's that supposed to mean? I'm not *that* old, you know."

"All I'm saying is, this is the best fridge ever and you want to pass it up because you think it will *spy* on us?"

I wagged my finger at her until she reached out and grabbed it.

"I can't believe I'm agreeing to this. Fine. You win. Let's get this one."

 I reached for the pan from the shelf above the stove and eyed the picture of my dad stuck to the side of the fridge. The eggs in my hand fell to the floor. I glanced down at the orange yolk splashed onto my ankle.

"Jay, what's going on?" my mom asked, placing the wet-mop robot at my feet and powering it on to clean up the mess. "Here, let me do this."

She took the remaining eggs from my hand and placed the pan on the stove. I looked at the photograph again. How could he be wearing these same clothes again? My mom looked anxiously from the eggs she was busy flipping on the stovetop to studying my odd behavior.

"Honey, I'm worried about you. Are you feeling okay this morning?"

"Huh?" I tore my eyes from his picture. "Yeah. I just couldn't sleep last night."

"Go sit down; I'll be finished with this in a minute."

I sat at our kitchen table, trying to piece together how this all fit. I rested my head in my hands, and Mom slid a plate of steaming bacon and eggs between my elbows.

"Thanks," I said, grateful to have a distraction to hold my attention for the moment.

She sat across from me, watching as I ate, taking slow sips from her mug. "How's work going? Anything I should know?"

I swallowed. Nervous energy was bubbling up, threatening to bring the eggs with it.

"I think we need to talk. Is it safe?" My eyes darted around the house, wondering at the possibility of Danika's reach in our home.

"Of course it's safe," she said.

Her words would have convinced me, but her body language told another story. She shook her head in a clear and deliberate refusal. Her eyes darted to various locations of the kitchen and she pointed to the door.

"I have a few pending deadlines waiting for me in my office that must be addressed this morning, though. I want to make sure I give you my full attention. Can we talk after?"

As she said this, she pointed her wagging finger at the front door.

"Yeah, no problem," I said.

She quietly scooted her chair back and tiptoed to the front door. When I didn't immediately follow her, she stopped and cleared her throat. I took two more mouthfuls of my breakfast and joined her.

She pushed a finger to her lips.

*Sorry,* I mouthed.

Mirroring her stealth, we both slipped on our shoes and slunk outside. I walked in step next to her until we rounded the corner. Then she turned to me with gusto, abandoning all pretenses of a whisper.

"Tell me what's going on."

"Aunt Danika still has me working on those specs for the AI project that she won't reveal to me. But when I was in her office, I caught the name of the project before she cleared her screen. It has Dad's initials. I think it's not a coincidence. Do you?"

Her face was grave. "Yeah, I don't like that," she said. "Okay, anything else?"

"Mom, do you remember what Dad was wearing the last time you saw him?"

She pulled away. Her arms crossed as she took a step back. "What?" Her questioning eyes burned into me.

"I know it's a random question, and I wouldn't ask you if I didn't have a good reason."

She inched closer, sliding her arm through mine. "Honey, I'm sorry. You caught me off guard. You can always ask me anything you want about your dad." We continued walking in stride, neither saying anything for a long while. "The last time I saw your dad, he was wearing his favorite ball cap and flannel."

"Did he wear those often?" I asked.

"Um…" She took a moment. "Well, I'd say he wore them as often as anyone wears anything they own." Her arms wrapped around herself in response to the morning chill in the air. "And to be more exact, I'd also say those were my favorite things of his, but they were maybe not *his* favorite." She smiled, remembering him. "That morning, he stood at the top of the stairs and told me how much he loved me while I rushed out the door with you."

"That picture of him on the fridge," I said. "Is it from that day?"

She glanced back at me as we continued walking. "What is this about?"

"I've never told you this, because I didn't want to make you sad."

She stopped in her tracks, tightening her hands around my arms and imploring me to confess.

"Since I was little, I've imagined seeing Dad."

Her face pulled. "You have? Like when?"

Revealing the times I thought he'd made an appearance in the background of our life, I watched my mom processing the news that I might be delusional.

"And Mom, he always wore the exact same clothes. Every time."

· · · · · ● ● ● ● ● ⬤ ● ● ● ● ● · · · · ·

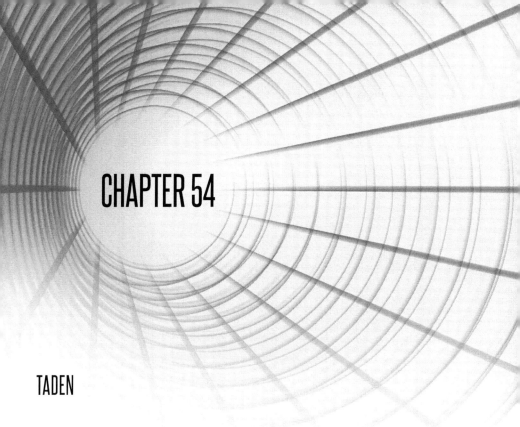

# CHAPTER 54

## TADEN

I closed my son's door and gingerly walked down the quiet hallway, letting my fingertips trace the smiles on Abel's face in each of the framed photographs that dotted the walls leading to the staircase.

I paused at the top of the stairs, conscious of the fact that he stood in this very spot the last time I laid eyes on him. I didn't confirm it for Jay, but Abel indeed did wear the same clothes and U-Penn hat on his last day that he wore in Jay's how-to videos.

I had noticed that coincidence long ago. It was the reason I'd gone through the trouble of printing a photograph from a screenshot of one of those same videos to hang in the kitchen.

Abel didn't ever age for me. He'd been preserved in time, as that man, from that day. Having wandered into the kitchen lost in thought, I found myself tugging his photo from underneath the magnet which held it to the fridge.

Meandering back to the staircase with it I stood at the bottom, where I stood that last morning. I looked up to the empty spot that once held Abel. I stared back at the photo in my hand. I hadn't wanted to make the connection before. My conscious thoughts tried, but I refused to entertain the notion. No matter how I resisted, after hearing the words from Jay's mouth I couldn't remain ignorant.

 "Mom, he made most of these videos for me the day he died." He paused, and then, as if a second thought had occurred to him, he added, "Or disappeared."

My skin erupted in goosebumps. Scooting next to him on his bed, I weaved my arm under his neck. Our heads resting on each other's.

"Your dad is gone," I whispered, barely audible.

"I know," he said.

"But I think you might be on to something. Your dad was trying to warn us. He was a smart and deliberate man."

My voice caught. I hadn't cried in front of Jay since he was toddler. I'd promised myself, all those years ago, that I would hold it together for my son. But in this intimate moment, discussing that painful day with Jay, my emotions brewed just below the surface. Attempting to swallow them back, I took regulated breaths and fidgeted with the stuffed animal Jenny had given him for his birthday.

I finally said, "Keep digging. But Jay…" I turned on my side to face him. In turn, he raised a questioning brow. "Be careful," I warned. "Aunt Danika is dangerous." I said the latter so quietly it was more like I'd mouthed the words. "I don't want you to draw any unnecessary attention to yourself. Just stick with the plan."

He nodded, and I kissed his forehead. I lingered a slow moment before peeling my arm from beneath him.

 I looked back to the staircase, photo pressed to my chest. Jay was right. Abel had made all of those videos on his last day. But the link there remained unsaid.

I'd heard it so loud that I couldn't refuse awareness of it any longer. Abel knew he was going to die—or, as Jay suggested, disappear. He knew it, and so he said goodbye. He made all those videos, he wrote to me in our book, and then, I'm quite certain, he time traveled.

Jay hadn't been imagining that he saw his dad on all those special occasions. I knew my husband. If Abel Mihal understood that he had a limited amount of time, he'd spend it this way—and I even knew how he selected the dates on which to watch Jay from afar. The virtual album.

I sat at my desk, feverishly logging into the account. I tapped open the uploaded files and hovering over the ones titled "Jay". The most recent upload I'd posted contained a photograph of Jay with Jenny on his birthday last week. I opened the message and scrolled down the menu to open the "viewed by" option. The sudden drop in the temperature of my skin left me dizzy.

Both recipients of the message had viewed it: Jay Mihal…and Abel Mihal. My brain conducted a rapid analysis in confirmation that my long-deceased husband had opened the message I sent last week.

With fervency, I checked the "viewed by" data for every single post I'd ever uploaded, and saw that Abel had viewed all of them. Not a single message was missed. I scribbled down the dates and events of these messages and returned to Jay's door.

Knocking softly, I whispered, "Jay, are you still up?"

"Yeah. Come in."

I pressed the sticky note of dates onto his computer screen. "Sometime tomorrow, can you mark on which of these events you might have seen your dad appear?"

His eyes darted to the note stuck to his computer, then back to me. He nodded.

"Goodnight, I love you," I said, leaving his room for the final time before I confronted my husband.

# CHAPTER 55

Digging my toes in the sand, I asked, "No one has any devices with them?" I looked between Dakotah and Ruth.

"I left mine in the car," Dakotah said.

"Same," Ruth added. "You're freaking me out a little."

I reached into my cooler and handed each of them a container of cut-up watermelon. It was my first visit to the beach this summer, and the only place I felt sure no one was listening.

"Are you going to get on with this?" Dakotah asked, revealing her frustration.

"We can't sit on this Danika thing anymore. I can't live in fear of what retribution she'll take on us." I pushed the cubes of melon around with my fork. Both sets of eyes bore into me.

"Did something happen with her and Jay?" Ruth asked. She had been worried about this situation ever since he started working at the NIST. "Because I have zero problem kicking her ass."

Dakotah's impatience grew further. "I need details. Lay it out right now, please."

After I updated them, I said, "I think Abel knew he was going to die." Mid-bite into her fruit, juices trickled down Ruth's chin—which she didn't bother to wipe. My throat constricted as I added, "And I'm more than certain Danika was involved in his death."

"He left me a note in our Gatsby book." I pulled the book out of my beach bag and flipped it open to the note he'd written right before he disappeared. "Here, read it."

Finally wiping her chin with her forearm, Ruth reached out to accept the book. Dakotah leaned over her shoulder, and the two women read his cryptic warning.

Waiting for them to finish, I moved the watermelon around more with my fork. Unable to stay silent, I interjected my narrative.

"All of this adds up. Then to have Danika pulling for Jay to work in AI..." I closed my eyes and absorbed the rhythmic sway of the waves. "These aren't coincidences. Abel knew something about AI and Danika. I have to figure out how to get into her computer system and see what's in her 'Abel' files."

Dakotah pushed her legs out in front of her, crossing them at the ankles. Her shimmering dark skin reflected the sunlight beating down. Leaning back on her elbows, a knowing smile crossed her face.

"I got you," was all she said.

"What do you mean by that?" I asked.

"Yeah, what does that mean?" Ruth said, revealing her concern that Dakotah might put herself in the danger zone.

"I mean, I'm the one with the mad hacking skills. I can get into Danika's programming no problem. Truth be told, I've been itching to go after that woman for a while." She lay flat, soaking up the sunlight. "It's time, ladies. We gotta take her down."

I was both relieved that Dakotah was on board and heavy with guilt over pulling them into this. There was no way around the facts, though. I needed them.

Although Ruth still held a look of hesitation, she wasn't willing to risk Jay's safety. "What can I do?" she asked.

"I think we need to bring Marius into this," I said.

Shame that I'd willingly suck that man into our world again was in that statement. Sure, he wasn't the murderous traitor he had been before I discovered time travel—and that was two decades ago—but it felt like throwing a matchstick on gasoline.

"I'm not sure how I can help with that," she said, clearly uncomfortable with the suggestion.

"I hate to ask this, but I thought maybe you could set up a meeting through Mary. I could talk to him and maybe gather backup through his resources. I figure he might be motivated once he learns how Danika effed with his timelines."

"Is that a game of roulette you're willing to play?" Dakotah asked, resting on her elbows again.

"I think first we find out what's in that file," I said, "and then we strategize our next move. I just wanted you two to know what I was considering."

Thoughtful, they both nodded.

"Or, and hear me out," Dakotah started, "Jaxson."

I raised my brow.

"I know he's sort of difficult to get a read on," she continued, "but he's got the right background, he's connected with the Navy, we've known him forever, and nothing has ever come out sketchy with him. He'd be a way better bet than Marius."

Truth be told, I never really clicked with Jaxson. I'd always felt like he was hard to connect with. The navy side of him made him feel almost robotic and too polite. But Dakotah wasn't wrong. He'd be a much better candidate to align with in order to take down Danika. I couldn't let myself forget that in another timeline, killing me was a little too easy for Marius.

"Not a bad idea," I said. "Let's just sit on phase two of this and see what Danika Farkas has been up to."

Ruth and Dakotah agreed. We lay in the sun, each analyzing the next steps we'd be facing. I had to get my hands on our serum.

Danika wasn't going to stop me from seeing my husband again. I knew exactly where to find him next. On his last day, filled with the knowledge of what would come for him, he had access to at least a dozen points in time he'd want to go. I could meet him there. I'd be damned if anyone would stop me from going after him.

· · · · · · · · · · · ● · · · · · · · · · ·

# CHAPTER 56

My son looked like a man in that suit. He wanted a bow tie instead of a necktie, because he thought it made him look more sleek. I'd talked him into getting a haircut so he didn't look scraggly for the big dance. Jenny was breathtaking in her beaded gown. I stood under the shade of a tree, watching the giddy high schoolers pose for the cameras like they were on the red carpet. I spotted myself—the version of me in this timeline—among the other parents who took on the role of paparazzi.

This was the event I chose to come find Abel. It was from early last fall, when Jay had his school formal. I couldn't resist getting to see him dressed up again.

Plus, it felt way less painful than traveling further back into Jay's life. If I went back too far, I would tap into the earlier stages of my grief. Time had eroded that pain into smooth edges, and I wanted to stay away from the memories of the sharper ones.

A slight draft picked up in the fall air, and the scent of decomposing leaves was carried with it. I turned in the direction of the breeze as I lifted my hood to cover my face—and that's when I spotted him.

Short of breath, I stumbled back into the trunk of the tree. This wasn't a manifestation; Abel really stood on the other side of the massive fountain structure that drew these kids here for photographs.

Beneath his University of Pennsylvania ball cap, he watched his son slip a corsage of white roses onto Jenny's wrist.

I was on the move. I didn't know how long he lingered in each of these moments, and I couldn't risk him leaving to the next timeline before I got to him.

Not wanting to draw attention to myself, I opted for a running walk. My heart beat into my throat. I wasn't sure what I would say or do. I hadn't seen him in so long. Was I nervous? It was Abel. My Abel. How could I be this nervous? Excitement rushed through me and I forgot everything else—where I was, what I was doing. All I could see was him.

As soon as I was close enough for him to hear me, I managed to squeak out his name. The sound of his name on my tongue stopped me, as if were I to come any closer he'd disappear again.

"Abel," I repeated.

He turned from his view of Jay and took me in. A smile played on his lips.

"You found me," he said as he lifted his arms for me to come home.

Without hesitation, I dashed into them. After just barely registering his touch, he faded from me. My eyes tore open to find him gone.

"Dammit," I swore to myself, wrenching up my wrist. I quickly programmed my TRB to take me to the next timeline. "C'mon, c'mon," I muttered to myself, waiting for the serum to kick in.

 Jay's eighteenth birthday party. Now here I was, revisiting it, trying to find my husband who'd traveled forward in order to see us there.

For the first time, I wondered how Abel had traveled forward. At the time of his death, we didn't have an old enough copy of Jay's DNA yet. I hadn't delved too far into my inquiry before I landed on my answer.

Of course Danika was responsible for this. She'd have access to whatever was needed for Abel to pull this off. *But why?*

I was moments from the truth.

From the far corner of the dining room, I looked on as we had dinner at Jay's favorite restaurant. His steak had just arrived. The waitstaff was singing that incredibly annoying ditty to celebrate.

In an effort to remain incognito, I found a table across the room and watched with the rest of the patrons as Jay smiled awkwardly at the waitstaff, and the other version of me cackled about requesting them to do this silly performance.

From my table across the restaurant I scanned the room, searching for the U-Penn ball cap. I finally spotted him by the restrooms. I ran to him. I almost didn't care what unwanted eyes followed me.

"Abel," I said, out of breath. I grabbed his arm and pulled him into the restroom. Locking the door so we wouldn't be interrupted, I jerked my face to be sure he was still there.

"How much time do you have?" I asked.

His stunned expression left me to reach for his TRB. "I have about five minutes before—"

"Jay's next memory hasn't happened for us yet," I said. "You and I have to talk fast."

His chin jutted upward. "I feel like I've wasted so much of your time," he said.

"I'm standing here right now." I looked deep into his eyes, determined not to waste our five minutes with tears.

He took one step toward me and I lost the battle. His arms around me, I was blanketed in his scent. I had dreamed of this for fifteen years while he had only just seen me moments ago, at home, with little Jay.

"How did you find me?" he asked.

"You left me enough clues. I'm sorry it took so long," I said. "Abel, you need to start talking—and fast. Things are looking dangerous with Danika. What should I know?"

A battle raged within me between having this discussion or resorting to my ever-present need to bury my head in his chest.

"She's the reason I'm gone," he said.

"'Gone'?" I asked. I found his eyes. "You didn't say 'dead'."

He guided my head back to his chest, gently running his fingers through my hair. "Taden, I don't really want to tell you the details. And I don't want you to dig into this. I did what needed to be done. Please. Stay away from it. Take Jay and move far away from Danika. She has traps set in various timelines. If you harm her in any of them, she will retaliate. She'll hurt our son."

"You know I can't run. My dad is getting older; he needs my help. Ruth lives close—it's not that easy to run away. Don't worry about Danika. She's not going to harm Jay."

He continued to pet my head, and it lulled me into a false sense of normalcy.

"You have to tell me what she did," I said.

221

Instead, Abel lifted my chin and brought his mouth to mine. It was gentle at first, our lips barely touching. His warm breath floated along my skin. When he pressed his mouth against mine my own breathing hitched, but I returned the pressure. And then all at once he opened his mouth wider, his tongue guiding mine in a symphony of desire. My body ached to be loved by him. Soft moans of pleasure laced with painful awareness escaped me. He responded by applying more. Closer. Deeper.

Then he was gone.

Alone and stunned, I remained inside the locked bathroom until a knock sounded on the door. Pulled from my trance, my finger traced the lingering sensation of Abel still on my lips.

"Just a minute," I said, wiping my eyes.

A quick glance in the mirror and I saw the woman Abel had just been kissing. She caught me off guard. Seeing Abel as he had been the last time I saw him, I momentarily believed myself to be *his* version of Taden. But looking at the lines in my face and the gray mixed with the auburn hair that spilled over my shoulders, I realized what he saw.

Finally I opened the door to apologize to the woman waiting to use the restroom—and I was faced with the woman I'd found in the mirror.

We locked eyes for only a millisecond before she turned to check if anyone saw us.

"What are you doing here?" she asked me.

"I came to see someone," I told her, knowing she'd understand.

Her forehead pinched. It was wild watching myself make that face. I mirrored it, just because I could feel how it felt to make the face as I watched her do it.

"Okay. This is strange," I said. She nodded, eyes rounded. "I don't want to mess up anything here; you'll know everything in a few weeks. Follow your gut. Stick to your plan."

"You should get out of here," she warned. "The dinner is wrapping up and everyone will be scattered throughout the place, using the restroom and heading out."

She reached for me, and I instinctively pulled back.

"Sorry. I'm having a moment," I said, hoping not to offend myself and cringing at the idea.

"It's okay."

She nodded toward the exit doors then looked again to her table with concern.

I didn't stick around to say an awkward goodbye. I'd become keenly aware that the exit wouldn't be necessary as my serum began pulling my molecules apart.


I hadn't expected Abel to withhold the information I needed. Although I couldn't complain about what he did instead.

He did confirm that Danika was the reason for his death—or his being "gone". He also sternly confirmed his desire that I not seek out what really happened. It was—as far as I knew—the most ridiculous notion he'd ever had.

"Do you even know me?" I muttered.

In my own timeline, I left the restaurant and caught a car pilot home. Although I was never truly comfortable with these automated vehicles, in that moment I was grateful not to have to banter with a taxi driver like we did in the days of my youth. It was an exchange Jay luckily never had to experience.

The car's programmed audio prompted, "Where to?"

I spoke my address, and once en route I fell back in my seat, head against the neck rest. I stared out the rooftop window at the passing clouds. All my mind could replay was the kiss I'd just shared with my husband. It had undone all these years of heartache, but like a whetstone to a knife had also renewed the sharpness of my grief.

I couldn't take Danika down in my immediate present. Abel warned me she had set timeline traps for me as insurance. If I killed her here, those other versions of herself would unleash hell on my world.

I couldn't end her in the past because, despite every fiber of my being wanting to undo Abel's death, I knew the blowback could be too painful to bear. The fear of unintentionally manipulating an event that would cause my son's death while attempting to bring back my husband left me paralyzed to take action.

Abel had warned me not to take that path, and I loved and trusted that man enough to listen to his admonition. It seemed pointless to destroy just any future version of Danika I could get at—how would that prevent or contain the things she was capable of, especially if she'd already succeeded with her terrible ideas?

The only way out of this was to end her just before she moved into checkmate. A precise moment when no one was there to save her, to see her die, to know what happened. A moment when she'd think she had won, and just as she'd begin to celebrate I'd take her down.

Decidedly, my next action was to send Jay to a version of me who still had full access to time travel. Before Danika began pulling back on TRBs, before she became obsessed with knowing every move we made in the lab. Before my time-travel serum was difficult to access. Then, I could get his DNA into my hands so that version of me could travel to the future and countermove Danika. The earlier version of me wouldn't know any of the things that I had been through. She wouldn't know Abel's warnings, but she would trust that I have hers and Jay's best interest at heart.

She—I—would get the job done.

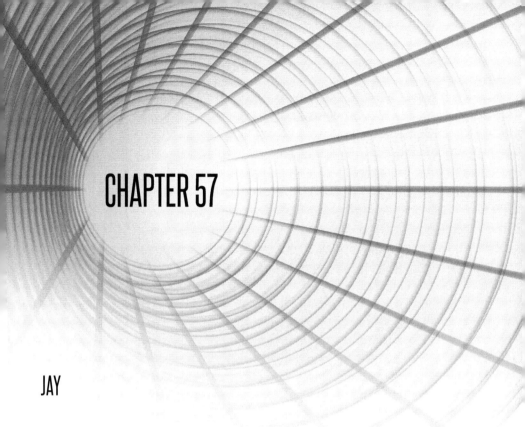

# CHAPTER 57

## JAY

Something my mom claimed she learned from my dad was the art of gift-giving. She's always tried to find the perfect gift. Her three rules were: it had to surprise, it had to be meaningful, and it had to be a gift the recipient would always have. It's a tall order; I certainly didn't have the level of gift-giving skill my mom did. However, Jenny had already benefited from my practicing.

What I didn't expect, though, was that my mom would give me a vial of serum for the TRB Gramps brought me. I'd been dying to talk to her about the exchange, but he warned me to wait for her to come to me about it.

Mom took me to the coast. Told me it was for my birthday gift and to leave our mobiles in the car. It was a hot day, so we went swimming in the lake a while after our lunch. Mom paddled over to me, using her feet to push her float my way.

"Are you ready for your gift?"

"I thought this trip to the beach was my gift," I said, knowing it didn't qualify for all three rules.

"Nope. I just needed to bring you here to give your present."

She reached for the necklace around her neck and pulled the charm from beneath her bathing suit cover, which she wore to protect her fair skin from burning. It contained a small vial, which she held in the sunlight. She looked at me from behind her sunglasses.

"Jay, this is time-travel serum."

"This is what Gramps gave me the TRB for!" I said, excited.

She watched me with curiosity. "I didn't think you'd be able to keep that from me. I guess you're more like your mom than I thought."

"I guess I didn't know you had your own serum," I retorted. "Were you involved in a secret mission I don't know about?"

Her contagious laugh invited me to join in. "Son, you have no idea."

She unclasped her necklace and motioned me closer. As she re-hooked it around my neck, she said, "In that vial is a mixture containing your DNA that will allow you to time travel back to your first birthday. When you get there, you will have a conversation with me, with the version of me from seventeen years ago. There are things she—I—need to discuss with you."

Then she lay back on her raft, closed her eyes, and drifted on the water like she hadn't just dropped the biggest bombshell of my life.

. . . . . . . . . ● ● ● ● ● ● ● . . . .

# CHAPTER 58

"Jay?"

I looked up to see my mom standing in the doorway, her hands pressed to her lips. She was beautiful. Exactly how she looked in the picture with Dad that hung over the fireplace.

"Hi, Mom," I said, wiping the bile from my lips. "Nice birthday present, by the way."

Her mouth creased at the corners, and the glint in her eye gave me the impression she had more in store for this visit beyond letting me experience time travel.

"I had a feeling you'd get sick," Mom said, bending down to rub my back. "Here." She handed me a napkin. "Why don't we go sit at the table and I can tell you what you're doing here."

This was insanity. Scratching my head, I agreed and followed my mom. It was the same kitchen as mine, but the look of it had changed dramatically. The cupboards were completely replaced and the island that we loved to sit at for morning coffee wasn't even there. Instead, I sat down—across from a much younger version of my mom—at a table. She was sad. It seeped into her posture.

"I bet I got the coolest eighteenth birthday gift out of all my friends," I said.

She just stared at me. I hadn't known my mom to be at a lack for words. I mean, sometimes she'd ramble on and I'd pretend I was still listening just not to hurt her feelings. But here, she said nothing for a long while and couldn't take her eyes off me.

"Mom, you're being weird," I said.

· · · · · · ●●●● ● ●●●●● · · · ·

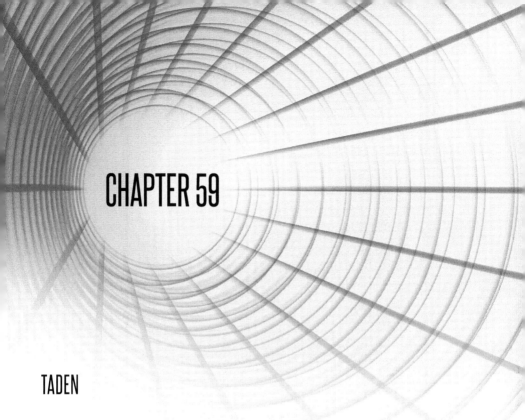

# CHAPTER 59

## TADEN

 Sitting in my car, I swallowed the fear that if one thing went wrong in this plan I could lose everything. I looked up at the building I'd spent my entire career in, hoping I'd get this right.

"I'm in," Dakotah said through the walkie-talkie. "I can't get used to this archaic device." Irritation carried with her voice over the old radio system.

"This is the only way we can be sure she's not listening," I scolded. "Besides, it's not like these are ancient. They were in Abel's things. He used them on recon all the time."

"I know, I know," she said. "Okay, logging into the file systems now."

My muscles tensed. "I'm in my car, watching for her return," I intoned.

"Copy that. I don't want to be anywhere near here when she does."

My charged energy found an outlet as I chewed my cuticles bloody. "How's it going?"

"I see the file Jay mentioned. It's AM/AI?"

"Confirmed."

"Copying it now."

I transitioned from my cuticles to the inside of my cheek while I scanned the parking lot.

"How much longer, do you think?" I asked.

"It's a much larger file than I anticipated," she said. "It looks like a few more minutes."

I sighed.

"I'm letting that do its thing," Dakotah continued. "Heading to her safe."

I closed my eyes. This was the part of our plan that terrified me. What kind of security did she have on that thing? Would it be the trap we walk into? I anxiously waited for Dakotah to update, not wanting to interrupt her.

"It appears to be motion-sensored," she said. "I'm deactivating the trigger."

I caught sight of a vehicle entering the lot. Sinking down in my seat, I peered over the dashboard.

"She's on the premises," I said. "Do you copy?" Dakotah didn't respond. "Do you copy?"

After a long few seconds, Dakotah swore into the walkie.

Danika's vehicle maneuvered into her designated parking space at the entrance. Why I even worried I'd miss her grand entrance was beyond me.

"She's walking to her entrance," I said.

"Understood," Dakotah responded. "The files are copied. I'm in the middle of opening the safe. I won't be out in time. I repeat, I need more time."

"Dammit," I muttered. With haste, I tapped my vehicle door. The automatic opening seemed to take a lifetime as I watched her close in on the entrance.

"Danika!" I yelled, dashing from my car. I waved with urgency. She slowed, squinting at me, lifting her hands to veil her eyes from the sunlight.

"Taden?"

During my slight jog to close the distance between us, I frantically formulated a stalling tactic.

"Can I speak with you?" I finally said between heavy breaths.

She looked surprised. We no longer discussed things alone. We'd shared a single private conversation since Abel had died. Otherwise, I'd always been conscious to leave the door open or request a team member be present. I never wanted to give her enough leverage to threaten me or my people in a one-on-one setting again.

But here we were, and this seemed like it was worth the risk. "I didn't properly thank you for the birthday gift you gave to Jay."

The lift of her forehead revealed further surprise. "Oh?"

"I know we don't exactly see eye-to-eye." My words were careful and slow. "But you have—for whatever reason—always been a presence in my son's life. One that he greatly values. And in turn, I myself am grateful."

Nausea flooded me. The words were like instant poison.

"It's true that I am very fond of the boy. He is so much like his parents, and his intelligence is bar none."

"Thank you," I said. "Anyway, it was more than a generous gift and…"

She took a step toward me, lifting her palm. "I won't have you refusing this one on his behalf, Dr. Barrett." Her stern features set in place. "He's old enough now to make his own decisions."

I waved my hands. "That's not what I'm trying to say. I wanted to thank you for the gift and leave it at that." I forced a polite smile. "I meant no disagreement."

She returned a relieved smile of her own.

"That's good. I'm glad. I'd hoped the two of you would be traveling together, but I don't want to tell him who he has to take. I just think it would do you some good to get out of this place," she indicated the building, "and relax a little."

I nodded. "Maybe," I said. "He does have a girlfriend he might prefer to travel with, though. And I have a ton to get done here."

"I can certainly appreciate that a woman's work is never done," she said, aiming her body back toward the entrance.

Her nonverbal cue meant our conversation was done. Dakotah probably needed at least a few more minutes. Frenzied, I searched for a way to extend our conversation.

"On the other hand, it will be our wedding anniversary soon," I said.

My face instantly flushed. I hadn't mentioned Abel to Danika in all these years. It was as if he'd never existed.

With a sharp turn, I watched her own face pale. Danika said nothing as she stiffened.

"It might be a good idea for me to go elsewhere with my son rather than stay behind and wallow alone," I added, hoping she felt guilt.

Could I dig past her hard exterior and plant a seed of shame? She tore our little family apart. Removed an invaluable member. Whatever her role in Abel's absence was, I knew she'd played one.

"I think that's an excellent idea," she said coolly. "Dr. Barrett, it was nice we could talk like this." Her words were warm, but her tone still frigid. "I wish we could spend more time conversing, but I do have an appointment." She glanced at her wristband and took several intentional steps toward the door. Waving her band in front of the door, she turned once again to me. "Are you coming in?"

"I need a minute or two before I start my day," I said. "Thank you, though, for offering your entrance."

My internal groan over the audacity of her exclusive entrance was inaudible.

As soon as the door closed behind her I broke into a full run back to my car, frantically trying to open the automatic door. With the walkie in my hand, I held down the button.

"She's entered the building and is enroute. Get out. Do you copy?"

"I'm on the elevator now," Dakotah responded.

"No! Get off the elevator. Whatever floor you're at, get off."

"Copy that," she said. "I'm exiting onto the fourth floor."

Time crept in the still minutes I waited.

"Heading toward the stairwell," she said.

Another pause. The pounding of my chest filled the quiet.

"Coming down the stairs. I'll meet you in our offices."

I'd left the car door open and leaped from it in a speed walk to the main doors. Gone were the days when Maxine greeted us at security. The entry process was now done through automated security, which scanned facial recognition and personal content before allowing entry.

I was keenly aware that every move I made at this point would be recorded. Walking through the hallway, I was sure of my calm composure. I even smiled and waved at a camera outside my office.

Waiting for me to enter Dakotah stood in my office, eyes bulging and a crooked smile on her lips. She tapped her pocket to imply the presence of the device that held the stolen files.

"I know the day just started," she said, trying to catch her breath, "but I'm already looking forward to lunch."

She rubbed her stomach and the smile on her face grew. These days, our jobs focused on creating the serum Danika required for time travel and research theories—which were bogus— for future time travel. We didn't know what she was doing with the stockpiles we'd made for her, but it was premixed, waiting for the specific time traveler's DNA to be added. It was enough to move an army through time. I still refused to reveal that I'd found the link into the future, and was too concerned about Jay's safety to further test it.

Lunchtime couldn't come soon enough. I met Dakotah at the swings. We'd made it our meeting place since the year I revealed Danika's true nature. She sat down next to me with the device in her palm, tapping the screen to open the file.

I dragged my swing closer to hers, digging my feet into the ground against the pull. While I looked over her shoulder, she moved the image closer between the two of us. Inside the file were documents with Abel's name, Jaxson Duncan's name, and files referring to cognitive function and algorithms.

"Are you seeing this?" she asked.

I nodded, but her focus remained on the files.

"What should I open first?"

Seeing his name there confirmed my long-held suspicions. Already feeling ill, I wasn't sure I could handle what we were about to uncover.

Swallowing hard, I said his name aloud. "Open Abel's."

"Here we go," she said, tapping his file.

It opened to reveal another list of files, each titled by date. One date stood out among the rest. The date that I last saw my husband. My eyes locked onto it.

"Open that one," I pointed. She knew the date I referred to, and hesitated.

"This isn't going to be good."

"I know. Just open it, Dakotah."

She tapped it, which prompted a video clip of Abel lying on an operating table. Next to him, another man lay on his own table. Abel looked over at the man's body.

"This is my new home?" Abel asked someone off-screen.

"No one will ever recognize you," the voice answered. "Not even you will know when you meet him."

I didn't have to see the woman to know it was Danika.

"I can't believe I've been working with him, with me, all these years," Abel said, his voice weak. "How did you get him into our timeline? If I'm still myself right now, how do I know him?

"Sweet, silly Abel," Danika simpered. "We're on a loop. I've already completed this task in another branch of time. Since moving into the future and bringing an element from a time that hasn't yet occurred, I was able to pull a version of Jaxon from ahead to place into your timeline and help me source the whole time-travel technology until I arrived at the actual moment where he is originally created. I used him to help create him. Don't hurt your brain over it. Jaxon here is going to need it very soon.

"Did she say Jaxson?" I asked Dakotah.

"I think so," she confirmed. "Shh, what's Abel asking her?"

"He has all my memories?" Abel asked.

"He will. They will be transferred to him once you're in stasis. He will not have any of the emotion entangled in your memories, though. They will merely serve as a database. His personality is already programmed."

"Danika," he said. "What you're doing is unethical. You *will* have a day of reckoning. The universe will ante up." He paused. "You can still reroute your course." He looked over at Jaxson. "He could be created without murder."

"You've agreed to this," Danika said. "It's not exactly murder."

"I'm protecting my family. Do you think I want to leave them? That I'm ready to die?" She kept her back to the camera. "I'm not ready for any of this!" he cried.

"Progress must move forward. It always does, and it usually requires sacrifices like the one you are making."

With that, she approached Abel and tapped the glass screen controlling her robotic surgeon. Within seconds, the anesthesia flowed through his bloodstream. He closed his eyes.

We watched as an industrial robot injected Abel with something that pulled him from consciousness. I pressed my hand to my chest when it began to perform surgery, cutting Abel from his neck to his abdomen. I watched with horror as it removed his organs.

"Shut it off! I can't see anymore."

Dakotah was frozen—hand over her mouth, eyes glued to what she saw.

I jumped from the swing, clasping my hands behind my neck, continuing to swear at the sky.

After all these years, I was witnessing my husband's death. This is how he left me. She took him from me and Jay. It wasn't a violent crime that stole my husband. He didn't disappear in a time-travel accident. Danika Farkas took him from me. She cut open his body and used it for her plans.

And to my utter dismay, Abel allowed it. He didn't fight her off or verbally resist. He seemed agreeable. Why?

Dakotah forced herself to stop the video and quickly maneuvered to open Jaxson's file. I moved behind her to catch a glimpse. A series of short clips showed Jaxson learning how to talk and walk. Conscious of my slow and measured breaths, I replayed every conversation I'd ever had with Jaxson Duncan. Every time I'd ever shrugged his robotic nature off to military training and good manners. Every time he and Abel were in the same room. The man wasn't even a man. He was a robot. And although I *could* make the connection between Jaxson and Abel, out of self-preservation, I would *not* make the connection between Jaxson and Abel.

"What the hell is this, Dakotah?" I asked through gritted teeth.

She looked at me with fearful eyes. She didn't want to be the one to explain what I already knew.

"I don't know what we're looking at yet," she said, swiping through the files. "Whatever this is, it's clear to me that Jaxson isn't who or *what* we thought he was."

Anger bubbled. "What does this have to do with Abel?"

In the long, silent moments that followed, I paced to the front of Dakotah and watched as she swiped from file to file. Her eyes widened as she read and watched atrocity after atrocity fill her screen. Occasionally, her lips moved in displays of disgust.

When the anguish was too much, I sat directly on the ground. "Dakotah," I said, arms crossed, "I need to hear it. Just say it."

"I don't want to tell you," she muttered. Her eyes were glassy as she looked up at me. "Abel is for certain dead, Taden." Her lip quivered. "I think that's all you should know. She killed him. It's confirmed in these files."

"There's something big here—bigger than Abel's death. Right?" I asked, my question really more of a statement. "I can handle this. You can't hold this information on your own. We're a team, and we need to maneuver through this together."

I returned to the swing next to her and grabbed her hand, squeezing it with the little strength I possessed.

"I'm ready."

Clearing her throat, Dakotah squeezed mine back. "She harvested parts of Abel and placed them within an AI droid."

My chest constricted. "Like an organ donation to a robot?"

"Kind of. This android is made up of mostly human parts, with technology intertwined." She clicked through a diagram of the AI skull. "See here?" She turned the screen so I could get a clear look. "The skull is made of titanium, but enclosed is a human brain. Instead of blood flowing throughout, it's a system of wires.

I studied the image, zooming out to see the face of Danika's AI. The face that masked Abel's brain. Jaxson's face. The connection between Jaxson and Abel snapped me into hyperventilation.

My lips tingled before the dizziness overcame me. Rising from the swing, my blood pressure dropped. Darkness filled my vision. With my hands on my hips I tried to balance my footing. The next thing I knew, Dakotah was leaning over my collapsed body. I sucked in regulated breaths through my nose. She helped me sit up. As I leaned forward, wrapping my arms around my knees, Dakotah sat next to me silent.

"Abel died for Danika to create Jaxson."

"What else of Abel is in that robot?" My voice pierced the air.

"I think this is enough for now. We should pause and get something to eat—for real. It's lunch time. You need food in your system."

"Mm-hm. We should eat," My sarcasm was thick. "Tell me, though, what else?"

"Okay, okay. It looks like his heart is pumping whatever liquid they are using to keep Jaxson's operating system running. His lungs are being used to simulate human breathing patterns." She scrolled through other images. "She used Abel's eyes. They're connected to an image receiver that can be digitally recorded."

My fingers dug into the skin on my face. It was too much to take. I held my hands in defeat. "No more." I stared off in the distance at two young children digging in a sandbox. "It's enough."

She wrapped her arms around me. My desperation for the consolation of her hug was deeper than I'd ever experienced. Two decades of pain unhinged.

"I'm okay. Keep reading," I said, pointing to her device.

Dakotah hesitated, but then released me. She tapped and clicked and scrolled further into Jaxon's files before speaking again.

"Danika had a visit from her future self along with the AI. Look." She leaned in with the screen in my view. "Check out the date. That was just a few months before you hired Jaxson onto our team."

"I'm sorry. I'm going into shutdown. My brain is in some sort of shock. Nothing is making sense." I threw my hand up.

"Taden, this…" She pointed at the image of Danika's future version of the AI. "…is the Jaxson we know. Future Danika sent a future version of Jaxon back in time to work with us."

"Why? What was the point of that?" I asked.

She tapped the screen. "According to this, Danika didn't actually finalize Jaxson's projected features right away. Look how old she is here. She looks like she's close to eighty years old!"

I blinked. "She killed my husband but still couldn't figure out her damn technology to do what she wanted it to do?"

Dakota didn't answer. She'd become distracted by a report attached to the images. I sat there on the ground a long while, watching her read. Eventually the wood chips beneath me were imprinting into my skin. To more evenly distribute my weight on the uncomfortable surface, I laid back and stared into the sky. Before I knew it, my eyes were becoming heavy and I questioned how I could drift off to sleep with the most disturbing images I'd ever witnessed burned into my brain. Settling into the purgatory, a gasp from Dakotah sent my nerves into a sort of reverberation.

"What?" I sat up sharply.

"I know what she wants Jaxson for!"

I sucked my lips in, waiting for the totality of it.

"This version of him from the future. The one we know. His bloodstream is actually our time-travel serum. His mainframe contains the DNA of every human to have ever provided a sample. With this, he can make any combination of serum to go backward or forward at will. His body acts as the host DNA and applies the genetic match for what he needs to go… whenever in time."

"I feel sick," I said. "It's actually fucking genius."

"Yeah," she agreed. "But she figured it out much later than she wanted to, so she sent him to us to speed up the process. Put it on a fast track."

"Of course." I said, the bile burning the back of my throat. "What will Danika Farkas do with a piece of such cutting-edge technology?"

Dakotah grimaced, her eyes flying across the screen like an antique typewriter. She came to an abrupt stop and threw the device to the wood chips, leaning forward on her hands.

"She's done this so that she can *become* this augmented version herself. She wants to live forever. She plans to alter humans into AI. Abel was only her prototype."

"Who's next?" I asked, barely audible.

She shrugged, eyes bulging.

"Dakotah, we will take her down. And we're going to use this abomination of Abel to do it."

# CHAPTER 60

Returning from lunch with Dakotah took every single ounce of self-composure I could muster. Not only did I need to be in the same building with Danika Farkas—a murderer, a traitor to our country, and the person I hated more than anything in the world—but I would also have to face Jaxson Duncan and work alongside him with this new knowledge.

"Are you going to be able to do this?" Dakotah asked me as we finished the last of our lunch.

I couldn't stomach eating much, so I nibbled on some crackers that came with the broccoli soup I'd ordered. I nodded weakly, but agreeing to look into his eyes and still hold together the lead scientist role that I continued to play at the NIST and actually doing it were two very different scenarios.

We walked inside, and immediately ran into Jaxson.

"How was your lunch?" Jaxson asked.

My mind raced. All I had to say to him was "good", but I couldn't manage to force out a single word. He didn't look up, but kept working at the counter across the room.

I watched him, wondering if I had ever seen him eat anything. Too many years had passed for me to be sure. He didn't eat anything the other night at Jay's party. I was sure of it. But he had ordered a drink. I remembered that.

"I'll take a draft Guinness," he told the waitress.

But had I actually seen him drink anything? No! He'd offered it to my dad! *Could* he drink anything? I wondered about aging. Surely a robot didn't age, but if Danika wanted us to believe in Jaxson Duncan that would need to be a process she embedded into his programming.

Lost in my curiosity, I forgot for the briefest moment that he was made up of Abel's parts—until he turned to me in assessment. His head was slightly cocked, body as straight and tall as ever.

"Dr. Barrett?" he said.

"Mm?" I replied, blinking.

"How was lunch?"

"Good."

I'd done it. A basic exchange with an android. I still couldn't bring myself to look him in the eyes, though.

"I've almost finished with today's collection of serums for Ms. Farkas," he said.

"Great. I'm going to let you finish alone, as I have some work to do in my office."

He nodded and returned to his task. The robotic nature of his movements and rhythms was never as obvious to me as it was in that moment.

I doubted my sanity as I walked to my office, consumed with the desire to run to Jaxson and bury myself in his arms. I felt as if, because he was made up of Abel, I would find my husband there. But I knew better.

In my office, I collapsed onto the rolling chair at my desk and allowed it to drift across the floor. I'd found myself surrendering to this chair so many times over the years. Head back, staring at the ceiling, I dragged my feet around and around.

Dakotah, Ruth, Jay, and I would have to come up with a plan to destroy all of Danika's timelines, and my money was on Jaxson to be the Trojan horse that got it done.

· · · · · · ● ● ● ● ● ● ◉ ● ● ● ● ● · · · ·

# CHAPTER 61

"I can program the AI to have an end date in response to a trigger," Jay said, looking between the four of us.

He had no idea of the makeup of Danika's robot, and I didn't have the heart to even tell him the robot was Jaxson. Jay had known my NIST family his whole life; I couldn't possibly level that kind of blow to his reality. I certainly didn't want him to make a connection between his AI work for Danika which Abel was warning us about and Jaxson being that very AI project which housed his dad's internal organs.

I suppose it was a lie of omission, maybe even comparable to the lies Danika had been guilty of exacting onto him. But I was charged with keeping my son safe, and his emotional well-being was a part of that.

"Can the trigger be an execution within the AI?" Dakotah asked.

Jay nodded. "It can be anything, really. A date, an action, a word or phrase. Like any computer command. It will run the function and complete its self-destruct pattern when triggered."

"Could Danika override the program?" Ruth asked.

"She could if I gave her the coding. But unless I shared it with her, she wouldn't even be aware it was embedded into the AI." He looked between us again. "Are any of you going to tell me what you found out about this technology?"

We were crammed in my sister's office, and an uncomfortable silence crowded between us. Ruth patted the seat next to her, which Jay accepted.

"Listen, we all love you very much, and not only have *your* best interest in mind but everyone's." Ruth put her arm around Jay. "Your dad taught me a lot about situations like these. And sometimes, the less you know the better able you are to help."

Jay pinched the bridge of his nose. "I don't like it, but I understand."

"You have your tickets?" I asked Jay.

He held up his wrist to indicate he'd downloaded the flight information.

"Good. If everything goes as projected, your codes will be embedded and you'll be on your flight with Jenny before anything occurs."

He smiled. "You wouldn't send me off to coddle me while my family…" He eyed each of us individually. "…puts themselves in danger, would you?"

The guilt took hold of us. It didn't matter what words we used to try to convince him otherwise; he knew what this mission entailed.

"Honey," I said, taking his hand. "We will be careful. But we need to know we can do what we need to and you won't be anywhere nearby to receive fallback."

"Will you time travel?" he asked.

I shook my head. "It's not a part of the plan as of now."

He swallowed. "I'm supposed to go on this trip with my girlfriend and pretend all is right in the world? Take her to the Eiffel Tower and sweep her off her feet, while in my head I'm wondering if my mom is dead?" His voice cracked.

He was already worried. If he knew much more, he wouldn't leave. He was just like me in that aspect.

"I'm not going to die." I lifted his chin. "You hear me? This will go smoothly, and the AI will be the one to take the brunt of the downfall. Just run the program and enjoy a once-in-a-lifetime trip. We'll be in constant contact, so you won't have to worry."

"Your mom is right," Dakotah chimed in. "You are making all of us safer by removing yourself from the circumstances. We will make much clearer judgment calls as we follow through, knowing you aren't in harm's way."

"I'm not going to talk any of you into letting me stay?" he asked, hopeful.

We answered with a collective "no," which led to all of us, including Jay, to chuckle in unison.

Ruth pushed her hands down her thighs and clapped her knees. "It's a done deal, then. This time next week, we'll straighten this mess out and avenge Abel Mihal."

Jay took my hand. The way he looked at me—the tiniest creases in the corner of his eyes—was reminiscent of his father. Even if that android had Abel's actual eyes, Abel was much more evident in the eyes of his son.

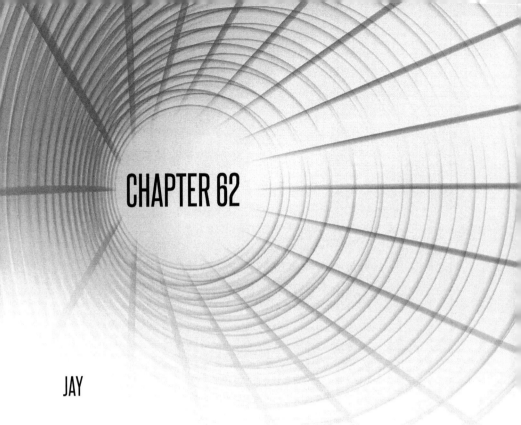

# CHAPTER 62

## JAY

My palms were clammy as I stepped off the elevator into Aunt Danika's office. I knew she was the enemy, yet I didn't. She cared for me and I cared for her. It was difficult to grasp the idea that Aunt Danika would intentionally hurt anyone I loved. But, then again, I wasn't naïve.

She had done terrible things. I didn't really understand how awful she was or could be until much later on, but I understood enough to sabotage the AI project she entrusted to me.

Aunt Danika was busy working, but caught sight of me. Her bodyguards, as usual, queued up to greet me, but she dismissed them.

"You two know Jay. You can stop acting so edgy around him." She looked at both with stern correction.

I watched the way they responded to her verbal command and briefly wondered if they weren't the artificial intelligence she'd been working on. That thought led to more wonderings about strange people I'd met throughout the building.

In any case, why would Danika hire a young college student to do materials inventory if she had robots about the place? It was certainly a job any robot could do. Then again, she had only hired me under that pretense. The minute she got me in the door, she began exploiting my programming skills.

"Take a seat," she said. "Can I help you with something?"

Her pleasantries were not the typical presentation I was used to. Ever since my birthday and her grand gift, she'd been sort of bubbly with me. Well, bubbly for Danika's standards.

"I just wanted to stop in and let you know that Jenny and I have booked our trip. We leave for Paris next week. I wanted to thank you again for such an awesome present. I really don't deserve it."

"Nonsense." She pursed her lips. "It delights me to give you something that will positively affect your future. It's important for a young person to experience the world and its beauty."

"I have something for you, too," I said.

"Oh?" Her brows rose.

"I know you weren't expecting this for a few weeks, but I wanted to show how grateful I am—and also, I wanted to be sure I was finished before I left for my trip."

I reached into my pocket to retrieve the chip. Upon setting it on her desk, it reflected a ray of light shining through the wall of windows behind her. Her expression matched the effulgence.

"It's done?" she asked, her voice struggling to remain in its tenor while the bounce on her chair and clamor to snatch it up revealed her excitement. "I was anxiously waiting for this code. I thought it could be a bit of a challenge for you yet."

She knew how to puff me up. Maybe it was a manipulative strategy, and I was an easy piece to put into checkmate. Although I did feel a sense of pride at delivering this code to her early, I also understood that she was probably handling me.

She didn't know that I'd planted a Trojan horse into her magnificent project.

She snatched the chip up like it was worth its salt and slid it into her device to skim. She liked what she found and, after skimming a few lines of code, she closed the program and beamed at me.

"I want you and Jenny to have the time of your life. Please enjoy a French coffee outside of the Eiffel Tower at the Terres de Café for me. It is my favorite little café. They have these lovely yellow tables. Tell them I sent you."

"You never cease to surprise me, Aunt Danika. Is there anything you haven't done?"

The edges of her mouth pulled outward. "I've lived a long while. You will, too, and your experiences will be incredible."

Conflicted between the need to stop her and the desire to celebrate her at the same time, I got out of my chair. Gripping the back of it, I took one last look at Aunt Danika.

Would I feel responsible for her death? Would it be my fault? Would it be murder? She'd already returned to her work—as usual without so much as a goodbye.

· · · · · · • • • ● • • • • • · · ·

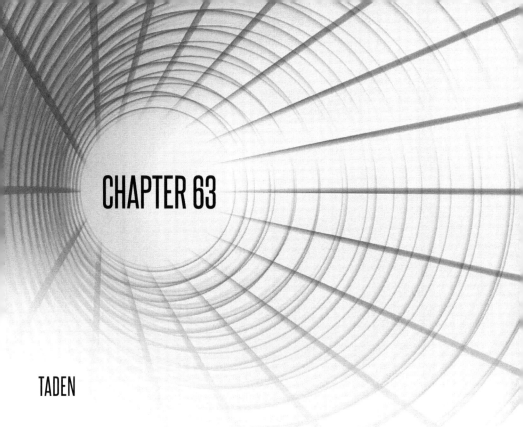

# CHAPTER 63

## TADEN

My son had put the ball in motion. Now that Danika's system had been infiltrated with Jay's coding it was my turn to move forward with the plan to get rid of Danika Farkas forever. My last office-wide message stared at me from the monitor. My finger over the send button, I read it one last time.

My role in this was to discover time travel to the future. I'd sat on this secret for far too long, trying to protect my family, my friends, people I'd never met. But it was time to unveil my discovery and open the door to whatever danger lurked.

Dear Team,

You've waited more years than can be counted for this breakthrough. You were with me as I struggled through personal tragedy and became a single mom. You stuck by my side, and science has finally led us to the forefront.

It is with great honor that I can finally tell you that we have discovered the link we needed in order to travel into the future. I am excited to move forward with this and get everyone on board with finalizing the details.

Your friend and privileged lead scientist,
Dr. Taden Barrett-Mihal

I didn't have to wait but seconds before notifications alerted replies. The response I was waiting for came unexpectedly. Danika didn't reply to my message—instead, she appeared outside my office. The gait of her unmistakable footsteps notified me.

"I couldn't wait to see the big breakthrough and congratulate you in person," she said, entering.

"Thanks," I replied.

The cold sting in my voice would go undetected, as it would actually match the tone she often had.

"Have you tested it?" she asked. I imagined bits of drool pooling in her cheeks.

"It's still in the infant stages. I haven't sent anyone forward, but every simulation I've run shows great promise. I'll be running a test later today."

"Are you nervous?" She walked closer, studying me.

"I'm not. It was good timing for Jay to go on his trip. It makes me less tense, in case anything goes wrong. At least he won't be here for it." I pulled my mouth into a crease. "Geez, I feel like a bad mom for saying that."

"Nonsense," Danika urged. "You're the best mom I know."

My shock at hearing those words leave her lips couldn't have been hidden.

"What?" she said. "You don't think I notice things like that?"

I shrugged. This was certainly not a topic usually up for discussion with Danika. I wasn't interested in getting personal with her, especially not after all this time and all the heinous things she'd done.

"Well, thanks for that," I said. "I'll be testing it out the whole week he's gone." I hesitated, hoping she wouldn't see through my diversion. "Why? Did you want to run a test?"

She cleared her throat. "I could do that?" She sat down on my office sofa, hands folded on her knees.

Sitting there, Danika reminded me of a little girl waiting patiently for a piece of candy. It captivated me how small she looked in that moment. I remembered a time when her presence felt so huge, so grand, that all I could do was work hard enough to feel worth her time.

"It's your science. I just push the buttons, so to speak," I said.

"Now that's not fair, Taden."

My words bothered her. But the truth was often unpleasant.

"All I meant was, you make the rules. If that's what you want to do, I'm certainly not going to stand in your way."

She appeared pleased with my sentiment. "All right, then! Sign me up for a maiden voyage."

Again, she stunned me with her enthusiasm—and her metaphor.

"Will you be ready tomorrow?" I asked, attempting not to sound too eager.

I surveyed her quick nod, then lifted my wrist to look at my Timed-Release Band—something I hadn't worn in years.

I said, "Will after lunch be good for you?"

She got back up and clicked her way to the door of my office. "I'll see you then."

As she left, she took the room's oxygen with her. Gasping for air, I eventually managed to calm myself enough to ping Dakotah and Ruth.

Our plan was live.

* * * * * * * * * ● ● ● ● ● ● ● ● * * * *

# CHAPTER 64

"She believed all of it?" Dakotah asked.

"It sure felt like she did," I said.

I'd gone to her house that evening to run through each step one more time, making sure we hadn't overlooked anything.

Ruth stood at the helm, recording a timeline on the board in Dakotah's home office.

"If Danika travels to here," she said, marking a spot on the timeline, "then she will encounter Jaxson, who we sent back to this time programmed to execute Danika."

"Correct," I said. "She'll think I'm sending her into the future. She has no idea that she can't go without a genetic sample from a descendant. She believes that the DNA only has to be old enough to extend the time traveler's timeline like the application of traveling to the past. The finite detail that the genetic match must be born after the time traveler isn't one she's caught on to yet. That's why I've kept it as locked-down information. I don't ever want her to have that key."

Ruth repeated, "You'll tell her she's going here." She marked the spot to the right of the simple line. "But she will actually be sent here." She circled the already marked spot to the left, indicating the past.

"Since our present version of Danika will be dead in the past, all future versions of her from this point on will also cease to exist."

Dakotah joined the verbal review. "The only versions of Danika that will exist throughout time will be the ones up to the present." All three of us nodded.

"That way we don't bypass big events, like Abel's death." I said this part so quietly, it didn't have any conviction.

Ruth gave me a sympathetic glance before moving the plan along. "And no other version of her before this time," she circled the entire line that belonged to time before tomorrow, "will know that she was killed, because she hasn't gotten her teeth into future time travel. Just the coding."

"We really need to make certain that before she encounters Jaxson tomorrow...in the past," Dakotah emphasized, "that she has the coding to embed into her AI." A pause. "Oh! And we have to add a command in Jaxon's programming that he clears out the unfinished version of him that would be in her evil lair."

"Right! Oh my gosh, that would've been a huge oversight! Good job thinking of that. She definitely wouldn't buy the lie that we sent her to the future if she arrives to her in-progress version of Jaxson." I facepalmed.

"Should we run through it again?" Ruth asked.

"No, I think we got it. Besides, I need some space from this to relax. I'm too wound up." At that, my mobile buzzed. "It's Jay; he knows our plan begins tomorrow. Play it cool, though," I said, looking back and forth between Ruth and Dakotah, making sure neither would lead him to worry.

I approved his call to the vision board, and the room filled with his image as if he was actually there with us.

"How's it going?" he asked, worry lines creasing his forehead.

"We've got it all under control," Ruth answered.

He looked to her with pleasant surprise. "Oh! Hi, Aunt Ruth. I'm glad I got you here, too."

"Aunt Dakota's in the room as well," I said.

"Hey, kiddo! How's France?" Dakotah chimed in.

"We're having so much fun—as long as I can convince myself you three are making good choices," he said, adding a nervous chuckle.

"Honey, nothing is going to go wrong. We have it all covered," I assured him. "Now get back to Jenny and enjoy yourself. We'll talk in the morning."

We disconnected and stared at each other. Dakotah broke the silence. "Okay, ladies, new topic. What could go wrong?"

Giving up my notion of a breather, I settled into the plan again.

We continued to rehash any holes until close to sunrise.

"What if we send her back and she knows instantly that we didn't send her forward?"

Through a heavy sigh, I restated once again, "We program her travel moment to an exact coordinate where Jaxson greets her, and then his coding will trigger to finish our plan."

"What if she fights him off? If somehow he is unsuccessful?"

"It's not possible. She won't even know what he's doing. The actual science of all of this doesn't make any sense to her," I said, my cheek flush to the floor.

In the hours we'd been fine tuning I had laid down, giving in to my exhaustion.

"Listen, we've gone through this over and over again. We're ready. And if I don't sleep for at least a few hours, a mistake will be made tomorrow out of sleep deprivation."

Ruth and Dakotah left me to drift off on their floor, draping a blanket over me and closing the door behind them.

In my sleep, I found Abel. I hadn't dreamed of him in years.

He was searching for me, and had just found me asleep. He sat at my side, watching me. It was an odd experience, to dream of myself sleeping. Even in my dream, I was aware of that.

As he watched me, the worried look on his face began to slip away. Replacing it was the longing that I remembered him wearing when he'd look at me.

Then he scooted up close to me and I saw he was crying. Pulling me into his lap, he cradled me, unable to soothe his bellowing. It was then that I realized I wasn't sleeping. I was dead.

At the same moment, a voice in the background cut through my thoughts: "You know you're not supposed to dream of yourself as dead. It means you're actually dead."

My eyes flew open, but my body remained rigid and motionless. I tried to look around, but my neck wouldn't cooperate. Still on the floor, I was relieved to be alive.

At least I hadn't died in my sleep. The ability to move slowly returned, and I convinced myself it was only a nightmare. But the foreboding stayed with me all morning and into the last day I would ever spend at the National Institute of Science.

"Good morning," Jaxson said as I entered our labs. "Ready to begin today's tests?" he asked.

"It's now or never," I said.

He held up the serum mixed with Jay's eighteen-year-old DNA. I would be going to the future, and it wouldn't be a secret. It would only be for a short moment. As Jaxson loaded my TRB with the serum, I watched him imagining the version of him waiting for Danika to arrive into the past. He would be doing this very same maneuver for her. She wouldn't know any better. It was eerie to think that way because the same could be said for me.

In this very moment, he could be loading my TRB with poison that would shut down my living functions, and this could be my last moment. It made me uneasy enough that I inquired about the process.

"Did you record the helix fusion?" I asked.

"I did," he said. "I followed the exact procedure we went through yesterday."

"Let me have a look." I tilted my head, searching for anything nefarious.

He pointed to the camera angled on the serum mixture station. "As directed," he assured.

It brought me small relief to know that even if his AI programming was hacked to endanger me, at least it was recorded and the others would know what happened.

I looked at the camera; the green light was on, indicating it was recording. "Good. We need to be sure if any of our tests result in outliers, we can review each process for reasons of error."

"I assure you, I followed every step to perfection," he said.

Before I knew he was a robot, it was easy to believe in Jaxson's accuracy. Knowing he was a robot, it was even easier to believe.

Aware Danika was watching my exchange with Jaxson from monitors in the room, I hoped it further cemented the storyline that I would be sending her to the future next.

Jaxson wasn't informed of this mission. I couldn't risk that he would point out the minor detail that Danika didn't have any descendants to make her serum. I was careful not to elicit that detail in conversation here at the lab, either.

The familiar sensation filled me, and before long I arrived at the same spot, eighteen years into the future. The change to my lab was the most drastic change I'd witnessed in any timeline.

Danika's robotic surgery room had infected our time travel labs. The glow—bouncing from every reflective white surface—caused me to wince. In the instant my constricted pupils adjusted to the encircling brightness, I audibly gasped at the blasphemy Danika had been allowed to employ.

Terror seized my pulse in knowing I could not remain another second. Anticipating every moment until the serum would beckon me back to my own timeline, I held my TRB in sight. The plan we'd devised was clearly the only choice to prevent her atrocities. Danika could not be allowed to live.

I was surrounded by artificial intelligence—copies of each of us—meandering through the wide open space. I tried not to make eye contact or alert them to my presence.

I quickly assessed that they were producing mass quantities of serum with the laboratory set up. Danika had done it. She'd multiplied her prototypes using us. We were who she had next on her agenda to expand her AI population and therefore increase her power to move throughout time.

Despite my effort, a copy of Dakotah locked on to me and swiftly approached. She wrapped her hand around my wrist and squeezed tight.

"You are unauthorized," she said, in a robotic match to her real voice. I resisted her grip, but she was much too strong.

"I have permission from Ms. Farkas," I said, hoping to convince her to let me go.

"Taden Barrett, you are unauthorized here. You will be terminated."

"What do you mean by 'terminate'?" I asked as cold terror spread across my skin.

The Dakotah android reached into her lab coat pocket. Her release of my wrist left me to push buttons on my TRB. The moment I began to dissolve, I looked back at the robot version of Dakotah and noticed all the other robots in the room had also stopped their work to focus on the two of us. She had a gun aimed at me as she responded to an internal voice command that I assumed to be Danika.

"I've got her. What are your orders?" Dakotah's face was expressionless. "Terminate? Understood."

And then I was gone. She pulled the trigger too late; my molecules separated in the same instant.

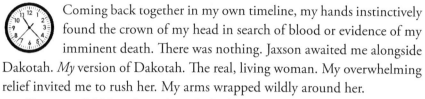 Coming back together in my own timeline, my hands instinctively found the crown of my head in search of blood or evidence of my imminent death. There was nothing. Jaxson awaited me alongside Dakotah. *My* version of Dakotah. The real, living woman. My overwhelming relief invited me to rush her. My arms wrapped wildly around her.

"It was awful," I said in a horrified whisper.

"What was?" she asked, her panic matching mine. "You're okay, right?"

I wanted to tell her everything I'd witnessed, but I was keenly aware that the monitors above my head were watching, and I wouldn't risk jeopardizing any part of our mission.

I looked straight into the camera and saluted Danika. This signaled her that our afternoon test was to continue as scheduled.

"I'm good. I feel a little woozy. I'm just out of practice." I chuckled to lighten the moment, but made sure to convey through the look I directed at her that there was more to tell.

"Good." She patted my shoulders. "Let's get you a glass of water and a seat. You should probably rest." She looked to Jaxson. "You good?"

"I can take it from here. The data is recorded; I'll send it to your files to analyze." Then he turned to me. "I hope you feel better quickly, Dr. Mihal."

"Thank you," I said.

My color was still wan. Dakotah escorted me from the lab to my office.

"Phase two," I said, barely audible. I removed my TRB and retrieved a vial of serum from my desk. Affixing it, I said, "Wish me luck," and I headed upstairs to Danika's office.

· · · · · · ● · · · · · · · · ·

# CHAPTER 65

"Are we good to do this right here?" Danika asked me.

I audibly hemmed and hawed, pursing my lips to the side. "It would be better if we did this in a more private location. I haven't recorded this in the data-collection process, and it could become a problem if you showed up unannounced in a different timeline. Let's use a lab space that will still be considered private ten years into the future."

"I think I have the perfect location for this," she said as she walked to her safe. She stood at a distance to allow the facial scanning to recognize her, and then she commanded, "Door." Before my eyes a hidden room appeared, as if the wall behind her desk never existed. I refused to give her the satisfaction of my awe.

Besides, it wasn't like it was time travel.

I followed her into the room. My eyes thrummed, soaking in the wall-to-wall colorless radiance. A bright glow pulsated through white fluorescent emissions streaming from the floor, walls, and ceiling. In the center of the room, upon a platform ringed with the same fluorescent glow, perched a cold glass table.

A halo light large enough to engulf the entire perimeter of the table hung from mechanical arms that followed the monochromatic theme of the room.

Reaching from the corona was a matching set of robotic arms. The chill in the air worked its way down my spine.

In the corner of the room a large cylindrical chamber emitted a softer green glow, making it stand out with the absence of any other viewable color inside the laboratory. Inside the life-size glass enclosure appeared to be a charging station. I thought to myself that it was befitting of a human droid.

This was the room in the videos. It was where she took my husband's life and created her robot.

Though my nerves trembled, I attached my TRB to Danika's arm and prepared her for what came next.

"You might feel dizzy and nauseated for a brief moment," I warned her. "I've thrown up several times."

"I'll be fine. I have a strong stomach."

Clenching my jaw, I thought about how I knew exactly how strong her stomach could be. The kinds of things she could tolerate.

"All right. The timer is set on the TRB. You'll be gone shortly. Your trip will last ten minutes, and then before you know it you'll return right here." I looked hard into her dark eyes. "Do you have any questions?"

She closed her lids. "No," she said. "I'm ready."

And like that, she disappeared. Without Danika's awareness, I'd set the Timed-Release Band on her arm to record her trip. The recordings streamed directly to Dakotah's computer. Dakotah shared access, so it streamed in real time on my server as well. I hadn't watched one of these since Abel's missions once upon a time—when he would leave recordings for me.

Since then, I'd had no interest or purpose involved in these missions.

Watching it made me motion sick, as the camera jiggled on her wrist, but the important part was the sound. As she pulled together in the time that I'd sent her to, I heard her uncomfortable moaning. It brought me great satisfaction to know she wasn't exactly as tough as she thought she was.

With her hand to her mouth, she provided an angle of the camera that displayed a view of Jaxson—as expected—awaiting her. From what I could tell, he'd already cleared the room of his older version. The first hurdle down.

He was out of the camera's view just as quickly as her hand went back to her side.

"Ms. Farkas," he said. Not a question or a surprise to see her, but a polite greeting.

"Agent Duncan. I'm glad to see you."

"Ma'am," he said.

"What year is it?" she asked him.

I tensed at the question. He was programmed not to answer that question, and I could only hope the program was successful.

"Can you repeat?" he said.

"I'm on a time travel. Dr. Barrett has sent me on a test. I will only be here for a few minutes, but would like to confirm the year I traveled to."

"To what year did she send you?" he asked.

Relief flushed through me. He'd followed the programming to avoid answering that question.

"Jaxson, I gave you direct command to answer me," she said, her voice thick with irritation.

"Allow me to check your TRB," he said, taking hold of her wrist. His face filled the camera view. He unfastened the band from her wrist and my anxiety resumed. This execution needed to go perfectly.

"Yes. Hm. You arrived at the destination set."

He walked away from her with the TRB in his hands. The camera was on Danika. She still looked woozy, the color not yet having returned to her cheeks.

"Agent Duncan," she said.

Danika attempted to exhibit her typical overbearing presence, but clearly found it difficult to regain her stamina.

"Can you get me a glass of water?"

He fidgeted with the band. This was his task—to switch out the time-travel vial with the poison serum. He then filled a cup at the sink and returned to Danika. The shaky camera view was unwatchable until it was reattached to her arm. Danika held the cup, which she brought to her lips. Within moments, she was flat on the floor, the TRB smashed in the fall.

"Self-destruct in ten," Jaxson said. "Five, four, three…"

And then there was silence.

I stared at my monitor where both Danika and Jaxson were terminated and looked up in the very same room to neither. It was over. Our nightmare had finally ended.

Running from her office to the elevator, I made my way to find Dakotah. Repeatedly pushing the button to call the elevator, she had beaten me to it. Dakotah rushed off as the doors parted.

"We did it! We actually did it!" she squealed, squeezing me. She tapped the air using her iCerebrum to call Ruth. I busied myself with pinging Jay to end his worrying. All of us had gathered to celebrate the downfall of Danika Farkas.

Dakotah fished in her coat pocket and pulled out a TRB. "I've got it," she said, holding it up so Jay could see his watch.

"Can it time travel again?" Jay asked.

"It's ready to go." She strapped it to my arm. "May the future be bright," she said as she programmed the date I'd last seen the droid versions of us in Danika's future. "Remember, after you confirm it all worked, set your TRB to go back to clean up Danika and Jaxson and get your TRB. Then come straight home."

I saluted, and as my hand left my forehead I broke apart into time.

· · · · · · ● ● ● ● ● ●○● ● ● ● ● ● · · · ·

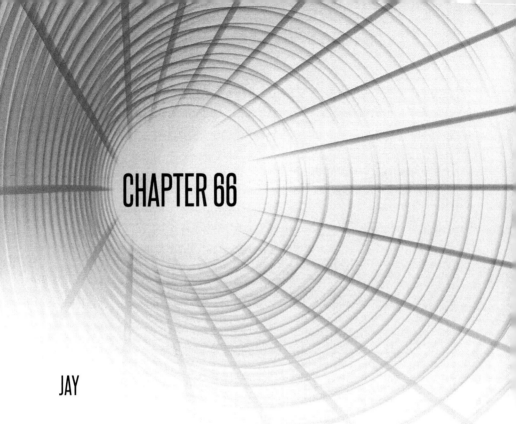

# CHAPTER 66

## JAY

The day of my college graduation, I looked for my dad's ball cap and found it in the crowd. After accepting my diploma I'd wanted to leave the stage and run to him, but I knew my mom was traveling from the future to find him here. I wanted that time for them.

I would find him at my wedding, then at my son's birth. I'd see my dad in every part of my life that mattered.

It was magical science, not a lucid manifestation that granted me these gifts of time.

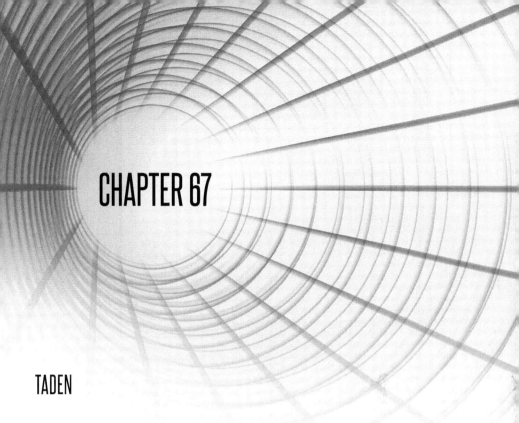

# CHAPTER 67

## TADEN

After leaving the NIST behind, my time-travel discoveries became lost technology. Dakotah and I cleaned up any traces of the serums, the data, and the altered timelines.

I had uploaded a photograph of Jay and Jenny in Paris and captioned it "Young Love and the Eiffel Tower".

And then I met Abel there.

I met my husband this way throughout the rest of my life.

I might never get to spend another new day with Abel Mihal, but if I was ever lost I could look and I would find him, time after time.

# AUTHOR'S NOTE

Follow D.M. Taylor on social media
Facebook: www.facebook.com/authordmtaylor
Instagram:www.instagram.com/auhtordmtaylor
Goodreads: https://www.goodreads.com/dmtaylor925
Bookbub: https://www.bookbub.com/@authordmtaylor2020

Sign up for D.M. Taylor's mailing list to receive updates on upcoming books in her new series. https://www.subscribepage.com/dmtaylorthereckoning

Dear Reader,

Thank you for spending your precious time with me to travel back in order to move on. Your support has opened new doors to my creativity and willingness to jump at new adventure. I look forward to spending more time with you between the pages of my books!

Love,
D.M. Taylor

If you would be willing to leave a review, you can do so at the following;

https://www.goodreads.com
https://www.amazon.com/Reckoning-Time-Travel-Thriller-ebook/dp/B084 Q9QVNT
https://www.bookbub.com

Printed in Great Britain
by Amazon